"We can all see what's happening here..." Ronnie rubbed Wade's arm consolingly.

There was no reason Wade should feel the impulse to cover her hand with his or to whisper to her. This was Ronnie "Bossy" Pickett!

"People always protest too much when they deny the truth," Ronnie said with a superior smile.

He'd always been partial to that smile and...

What had come over him? Ronnie had said herself fifteen years ago that they were too much alike and not romantically compatible.

Wade turned his gaze away from Ronnie. "There is no truth and no denying. I'm a bachelor now and I'll be a bachelor until the day I die. Now, if you'll excuse me, I've got to stow my competition gear and then help my brothers manage stock for the rest of this rodeo."

He walked away from the would-be matchmaker.

But he could feel her gaze upon him...

Dear Reader,

We moved when I was about twelve. Twelve was an age of transition for me. My body was changing. My outlook on the world was expanding. And suddenly, boys weren't just on the playground to compete with. And our new house? It was right around the corner from a foster home for boys. There were kids of every circumstance taking shelter in that home.

I had those boys in mind when I began creating The Cowboy Academy miniseries. It features a group of now-grown boys who were fostered at a ranch owned by a childless couple. First up, in *A Cowboy Worth Waiting For*, bronc-riding single dad Wade Keller is trying to put his life back on track after his wife's death. It's been two years, but he can't get out of his funk. Enter Ronnie Pickett, his wife's best friend, a plucky girl he once had a crush on and a woman who's trying to start a matchmaking service for rodeo competitors and fans. And her idea for her first client? Him!

I hope you come to love the cowboys of The Cowboy Academy as much as I do already.

Happy reading!

Melinda

HEARTWARMING

A Cowboy Worth Waiting For

———

Melinda Curtis

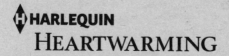

HARLEQUIN®
HEARTWARMING™

Recycling programs
for this product may
not exist in your area.

ISBN-13: 978-1-335-58491-5

A Cowboy Worth Waiting For

Copyright © 2023 by Melinda Wooten

For questions and comments about the quality of this book,
please contact us at CustomerService@Harlequin.com.

Harlequin Enterprises ULC
22 Adelaide St. West, 41st Floor
Toronto, Ontario M5H 4E3, Canada
www.Harlequin.com

Printed in U.S.A.

Award-winning *USA TODAY* bestselling author **Melinda Curtis**, when not writing romance, can be found working on a fixer-upper she and her husband purchased in Oregon's Willamette Valley. Although this is the third home they've lived in and renovated (in three different states), it's not a job for the faint of heart. But it's been a good metaphor for book writing, as sometimes you have to tear things down to the bare bones to find the core beauty and potential. In between, and during, renovations, Melinda has written over thirty books for Harlequin, including her Heartwarming book *Dandelion Wishes*, which is now a TV movie, *Love in Harmony Valley*, starring Amber Marshall.

Brenda Novak says *Season of Change* "found a place on my keeper shelf."

Sheila Roberts says *Can't Hurry Love* is "a page turner filled with wit and charm."

Books by Melinda Curtis

Return of the Blackwell Brothers

The Rancher's Redemption
The Blackwell Sisters
Montana Welcome
The Blackwells of Eagle Springs
Wyoming Christmas Reunion

Visit the Author Profile page
at Harlequin.com for more titles.

To those who need the foster system and those who help make the system live up to its potential.

CHAPTER ONE

"WADE KELLER, you need me." Ronnie Pickett's pert little nose was thrust high in the air, and her silky black hair swung from beneath her black cowboy hat.

Wade Keller's chest heaved, and it wasn't because he'd just jogged out of the arena after a semi-successful bareback bronc ride at a rodeo north of Tulsa. Ronnie's words yanked the rug from beneath his widower feet.

"I'm starting a matchmaking service. Now, you need a wife and Ginny needs a mama," Ronnie explained matter-of-factly, smiling kindly at Wade's ten-year-old daughter. "I'm going to find you the perfect woman."

Gaping, Ginny stared up at Ronnie with an expression that was half-worshipful and half-shocked.

Ronnie had that effect on people. She was a force to be reckoned with when she set her mind to something. Wade just hadn't expected her mind to be set on finding him a wife.

"Ronnie's right." Wade's father beamed at her as if her conclusion had flipped a light on in his nearly bald head, currently covered by a wide white Stetson. Frank Harrison was actually Wade's foster father, although sometime during the past twenty years, Wade had stopped attaching the "foster" label to him or any of his other foster family members. "You should hear Ronnie out."

And marry again?

Wade shook his head. Normally, he gave credence to his father's opinion, but not today. He stared Ronnie straight in her big dark eyes and said, "Not interested."

Wade's score from his ride on Graveyard Express was announced. As he'd suspected, it wasn't going to be high enough to put him in the money. His rhythm had been off. He'd been lucky to stay on for eight seconds but not lucky enough to place.

Another waste of a Saturday entry fee.

He couldn't afford to lose anymore. Disappointed and annoyed, Wade took Ginny's hand and tried to move past Ronnie.

She stepped in front of Wade, cutting him off. "Not so fast." Ronnie tossed her hair over her shoulder as if she were a bronc tossing off an inexperienced rider. "You've been avoiding me, and that's bad because you need me."

Wade hesitated, struck by those three words once more: *You. Need. Me.*

Do I need Ronnie Pickett?

Currently, Wade was on a dismal losing streak. Some would argue that he needed something. But was matchmaking Ronnie—and a second wife—the answer to his prayers?

He took stock of the petite woman in front of him. Never one to shy away from color, Ronnie was dressed like a Valentine's Day card—shimmery red boots, a bright pink flowered button-down and blue jeans with white flowering vines climbing up her seams. She was the polar opposite of his wife in practically every way—louder, more colorful, more assertive. And wherever she went, a well-meaning accident was sure to follow.

Do I need Ronnie Pickett?

If forced to decide right now, he'd have to say no.

And so, he said just that, *"No."*

"But—"

"Whatever you're selling, Miss Ronnie—" he gave her a stern look "—I'm not interested."

Ronnie put her hands on her slim hips. She'd been bold in high school and emboldened by every rodeo win in her short barrel-racing career. He could remember a time when a dare combined with her magnetic, brash character and dark, silky locks had enticed him to ask her to Clementine High School's junior prom. She'd thanked him for asking and told him they were too much alike to be a couple. And then she'd pointed out that her shy, quiet friend Libby worshipped the ground he walked on and was just what he needed.

And oddly enough, she'd been right. He and Libby had become a couple. After high school, they'd gotten married. They'd been well-suited. He'd been happy until Libby passed away.

A lump tried to fill Wade's throat.

Didn't mean Ronnie was right about him needing a wife and mother for his little girl. After losing his parents when he was in middle school and losing Libby two years ago, Wade didn't think he could take any more heartache. Love was risky.

While he'd been sorting through his thoughts, Ronnie's mouth had been moving. It was only her last words that sank in. "Wade Keller, do you want to be lonely in your old age?"

Thirty-two wasn't old. And living on the

Done Roamin' Ranch was never lonely. Many of his brothers still lived and worked on the D Double R.

Wade pushed his hat back, stared Ronnie down and got right to the point. "I don't mind being alone."

Wade's father chuckled the way he did sometimes when he thought one of his sons said something illogical. Given the number of cocky, full-of-themselves teenage boys Frank and Mary Harrison had taken in as fosters at the D Double R over the years, Frank's life had been filled with laughter.

Wade set his jaw. "I'm too busy to go looking for a woman." He had his plate full helping his parents and brothers run their rodeo stock company, competing in bareback bronc riding and raising a little girl.

"I know you're busy. That's why I can do the searching for you." Ronnie bent her knees until her face was level with Ginny's. She fussed with the set of his daughter's cowboy hat. "You want your daddy to be happy again, don't you, Ginny?"

Talk about low blows. Wade frowned.

Ginny nodded slowly. "Daddy doesn't tell me jokes no more."

"*Any more*," Wade corrected automatically.

"You lost your heart for dad jokes?" Ronnie rose to her full height, which meant the top of her black hat barely reached Wade's shoulder. Her nearly black eyes sparkled the way they did when she thought she was winning. "This is serious, Wade. You can't go pining away like this."

The way she teased him…

It reminded Wade of the experiences they'd shared as kids, including times most wouldn't call good but ones he cherished, nonetheless.

He didn't want to revisit those memories.

"Mary and I have been telling you to date since last summer." Wade's father upped the ante with his two extra cents. "Ginny needs more than just a daddy to look after her."

"She lives on a ranch with her grandparents and a passel of uncles." If anything, Ginny had too many cooks in the parental kitchen.

"But she doesn't have a mama," his father insisted, as if two parents were necessary, like two wheels on a bicycle.

"A mama would buy me dresses I like," Ginny said, wide-eyed and sad-faced, clearly trying to help play Wade into Ronnie's meddlesome hands. "And teach me other girl stuff."

"That's enough from you two," Wade grumbled, feeling outnumbered.

"We can all see what's happening here." Ronnie rubbed Wade's arm consolingly.

Her touch was soft and friendly. There was no reason Wade should feel the impulse to cover her hand with his or draw her closer. This was Ronnie *bossy* Pickett!

"People always protest too much when they deny the truth," Ronnie said with a superior smile.

He'd always been partial to that smile and…

Yowza! What had come over him? Ronnie had said herself fifteen years ago that they were too much alike and not romantically compatible.

Wade turned his gaze away from Ronnie's glossy red lips. "There is no truth and no denying. I'm a bachelor now, and I'll be a bachelor until the day I die. Now, if you'll excuse me, Miss Ronnie, I've got to stow my competition gear and then help my family manage stock for the rest of this rodeo."

He walked away from the would-be matchmaker. But he could feel her gaze upon him, as unsettling as her touch.

MOST PEOPLE ATTENDING a rodeo were spectators, a level removed from the action.

Veronica Pickett wasn't competing any-more, but she was no spectator sitting in the stands eating popcorn. That was something she couldn't bear. The dust, the noise and ex-citement of rodeo life had been a part of her DNA since she was a little girl watching her daddy compete in the bronc riding event.

She'd followed in his footsteps. Sort of.

She was a former barrel racing title holder, former rodeo queen and current spokesperson for Cowgirl Pearl Fashion. She lived for the action in and out of the arena. When Ronnie showed up at the rodeo nowadays, she spent a little time doing meet and greets for Cow-girl Pearl, checked in with her friends who were competing, and then had all the time in the world to be a spectator.

If only she was the spectating type. She couldn't sit still. She was a fixer. And what she liked to fix most was other people's love lives. She had a track record to validate her matchmaking skills. But it was only recently that she'd decided to use that talent to make sure Wade didn't wallow in the grief of Lib-by's dying from a brain tumor.

Before Libby passed, she'd asked Ronnie to watch over Wade. If only the stubborn man would make that easy. He'd become something of a recluse. For nearly a year, she'd been trying to fix him up, but he'd rejected every invitation she'd extended for coffee or dinner. It was time to go to extremes.

After much thought, she'd come up with a plan. Everyone knew she had a love of, and a knack for, matchmaking. Everyone also knew she had a history of starting businesses that eventually failed—a bothersome reputation, but the truth, nonetheless. What if she leveraged the two? No one would be too surprised to learn she was starting a matchmaking business. And no one would be too surprised if that business failed…after she found Wade a wife.

But darn that Wade Keller. He'd turned her down.

Was my pitch all wrong?

Perhaps it needed refinement. She sometimes conducted herself like a bulldozer when a broom would do, especially when she was nervous.

What she needed was another run-through of her pitch.

Ronnie planted her fancy red boots in the back corridor of the auditorium where the rodeo was being held and raised a hand to stop a handsome bull-riding cowboy. "Cord, didn't you get dumped last month by Mitzy or Mandy or Molly someone?" She couldn't remember the woman's name.

"Millie." Grinning, the lean blond cowboy grabbed hold of Ronnie's elbows. "Are you finally asking me out? Because the answer is *yes*!"

Ronnie gently pinched Cord's cheek, trying to say without sayin' that she was too old for him. He was barely out of high school, and her thirtieth birthday was fast approaching. "I'm starting up a rodeo matchmaking service. Are you single or not? I've got a list of cowgirls looking for love."

Or at least, she hoped to have one by night's end. Currently, she only had two women on board.

"Love?" Cord scoffed, rubbing his cheek without losing that mischievous grin. "Who needs love when I can offer charisma?"

"You mean a good time?" Ronnie softened her words with a gentle smile. "Reputations travel fast on the circuit, Cord. Good-time cowboys are usually popular with the ladies only if they're winning." And Cord hadn't been lately.

"You're full of low blows today, Ronnie." Wade passed by. He'd shed his competition accoutrements—his bright orange leather-fringed riding chaps, his wrist wraps, elbow support and such. He looked like any regular working cowboy as he headed toward the holding pens, presumably to help his family continue the smooth flow of stock the rodeo relied on for bull and bronc riding, steer roping and steer wrestling competitions.

Wade had an athletic build with dark brown hair and deep brown eyes that were easy to get lost in since they didn't do a good job of hiding the pain of his past. Two years ago, he'd been the points leader in the bronc riding field in the Prairie Circuit. Now, as a widower, he was trying to work his way back to the winner's circle. But he was as out of sync with life as he was with the broncs he'd drawn to ride.

Distant. Unapproachable.

Or just uncatchable, if the pace his long legs set was any indication.

That man's a challenge.

And she wasn't sure she was up to it.

The pressure of Ronnie's promise to Libby wrapped around her chest, making it hard to breathe.

"Low blow," Cord said, repeating Wade's sentiment with a chuckle. "Look at me. I have no need to swipe those dating apps. And I won't hire a matchmaker unless someone like Wade Keller is on your roster and blissfully happy because of it."

My sales pitch really stinks.

Ronnie held on to her smile, trying to look as if she had a secret where Wade was concerned. "I'll get back to you on that Wade Keller thing. But you'd best sign up soon, or you'll be dateless on Valentine's Day." Which was less than a month off.

Cord laughed again. "Honey, I'm never dateless." He spun away, heading toward the chutes.

Behind Ronnie, Wade's brothers from the D Double R herded bulls through a funnel toward the arena and cowboys waiting for a ride. The crowd noise increased, shouts mingling with applause until Ronnie couldn't distinguish individual voices of those walking past.

She stepped out of the flow of foot traffic to give herself a pep talk. Optimism and determination had always been her superpowers. Admittedly, things didn't always go her way or as planned. But Ronnie was good at bouncing back and landing on her feet.

I will find Wade a wife. She hugged that

thought, drawing several deep breaths as she focused on another mantra: *Count your blessings*.

She had two women interested in dating Wade. All she needed...was Wade.

I can convince him.

She'd find a moment alone with the former bronc riding superstar to persuade him to date again. She knew that would be a tough order. Since Libby died, Wade wasn't just avoiding her but everyone. He didn't hang around for idle chitchat, not at the rodeo or in their hometown of Clementine, Oklahoma.

"You look like you just lost the rodeo queen crown." Bess Glover separated herself from the stream of cowboys and cowgirls passing by. Ronnie's BFF flicked the brim up of Ronnie's black felt cowboy hat with one finger. "That is, you look the way you did that time you lost the rodeo queen crown *to me*." She laughed warmly, softening the tease.

"I would have earned the crown first if I hadn't started dating Quinn Lachey during rodeo week." Quinn was a very short-lived footnote in her dating history. Ronnie absently straightened her hat, drawing Bess to her left but keeping her gaze on her friend's face. "Quinn can charm anyone. It was a minor error of judgment on my part. I should have known better, but his sweet-talking was awfully sweet. I couldn't resist." After she'd lost, Quinn had broken up with her, claiming Ronnie was too high maintenance.

More like my standards were too high.

Bess rolled her eyes.

"I learned my lesson." And she'd won the next year. Ronnie gave Bess an assessing look, from her tame red locks to her spotless brown cowboy boots. "You haven't agreed to sign up for my matchmaking service."

"That's because I'm your friend. And friends don't enter into financial agreements with friends." Bess and Ronnie had known each other since grade school, same as Ronnie and Wade. Nowadays, Bess was a teacher and Clementine High School's rodeo coach. She had boxes and boundaries for everything, including, it seemed, friendship.

"I know the type of man who'd be perfect for you," Ronnie told her. Someone who'd help Bess cut loose sometimes without worrying about being judged or being seen as imperfect.

Wade Keller!

"I have too much on my plate right now to date," Bess said. She turned and stepped into the path of one of her former rodeo team members, now a barrel racing contender.

"That's the excuse everyone gives," Ronnie muttered, crossing Bess off her list of potential candidates for Wade.

Bess and her former trainee talked a few feet away, but their words were lost to Ronnie in the buzz of the crowd noise.

Ronnie waited for Bess to finish. She wasn't good at waiting. She was go-go-go, which made Wade's roadblocks that much more frustrating.

"But I won't give up, Libby," Ronnie said softly.

Her older brother Hank appeared at her side, waiting to speak until she looked at him. "Are you okay? You're talking to yourself."

"I'm fine. I haven't broken anything today or made a mess of this." Ronnie mustered an enduring smile as she extricated her arm. Admittedly, she wasn't the most nimble on her feet, she did sometimes rush into things without thinking, and her enthusiasm occasionally resulted in what some might call disaster. Her childhood had been a string of mishaps and misunderstandings. But Ronnie had found her stride as a barrel racing competitor and in the rodeo realm. For the most part, she was adulting with flying colors. If only her family didn't still treat her as if she'd only thrive within their overly protective embrace. "Did you make that heifer stock trade?"

"Yep." Hank had a faraway look, as he often did since he'd taken over running the Pickett Ranch while their father served in the state house. And then he seemed to come back to the present, smiling again at Ronnie. "Are you ready to go?"

"Not yet. I've still got business to conduct." There were lots of events yet to be run, and she wanted the chance to recruit more potential matches for Wade.

"Fair enough." Hank leaned closer to Ronnie to say, "Be ready to go in two hours. We want to beat the traffic." He stalked off, disappearing into the throng of cowboys streaming toward the stock pens.

"Did Hank sign up to be matched?" Bess asked, taking Hank's place next to Ronnie. "He should. You've been successfully playing matchmaker since we were kids. Look at Wade and Libby, Pascal and Mina, Jacqueline and Monte." She ticked Ronnie's triumphs off on her fingers. "Dan and Tilly, Ebony and Lucas, Trixie and Gerald. Do I need to go on?"

Ronnie shook her head.

Bess grinned. "That's because you know and everyone else knows about your expertise."

"You think I can do it?" Ronnie asked, a bit breathless by her friend's support. "Charge for matchmaking?"

The thought gave her pause. Her plan had been to find someone for Wade using the launch of a matchmaking business as a cover. But do this for real?

"Yep." Bess scanned the passersby. "But you need to build your client list the way I build my rodeo team roster. First, recruit one standout, someone everyone respects and secretly aspires to be."

Wade Keller.

A man as stubborn as the day was long.

"And two solid athletes that are hard workers without big egos," Bess added.

John Garner and Tuf Patterson.

Two other popular, as yet unmarried, competitors on the circuit.

She ruled out Cord. He was already in love—with himself. Ronnie saw that now. She had to sign people ready to settle down.

If I do this... I need to refine my sales pitch.

Ronnie wasn't sure she wanted a matchmaking business for real. There was always the chance that she'd muck up the business side, and then she'd be unable to make matches casually. Not that there were many of her friends left single who were interested in finding love. Not that she could find fault with her friends who wanted to remain single. She was of the same frame of mind.

"Find your standout. And then their friends will all want to tag along," Bess said decisively. "Now's the perfect time to build the foundation of your team, Ronnie."

"Right. Here I go." Ronnie marched off, if not to start a matchmaking business for real, at least to find a woman Wade could spend the rest of his life with.

CHAPTER TWO

"YOU KNOW THE DRILL, Tornado Bill." Wade whistled shrilly, riding at the flank of a bull that had just thrown young Cord to the dust. He guided Tornado Bill toward the gate with the chute leading back to the paddock and the cattle truck that would return him to the D Double R, the Done Roamin' Ranch.

Wade Keller, you need me.

Ronnie's words kept playing on repeat in his head.

You need me.

Those three words shouldn't have made Wade smile. But here he was, having lost his event and grinding through the dust and noise of rodeo stock management with a long drive home ahead of him later.

You need me.

He grinned.

"That's the last of the bulls." His older brother Chandler closed the gate after Tornado Bill passed through. He was the D Double R's ranch foreman and had been in charge since Frank had stepped back from the off-ranch operations a few years ago. "What are you grinning for? Cord eating dust?" Chandler glanced back toward the young cowboy who was limping out another gate, the last bull rider before the chuck wagon races.

Wade wiped the smile from his face and reached for a quick excuse. "I...uh... I like that Tornado Bill is building a mean record."

The harder bulls were to ride, the more popular they were on the circuit because a cowboy could earn big points if they stayed on until the buzzer.

"Are you sure that's why you were smiling?" Griff, another of his brothers, rode up to Wade. He was burly with a slapdash attitude and often served as the pickup man, getting bull and bronc riders to safety. "I saw you with Ronnie Pickett earlier. I hear she's turned her hand toward the art of love. If you're smiling, that's good. It's about time you put yourself back out there."

"That is *not* why I was smiling."

"I bet it is." Tate, one of Wade's younger brothers, leaned on his saddle horn not far away. "Ginny told me Ronnie's going to find her a new mama."

His family laughed. Even Dad and Ginny, sitting in the nearby stands, seemed to be amused. Not that they could hear. Heads bent together, watching something on Dad's phone, the pair was smiling. It was good to see Dad smile considering he seemed a bit adrift lately.

Wade pointed at Tate and Griff. "Don't you two need to load bulls in the transport?"

"Oh, there's something going on here, all right." Chandler chuckled. "Giving orders is my job, Wade, not yours." And then he gestured at Tate and Griff. "You guys need to load bulls. Get on with you." Chandler returned his attention to Wade. "You and Ryan need to load the near chute for steer wrestling. That's the next event after the chuck wagon races. And Wade…"

About to do Chandler's bidding, Wade held his horse in check. "Yeah?"

"You and I and the rest know too well that sometimes you need to start over." Chandler was the oldest of the men Frank and Mary Harrison had taken in as teenagers. He was also the most likely of the brothers to dole out advice, wanted or not. "It's okay to smile at the possibility of dating. A little luck on your rides and a little love at home, and you'll be back on your feet."

Wade frowned. "One doesn't necessarily feed the other." Love and luck didn't blend into a recipe for a happy life. "And luck is hard to come by."

Chandler shrugged. "Sometimes the luck you need turns up when you least expect it."

"Wouldn't that be nice?" But not only did Wade no longer believe in love; he didn't believe in luck, either.

"IN FACT, I do know Tate Oakley." Ronnie had been smiling so long and so hard for so many ready-for-love cowgirls that her cheeks felt like they might crack and tumble into the path of the chuckwagons being pulled by teams of six horses around the arena. "And yes, Tate is single. But what about Wade Keller?"

"Oh, Tate is the more handsome of the two." Sarah gushed. She was a barrel racer with a steady track record and had the shine of a woman enamored with the idea of love.

The crowd cheered on their favorite rigs as they passed by, which prevented conversation and gave Ronnie time to think about Sarah's idea of the ideal mate.

It wasn't Wade. And Tate was a bad choice.

He was dangerously handsome and a total heartbreaker, like Cord.

And speak of the devil, there was Tate, sitting on a top rail over by the catch pen gate next to Wade and a half dozen other D Double R cowboys. They were a handsome crew.

The image of all those good-looking cowboys in a row reminded Ronnie of being on the high school rodeo team. She'd been a freshman and Wade had been a junior, but somehow they'd gravitated toward each other. Even as a teen, he'd been a man of few words. And since a failed summer episode involving a cheerleading tryout where she'd failed to uphold the bottom of the human pyramid, Ronnie had been happy to be with kids who always looked for the silver lining and didn't belabor the point that she'd ended up at the bottom of the pyramid pile.

"What is it you're looking for in a man?" Ronnie prompted Sarah when the chuckwagon race came to a close and the applause died down.

"Well, if I say cute, I'll sound shallow." The glow faded in Sarah's eyes. "I want someone nice and... A guy with a good sense of humor... A man with goals in life and a willingness to try hard to… Someone who hasn't worked himself into a hole."

"A hole?" Ronnie had been filling in blanks but wasn't sure she'd heard Sarah correctly on this last bit.

"A hole." Sarah turned to face Ronnie, an earnest expression in her eyes. "Guys who gamble on themselves at the rodeo, even though they never win, dig a financial hole. I met someone last year who put every entry fee on a credit card and hadn't won in over a year. He threw tens of thousands of dollars toward an impossible dream."

"He didn't know when to quit." Ronnie glanced toward Wade once more. He'd had a good five years or so at the top of his game. He might have saved money to pay for all his entry fees nowadays. But how much longer could that last?

She made a mental note to ask him.

All for the sake of finding him true love, of course.

"Knowing when to throw in the towel shows maturity." Sarah stared toward Wade and his brothers. "But I'm not sure I want a man whose been married before and has kids."

Ronnie sighed. "You shouldn't count someone out without good reason, Sarah. Tell me a little more about yourself." And why Wade wouldn't be perfect for you. "You said you live on your family's ranch. Is it self-sustaining? Or do you work elsewhere? And what about your hobbies?"

"I'm a receptionist in a dentist's office and I raise ducks."

Ronnie stared at Sarah open-mouthed, waiting to hear more. When nothing seemed forthcoming, she prompted, "Excuse me for asking, but are ducks a thing? Like are they trendy, or do you breed them for eating or..."

Sarah seemed to draw in on herself as if she were embarrassed. "I just like ducks."

"No need to apologize for your passions." Ronnie pondered the meaning of Sarah's hobby and how she'd frame it to Wade. Meanwhile, she caught sight of the man himself mounting up.

Wade has a fine look to him in the saddle. Tall. Sturdy.

She bet if she stood nearby and caught his eye there'd be a gleam in his gaze that said, *I'm not going to tell you everything, Ronnie Pickett, including how lonely I am.*

She remembered that exact same look when she'd confronted him earlier, and it made her heart ache.

If she told Wade about Sarah's duck interest, he'd find her candidate wanting. Although, increasingly, Ronnie was feeling that Sarah wasn't right for Wade. She was too gentle.

Like Libby.

Wade didn't need another Libby. He needed a strong, vocal woman to draw him out and remind him of all the joy to be found in life.

Still, she was reluctant to give up on Sarah.

"I don't suppose you raise chickens, too?" Ronnie turned back to Sarah. Chickens got a lot of respect in the ranching community, certainly more so than ducks.

"I raise what I like. And that's ducks. My daddy says I should sell them, but I don't. My flock just keeps getting bigger."

For the love of Mike. She's a duck hoarder.

The voice in her head suddenly sounded like Wade's.

Ronnie tsked. "There's nothing wrong with keeping ducks." In fact, Wade had designated ten acres on the D Double R to rescuing retired rodeo broncs, including the infamous Jouster.

"Do you think there's something wrong with my duck habit?" Eyes wide, Sarah had her feathers ruffled and wasn't letting this go. "Is that why guys don't call me back?"

"No. Not at all," Ronnie rushed to reassure her. "You just haven't found the right man for you. And as for me, I'm trying to find the proper frame to present you to eligible men." She touched the younger woman's arm. "How does this sound? *You'll love Sarah. She's a rancher, born and raised, with experience breeding stock.*"

"We don't refer to ducks as stock." Sarah's shrill voice indicated the duck hobby was a sore subject.

Message received.

Ronnie rushed on, hoping to salvage something. "Have you raised horses or bulls?" Or both?

"Of course, I have. But no one would call a duck *stock.*"

"Understood." Ronnie clung to her smile. "What about… *You'll love Sarah. She's a rancher, born and raised, with experience breeding stock and fowl.*"

"I like that." Sarah sounded slightly less ruffled. She settled back in her place on the bench.

"That's what I'll say then." Ronnie caught sight of Bess walking past. After promising Sarah she'd keep in touch, she excused herself.

Bess took one look at Ronnie's face and said,

"No one claimed starting a matchmaking business was going to be easy."

"Do I look demoralized?" Ronnie checked her cell phone to see if any of the women she'd approached today had messaged her. *Nada.* "I'm going more for a carefree demeanor, one that says I don't desperately need clients." Even if they were only clients for Wade.

Bess studied her features again. "I think anyone who doesn't know you well would buy the carefree demeanor."

"Good answer." Ronnie spotted Wade talking to Chandler across the ring. "I'm going to need something more than a carefree demeanor if I want to find a wife for Wade. He's reluctant to be matched."

"Is he?" Bess followed the direction of her gaze. "Blackmail would work."

Ronnie sighed. "If only I had something to blackmail him with."

And if only I was the blackmailing type.

"DAD, THERE'S NO rodeo next weekend, right?" Ginny's small, tired voice came from the back seat of the truck Wade was driving home from the rodeo.

"There is a rodeo next weekend, sunshine. But I'm not competing." The funds Wade had allocated for entry fees were nearly empty because he wasn't winning. He made a slow turn toward the highway, mindful of the stock trailer full of horses he was towing. "I'm just working."

"I want to stay home at the ranch with Grandma Mary." Ginny had her pillow against the back-seat window and a fuzzy blanket over her. It was long past her bedtime, and she sounded two ticks shy of sleep. "I want to play with my friends in Clementine."

"You can take next weekend off with Tate and Griff, son," Wade's father said from the passenger seat. His white cowboy hat sat on the dash in front of him next to Wade's dingy straw hat. "You've been burning the candle at both ends, competing and working stock."

"Meaning that's why I haven't been in the money?" Wade tried not to snap, but he was afraid he failed.

"I can't tell you why that is, son," Dad said evenly. "But it might do you good to get out and cut loose. Forget about all that pressure you've been putting on yourself to win and just hang out in your own skin."

Wade Keller, you need me.

Given Ronnie's matchmaking proposal, his father's suggestion sounded suspicious. "Did you talk to Ronnie after I turned her down? You know I'm not looking for a wife." He glanced back at Ginny, hoping she wasn't awake.

Her eyes were closed, and her mouth was slack-jawed. She was out.

"I didn't talk to Ronnie." His father had the patience of a saint, which was why he'd done so well taking in teenage boys for two decades. Unlike Wade, his voice and demeanor showed no signs of irritation. "And I'm not saying you need to replace Libby, but—"

"No one can replace Libby." She'd been a good woman, a loving wife, a doting mama.

"—what I'm saying is that it might do you good to hang out with someone other than your family for a change."

Wade made a sound of dissent as he brought the rig up to freeway speed and merged into a lane. "I don't need time off."

"Maybe not. But I'm taking you off the work roster for next weekend."

"That's not necessary." He didn't like being grounded. "Taking time off isn't the answer to my problems. Not that I have any," he added quickly. He should have left it there. But it was late, and nothing had gone his way today. "Why do you think idle time is what I need? You reduced your workload and look how unhappy it made you."

"What's this nonsense?" Dad half-turned in his seat, the tiniest trace of exasperation slipping through his tone. "I'm happy. Ask your mother."

"You're bored," Wade said with mic-dropping emphasis. "You putter around the ranch asking us if we need help with anything. All those heavy sighs you make when we assure you no help is needed don't sell the impression that you're in blissful semi-retirement. You have no more wayward teens to take in and straighten out." Tate and his twin brother Ryan had been among the last. "No more stock to manage on rodeo day." Not since he'd handed over that responsibility to Chandler. "You don't know what to do with yourself."

"I'm happy," Dad repeated, albeit curtly and without further explanation. "Take the time off before I pull you from the roster for two weeks instead of one."

With effort, Wade kept his mouth shut.

But inside, he had a lot to say, and he was thinking of saying it to Ronnie.

The last thing I need is a wife.

CHAPTER THREE

THERE WAS NOTHING as freeing to Ronnie as riding fast.

Only five dating candidates for Wade. Grr.

After yesterday's rodeo fiasco, she sought solace in barrel racing in the Pickett Ranch arena on Sunday morning, riding Yanni, her palomino gelding, as if they had a time to beat.

And Wade still didn't agree to be matched. Grr.

The sun was bright, but the January morning air was cold on Ronnie's heated skin. Frustration had been building since yesterday. And she could trace it back to her little white lie that she was starting a matchmaking service. Wade hadn't bought into it, as had some women, while Bess thought she should open the business for real. And Ronnie felt caught in the middle. What if she recruited a larger dating pool for Wade? And what if he fell in love with the first woman he started dating? What was she supposed to do with the rest of the women?

Stay the course, Ronnie. Worry about the women when Wade finds true love.

She guided Yanni back to the start position, patting his damp neck.

Yanni was a pro at hunting barrels. And he loved it as much as she did. She needed to ride him more often. *If* she did start a matchmaking service, she'd have less time to spend riding him.

Don't get ahead of yourself.

But *things* were tangled inside of her like the power cords beneath her secretarial desk at the elementary school. She hated uncertainty.

"Yah!" she cried, cuing her horse into action.

Yanni sprinted to the first barrel, keeping his compact body low and tight as they circled it. He stretched and practically flew to the next, eating up that twenty-five feet with long strides. They made a snug pass around the second barrel. And then they were tearing it up toward the third, so in sync after years of practice that Ronnie just knew they were making winning time.

Practice always pays off.

In a heartbeat, they were past the third barrel and dashing toward the finish.

That's what I need. Matchmaking dress rehearsals.

The question was: *Where and with whom could she perform dry runs on?*

I'd have plenty of practice if I started the business for real.

"Argh!" she cried, reining Yanni in.

Over at the gate, Hank waved her down. "Aren't you supposed to be packing?"

"I'm packed." Today was moving day. Ronnie had been boxed up for months, prepared to move into the house she'd inherited from her Great Aunt Didi.

The sweet spinster had left Ronnie her home, even though Ronnie hadn't always been the perfect relative. But Didi understood and accepted young Ronnie's foibles. One time, she'd helped Didi weed the garden and accidentally pulled out her prize geraniums. And what had Didi said when she'd found out? She'd given Ronnie a hug, thanked her and said, "I was stuck in a rut with those flowers. Now I can move on to something new."

And now, so could Ronnie. She flung herself out of the saddle, suddenly excited. "Are you ready to help me move?"

"No." Hank wouldn't look at her. In fact, he tugged his hat brim low.

Some of Ronnie's elation drained. She thought she knew why Hank was balking. And the reason didn't make her feel better. "Is Mom in the house crying?"

Hank fidgeted, looking uncomfortable. "Mom says she can't bear for her baby to leave."

"Don't ask me to reschedule moving anymore. I need space." Freedom from her family's protective embrace. They thought she was a disaster waiting to happen. She was cleaning up her own mistakes now. Ronnie slipped Yanni's reins over his head and led him toward the barn, planning to remove his saddle and then cool him down on the walker. "She's ready for grandchildren, Hank. Hint hint."

"I've got things to do before I settle down," Hank said flatly, which was his pat answer. "Would it be so bad to wait a little longer to move?"

"I've already postponed two times for her." Ronnie wasn't letting Mom have her way today. It was the one thing she could control.

Hank said something too low for her to catch, something that might have had to do with Pickett folk and their stubborn natures. He pointed back toward the barrels. "You only race when you're upset. What's bothering you?"

Everything...

Nothing...

She stopped, faced her brother and voiced the question that had kept her awake last night. "If everybody is looking for love, why aren't they open to matchmaking?"

"Think of it like this. There are lots of ways to buy a car. Your way of selling them a car might not be their way of buying a car. And maybe others aren't looking for a car, period." Hank gave her a wry grin. "*I'm* not looking for a car. Or for love."

"Not yet anyway." Ronnie made a frustrated sound, staring at the clear blue Oklahoma sky. Was that the problem? Wade wasn't ready for love again? It had been two years. "Of those who *are* looking for love, why wouldn't they want a little help finding it?" Why didn't she have twenty candidates instead of five?

Hank chuckled. "That question is above my pay grade."

Yanni nudged Ronnie and plodded forward. He knew there were oats in his future.

"Lot of help you two are." She led her horse

through the gate, letting Hank close it behind them.

Over at the main house, two of the ranch dogs were sunning themselves on the porch. Brisket, their elderly chocolate Labrador, and Barstow, their shepherd mix.

Her brother trotted to catch up, touching her arm. "Love isn't like baking cupcakes. There's no recipe. And if it were me, I wouldn't pay for something when I don't know what I'm getting."

"That's deep." She nodded. "And fair." Demoralizing, too. It applied to both Wade and the women.

They entered the barn. It was a two-story structure built nearly a century ago by the first Picketts to own the property. The beams were hand-hewn and rock-solid. The siding and roof had been replaced a few years ago, along with the stalls and doors. It was just the beams that said the family had endured and would continue to endure.

At least, if Hank and their brother David finally settled down and had kids.

Ronnie sighed. Maybe she'd been wrong about Hank. Maybe he was too busy with the ranch. Maybe he hadn't met the right woman.

She looped Yanni's reins on a hook in the

breezeway, thinking of Sarah, who was nesting in her own way. "What's your opinion on ducks?"

"Is this an ecosystem question?" Hank loosened the gelding's girth strap. "Are ducks as good for the habitat as bees?"

"No." She struggled to keep her tone neutral. "I'm just asking you if you like ducks." Hank and Sarah might hit it off.

"I prefer turkeys. They're wild. I don't have to feed them or protect them from predators, but I can still have one for Thanksgiving dinner." Hank hefted her saddle and spared her a grin before he disappeared into the tack room.

"That was a matchmaking long shot," Ronnie muttered, switching out Yanni's bridle for a halter and lead rope. "Too bad. They'd have made adorable babies."

She led the gelding out to the circular walker on the other side of the barn, fastened his lead rope to it and set the motor on low. She moved back, making sure everything was working properly and the gelding was settled in.

"Were you trying to set me up with a duck breeder?" Hank joined her. "Is all this matchmaking for other people really necessary? Don't you want to find someone of your own?"

"Who would want me?" Ronnie asked absently, although recently she'd spent far too much time pondering the answer to that question.

Hank grabbed her by the shoulders. "*Who?* Guys ask me for your number all the time."

She scoffed. "Like you'd give out my number. Admit it, you and Mom would prefer I stay single and on the ranch forever."

Her brother's dark brows lowered. His expression turned fierce. "That's not true. We want you to be happy."

Yanni's ears twitched as he walked past.

"Then why don't you give out my number?" Was it because he thought she was a walking catastrophe maker?

Still holding on to her arms, he said, "It's because the guys who ask for your number aren't good enough for you."

She shrugged him off, annoyed. "Sounds like you're running a matchmaking service of your own."

He widened his stance and put his hands on his hips. "Is it wrong to want the best for my kid sister? Have you ever considered that Mom would be happy to see you move out if you were getting married and settling down for good?"

"You mean she'd be happy to pass me from one keeper to another?" Ronnie's fingers curled into her palms. "Let me be clear. I'm not getting married." *Ever*.

Some of the bluster drained from Hank, like an inflatable lawn holiday decoration that had been unplugged. "You… You're a matchmaker who doesn't believe in love?"

"Yes. *No*. I mean, I don't believe it's in the cards for me." For others, for sure. But for a woman who was something of a jinx…no. "I know who I am on the inside, but when it comes to romance…"

Hank nodded. He knew.

It was like there were two separate Ronnies—the woman the world saw and the woman Ronnie believed herself to be. There was the Ronnie in her head, the one who planned romantic picnics. And then there was Ronnie out there in the world, spreading her picnic blanket over a fire ant mound. After her last date had called her a menace and was trying to sue her for damages, she'd come to a decision. Men were safer without her.

She turned to leave, needing a moment to let go of the upset inside of her.

Hank caught her arm. "*Why?* Why would you think that?"

"Need you ask?" She gave a sad little laugh as she extricated herself. "If my own family doesn't think I'm capable enough to live on my own, what could I bring to a relationship but trouble?"

"You aren't trouble," Hank insisted.

"If that's true, you would have gotten married by now." It was suddenly all so clear to her. And so demoralizing.

Dad was a state representative, spending weeks at a time in the capital, leaving the ranch and family matters, including the care of Ronnie, in Hank's capable hands. Her older brother was the one Mom turned to when she and Ronnie bumped heads. He was the one sent to make peace or make Ronnie see reason.

"It's time I got out of the way of your happiness," she said softly.

Hank scowled but didn't argue, confirming her hypothesis.

Ronnie wanted to saddle Yanni once more and gallop to the far end of the ranch. But Hank would worry. Perhaps there was an upside to this…

"You don't need to hover over me, Hank. But I do need something from you." She smiled sweetly, an idea forming in her head. "I need a favor—some cowboy clients to match with the cowgirls I've got signed up." Because she suddenly wasn't certain any of the five women she'd recruited would be right for Wade.

I can match them to Hank's friends.

"You want to…" Hank took a few quick steps back. "Don't look at me."

"I am looking at you." She followed him, matching him step for step. "You and your single friends."

"No." Hank stopped, holding his ground, chin thrust out.

"I'll settle for referrals to your friends. And if you don't give them to me, I'll tell Nan Ingersoll that you want to get back together." Nan was sweet and had been hung up on Hank for a long time in the worst way.

"We were never together!" Hank cried, as if she'd prodded a sore spot. "It was *one* date!"

Ronnie's smile broadened. "Oh, but it must have been a doozy of a date. Nan always talks about you when I see her around town."

Hank lowered his hat brim, which did nothing to hide his frustrated expression. "I'll tell Mom you're ready to move today."

"And your friends?"

To his credit, Hank didn't stomp away. "I'll mention it to them. I can't promise more."

"Good." Impulsively, Ronnie hugged him. Things were looking up.

Not to mention, she had a knack for blackmailing after all.

"DAD, DO I have a college fund?" said Ginny.

Wade choked on the buttermilk biscuit he'd taken a bite of on this early morning. He coughed and reached for his water.

Beside him, Chandler slapped his back, nearly causing Wade's water glass to spill.

Wade brushed his brother's hand away. "What makes you ask about college funds, sunshine?" Because heaven knew no one in his biological family had ever gone to college.

It was Sunday breakfast. His mother had laid out her usual big spread to fill them up before they attended church. Her grown boys may not live in the main ranch house, but Sunday breakfast found them all in Mom's kitchen. No one wanted to miss Mary Harrison's sausage, biscuits and gravy. The price of breakfast was a seat in church afterward.

"A lady at the rodeo yesterday said her husband was wastin' her kid's college fund 'cause he was losin'." Ginny sat in the chair next to Wade, wearing her best Sunday dress and swinging her feet. She grinned across the table at Griff and Tate, who were starting to laugh. "Did you waste mine, Dad?"

His brothers' laughter died away.

Wade's father looked up from his plate. His mother turned from her position at the sink.

All eyes were on Wade.

"I…uh… I haven't started a college fund for you yet, sunshine." The biscuit in his hand crumbled. "I thought I'd wait and see if you wanted to go."

"I do." Ginny beamed at him. "I want to be a lawyer and sue folks for being mean."

Griff and Tate started laughing again. Dad smiled and sipped his coffee. Mom wiped her hands on a dish towel, looking thoughtful.

"Sunshine…" Wade laid his arm over the back of Ginny's chair. "Lawyers don't just sue people. Some of them write and review contracts. Or make laws. Or ensure that folks get treated fairly."

"So…you like lawyers?" At his nod, Ginny swung her feet faster. "Good. Makes me happy since I'm gonna be one."

"I like a child with ambition." Mom's short silver hair was tamed and curled today, and she wore an apron over a blue dress.

"You better start saving, Wade," Chandler managed to grin and shove a bite of gravy-soaked biscuit in his mouth at the same time.

"Are you saving for your kid, Chandler?" Wade asked, treading in treacherous waters since Chandler was only recently divorced.

Chandler sat back and finished chewing his food before answering. "Sam is four. And he'll probably be a cowhand, like his father."

"I thought Ginny was going to be a working hand and love rodeo, too." And look how that came back to bite Wade.

"Nope. Lawyer." Ginny stabbed a piece of sausage with her fork.

"Who inspired you to be a lawyer, sunshine?" Yes, to whom did Wade owe this debt of gratitude? He grit his teeth, trying not to panic over college tuition he would need for seven years or so.

"I saw lawyers on a show Grandpa let me watch on his phone yesterday." Ginny grinned at Wade's father.

"She asked me what folks went to college for." Dad carefully wiped gravy from his chin. "I thought you'd be proud of me for finding a video on my phone speaking to kids about different types of college education."

"You know he's right," Mom chimed in.

"Your father can barely figure out how to email on his phone."

"He can barely send a picture on our text loop," Griff pointed out.

"And don't get me started on him accessing his recorded programs on television," Chandler added.

"All right. All right. You've all had your fun." Dad eyed Wade. "What's the big deal? It's not like being a lawyer is a bad thing. Who knows? Ginny could be a judge someday."

"A judge," Wade said vaguely, glancing around at his brothers. No one seemed to be joyous anymore. They'd all had dealings with judges and court-appointed lawyers when they were young when their family situations fell apart for one reason or another. He'd bet none wanted to deal with the legal system any more than they had to.

But there was Ginny, his pride and joy, eyes full of dreams.

"I guess I'll open up a college fund," Wade said with forced optimism, wondering how big this fund would need to be. "I'll call Dix over at the bank." One of his brothers who didn't work on the ranch.

After their plates had been cleared and the dishes done, the family loaded up into trucks to head into town for the late morning service. The day was clear and the air crisp. Sunlight bounced off the white walls of the main ranch house and the original old farmhouse.

"Wade." His mother carried her brown jacket and a picnic basket down the front porch steps. "Can you drop this off after church?"

"Sure. To who?" He took it from her.

"I heard from Nell Pickett that Ronnie's finally moving out." Mom patted his arm. "Nell hasn't let her go easily. I bet she could use a pick-me-up."

"Nell? Or Ronnie?" Wade chuckled.

"Ronnie." Mom gave her head a shake.

He stopped laughing, not liking to hear that Ronnie was having a hard time, even if he'd been avoiding her since Libby died. "Where's she moving?"

"Didi's old place in town."

"The pink palace on King Street?" Wade grinned. The bungalow had once been painted a too-bright shade of pink, a color hotter than a fluff of cotton candy. It was fitting that colorful Ronnie was moving in.

His mother explained what she'd packed inside the basket, going on and on about ingredients and such.

"Hang on." Wade extended the basket back to her. "Why aren't you taking it over? You don't have an ulterior motive, do you? Have you heard Ronnie's started a matchmaking business?"

Mom scoffed, ignoring the basket as she slipped her jacket on. "'Course, I heard. I'm just being neighborly, and you know how my back stiffens up after a long service spent sitting on those hard wooden pews. You'd be doing me a favor."

Wade nodded. He knew.

But across the ranch yard, Griff, Ryan and Tate were pointing at him and laughing.

CHAPTER FOUR

"I DON'T LIKE you moving out, Ronnie."

Carrying a box of framed photographs, Ronnie walked quickly ahead of her mother Sunday afternoon and entered the little bungalow in Clementine.

Outside, the house was a faded pink color with white trim. Inside, there was faded pink flowered wallpaper on the living room walls. Faded pink. It was a theme. Faded pink plush carpeting. Faded pink antique chair and love seat with wooden arms. Faded pink Formica countertops. Faded pink sink, toilet and bathtub. Pink had definitely been a theme of Great Aunt Didi's. And when Ronnie was little, she'd admired all that color.

Not today.

Ronnie set the box down on a faded pink wingback chair, sending dust motes in the air. "Mom, Great Aunt Didi wanted me to have her house. She loved this house. *I* love this house. I'm not going to sell it." She was going to sift through all Great Aunt Didi's things and give the house some much-needed attention, paint, restain the floors and such, and deal with the more expensive repairs, like the kitchen and bathroom remodels, later.

Ronnie made her way toward the small kitchen.

"My point is that you don't have to move in." Mom practically shouted from behind her. She trod on Ronnie's heel. That's how closely she followed her, physically and emotionally. "You could rent the place out."

Mom blew everything out of proportion. And this was why Ronnie refused to tell her mother about her recent decision not to get married. If she knew, she'd have done more than cry about Ronnie moving out. She'd have found a way to keep her at home.

Sunlight and shadows undulating on the wall from movement at the front of the house had Ronnie turning.

Her brothers came through the open front door carrying cardboard boxes marked *Bedroom*.

"It smells like old lady in here." Hank turned into the hallway.

"That's *Eau de Old Maid*," David joked before following him. "Which Ronnie is soon to be."

"Twenty-nine isn't old," Ronnie protested, ignoring the "old maid" part.

David turned, grinning at her from the hallway. "But thirty is over the hill."

"Ha! You're thirty-three," Ronnie called after him.

Mom wrapped her arms around Ronnie as if she wasn't going to let her go. "All I'm saying is that you don't have to move out."

"Mom." Ronnie patted her arm before stepping clear. "I need my own place."

My own space to breathe.

Mom looked stricken. "But why? The boys still live at home."

"In the bunkhouse and the foreman's cabin," Ronnie countered. In other words, they had their own places, because the Pickett Ranch no longer employed outside hands. Technology had done away with the need for more than seasonal cowboy hires. Ronnie turned her attention back to the kitchen, knowing this was an argument she could only win by outlasting her mother.

Ronnie opened a cupboard near the stove. It was full of spices in faded red-and-white rectangular tins. "These are ancient."

"I'll throw them away." Mom elbowed Ronnie aside and began emptying the cupboard. "These old spices aren't safe. Why are you moving in when you haven't gone through all Didi's things?"

"I'm working on it. I spent my Christmas vacation clearing out the carport and back patio stuff." Great Aunt Didi had been on her way to becoming a hoarder. She'd never gotten rid of anything—broken lamps, ancient fans, outdated microwaves. The list went on. And now that the first batch of items had been cleared, Ronnie planned to move the rest of the things she didn't want in the house out to the carport.

Her mother removed the lid on the small cumin canister and dumped the contents in the sink. "I still say it's safer for you to live at home."

"You make it sound like living here in town is dangerous." Might just as well approach the issue head on.

"It could be." Mom angled her head so Ronnie could see her face. "Clementine is lovely, but I can't keep my eye on you here."

Ronnie took her mother by both hands. "I'll be fine. There aren't any stock here to run me over." Yes, that had almost happened a time or two. Ronnie tended to get lost in her own thoughts. "There aren't any prairie dog or gopher holes in the yard." Nothing for her to trip over. "I know most of the neighbors. No one will sneak up on me without me seeing. I'll be fine."

Her mother covered Ronnie's cheek with her palm. "How are we supposed to take care of you?"

That's the point.

Much as Ronnie loved her family, she didn't want to be coddled or stand in the way of someone else's happiness.

Maybe I'll set Hank up with someone as a way of making amends.

Ronnie gave her mother a bright smile. "Your little chickadee had to fly the coop sometime."

Mom shook her head. "Who will help you with this matchmaking business? Are you going to the Buckboard next weekend? It's so loud there. I should go with you."

"Uh…" *Oh, no.* Forget that she was waffling about matchmaking beyond Wade. Saturday night at the Buckboard was her girls' night out. No mamas allowed. Before Ronnie could formulate a reply, her brothers crowded into the kitchen.

Hank tsked. "You do realize all Great Aunt Didi's clothes are still in the closet of your bedroom."

Ronnie nodded. That was an easy enough fix.

"And the bathroom faucet doesn't work." David frowned. "This place is a money pit. Are you sure you can afford it?"

"I'll get by." Ronnie shooed them toward the front door. "Quit *lollygagging*." A favorite phrase of Great Aunt Didi's. "I know there are more boxes outside, and it's supposed to rain later." The clouds were already moving over the plains.

David passed through the open door to do as she'd asked. He paused. "Hey, Wade and Ginny Keller are here." Then he moved out on the porch, followed by Hank.

"Wade?" Ronnie glanced around her living room. Although she was fond of the place, it was dated. And pink. Faded pink. She was used to it as the work-in-progress it was, but she worried what Wade might think.

"Hi." Ginny stepped inside tentatively, carrying a vase of red carnations and glancing around with wide eyes. She wore what looked like her Sunday best—a bright green dress beneath a yellow coat. "Grandma Mary sent us with flowers and food because Miss Ronnie is broke and sad."

Mom denied that even as she rushed forward to take the small vase of flowers Ginny was carrying.

"Miss Ronnie isn't broke." Wade entered. He wore dark blue jeans and a forest green shirt beneath his heavy blue jacket. "We brought food because Miss Ronnie's got too much to do on moving day and won't have time to make dinner. This is from Mary." He set down a picnic basket on the kitchen counter. "She made her chicken-and-broccoli casserole plus some other things. *We* brought you flowers." His voice boomed into the room.

That was one thing Ronnie appreciated about Wade. He had a voice that carried naturally. But she did notice an omission in his little speech.

"I'm not sad," she told Ginny, pointing at the flowers Mom had set on a coffee table. "It's a happy day."

"I'm the sad one." Mom waved to someone outside that Ronnie couldn't see, adding, "I see your friend Izzy on the sidewalk. I need to say hello." She probably wanted to make sure Izzy, who lived next door, helped keep an eye on Ronnie.

Doesn't Mom realize Izzy's on my side?
Ronnie sighed.

"Dad…" Ginny turned to Wade, brown braids swinging. She was beaming to beat the band. "Dad, can I go say hi to Lila?" She was one of Ginny's best friends and lived down the street.

Wade waggled a finger at his daughter. "Okay, but don't stay long."

Ginny darted out, leaving Wade and Ronnie alone.

Wade turned to Ronnie with an indecipherable look in his eyes.

If I stayed on the ranch, I wouldn't get looks like this from Wade.

Or anyone else for that matter, considering how Hank made sure she had no dating life.

Not that I'm looking to date. Or looking to date Wade.

Wade cocked a brow. "You got something to say?"

That arched brow. His intense regard. That curl to his lips.

His lips.

Ronnie's heart fluttered for no reason other than the curling of Wade's lips.

His smile broadened.

"Nope. Nothing to say." Mortified that he'd

caught her mooning over him—because he was one of her closest friends and off-limits—Ronnie spun around and returned to the kitchen, setting the picnic basket on the counter. "Tell Mary I really appreciate her thoughtfulness." She removed a casserole dish, cornbread muffins, and a pan of brownies from the picnic basket. She tucked the casserole into the refrigerator. Luckily, the one thing she and her mom had done when Didi passed in November was clean out the fridge.

She handed the picnic basket back to Wade, who was no longer smiling.

He's as nervous about being here as I am about his smile.

And she wasn't sure why.

In the small kitchen, Wade stood close to her. He shifted his weight on the salmon-colored linoleum, as antsy to bolt as a green-broke stallion.

She suddenly remembered her mission to find him a wife. "Do you have any plans for Saturday night?"

"I plan to stay at home." Wade shrugged, mouth quirking a bit, as if he fought a frown. But he didn't stop staring into Ronnie's eyes.

Her heart pounded a little faster. He was her kind of good-looking and she wasn't immune. "It's been a cold winter for you, Wade, and I predict it's going to be a cold spring."

His brow clouded.

"You won't be able to find a wife to keep you warm if you never leave the house."

"Ronnie Pickett." Wade leaned forward, invading her space. "What are you suggesting?"

His voice was no longer booming. She imagined what she heard was his bedroom voice—deep, gruff, capped off with an unflinching stare that was equal parts mischief and mayhem.

Oh my.

"I…uh…" She cleared her throat, trying not to give an inch. "I'm suggesting a night at the Buckboard."

"So you can fix me up with someone?" Wade straightened, crossing his arms over his chest.

Was she that transparent?

"Nope. Not at all." *Think, Ronnie. Think.* "This is your chance to prove to me that you can get a woman back in your life without my help."

Oh, that was good.

He scoffed, giving her that half smile of his she'd known so well back in junior high and high school, the one that said she wasn't putting anything over on him.

She nudged his shoulder playfully, not that he budged. "All you have to do is show up and ask a woman to dance, and I'll stop bothering you about becoming a client of mine."

That was even better.

"I don't need to prove anything to you, Ronnie." He was still half-smiling.

And her heart was still beating too fast. "No. But you want to, don't you?"

RONNIE PICKETT WAS as unsettling as an unexpected summer storm.

Wade stomped out Ronnie's door and headed for his truck, blaming his irritation on him being chosen by his mother to deliver a housewarming gift to Ronnie, despite Mom knowing Ronnie had set her matchmaking sights on him.

And then I bought her flowers.

He'd known that had been a bad idea, but he'd been unable to resist trying to lift her spirits. It would be hard for her to gain some independence from her close-knit family. He shouldn't have bothered. Because now he had Ronnie's dare to deal with, and he didn't have an excuse not to show. Dad had given him next weekend off.

Ronnie and that dare.

He hunched his shoulders, telling himself he did so because of the rising wind.

When he was in high school, he'd had no problem taking on dares from his foster brothers.

Wade, I dare you to ride that bull that gored a cowboy last weekend.

Wade, I dare you to rope that wily stallion.

Wade, I dare you to ask Ronnie Pickett to the junior prom.

That last dare… That had been an easy one to take. He'd been fascinated with Ronnie since they'd met in middle school.

Back then, he and Ronnie had both been out of school for a week—her because her volcano in the science fair had been overstocked with a combustion agent, had rocked the sprinkler system controls on the other side of the gymnasium wall and then flooded the school grounds, him because his parents had died. Someone thought it would be a good idea to put them into a special after-school pilot program to help them catch up on their studies. He'd been in eighth grade and she in sixth.

School aides had whispered around them the first few days. At first, he'd assumed all the whispering was about him. His paternal uncle and grandparents had declined to raise him. Everyone expected the same answer from his mother's side of the family since they'd washed their hands of his mother when she'd run off with his father. Wade had heard quiet conjecture about him being too much like his father to take in. But those school aides had also whispered about how everything little well-meaning Ronnie tried to accomplish ended in mayhem and destruction. They'd used phrases like "last straw" and "she's got to learn" and then hidden away the breakables in the room. The little sprite sat at the desk next to his, bent over her work, and sniffing occasionally as if trying not to cry. Earlier, he'd handed her a tissue and felt he should point out that she hadn't intended to cause any damage and that no one seemed mad at her. More like they thought she needed to learn to be more careful. But the sniffles and the air of gloom prevailed.

"We've got two choices, I suppose," Ronnie had unexpectedly spoken to him when they were left alone one afternoon. "Go around like the sad sacks they've made us out to be.

Or just keep livin' like we have been. I say, we live. There's no way back, anyway."

"I can't keep on living like I have been," Wade had snapped. "My parents are gone." He'd been moved to the D Double R as a stop-gap measure until the court and his family decided what to do with him. "At least you have parents."

"I like your voice," Ronnie said, not at all put out by his anger. She looked him right in the eye. "And I haven't seen you trip once or mess up a thing. My daddy says the Harrisons at the D Double R are good people and will keep you. That's what you want, isn't it? Someone who wants to keep you?"

It was. Wade's anger faded. It was the first time anyone had phrased things that way. It was as if the hammer that had been pounding in his temples non-stop, suddenly disappeared.

And all by a spitfire of a little girl. He'd been fond of her ever since. And he wasn't at all surprised that she'd grown up to be a spitfire of a young woman who still sometimes left havoc in her well-intentioned wake.

But that didn't mean Ronnie had him wrapped around her finger.

Ginny came running up the sidewalk from

her friend's house, waving her arms as if she'd sprouted wings. "Dad, can we live in town? On this street?"

"Live here?" Wade glanced back at Ronnie's washed-out pink house with its sagging front porch and crookedly hung mailbox, thoughts of the past dissipating.

He'd always aspired to live in a big, grand house, the one his father had always promised he'd have someday when he became a bronc riding champion. His father had died before that happened. And similarly, Wade had always promised Libby they'd live in such a house someday when he won enough. She'd died before that became a reality. He still carried guilt over it.

Wade was determined to own that large house on a matching piece of land, even if he was currently running in the red, having lost his sponsors when he lost his winning touch riding stock.

And then there was that college fund he'd promised Ginny.

"We're not living in town." Wade walked to the driver's side of his truck, bidding farewell to the Pickett brothers, who were almost done unloading a single vehicle that had been carrying Ronnie's possessions, few as they seemed to be.

"See you Saturday night, Wade?" Ronnie leaned against the rickety porch railing, daring him to show at the Buckboard.

Wade shook his head and got in the truck. He wasn't the honky-tonk dancing type. Never had been. He'd been with Libby from age seventeen until age thirty. They hadn't spent much time at the Buckboard or places of its ilk. Libby had been a homebody.

"Is Miss Ronnie coming over for family poker night on Saturday?" Ginny climbed into the front seat. "Cool."

"She's not coming," he said gruffly, struck by a thought. "And you shouldn't be playing poker with me and the boys. Not if you want to be a lawyer."

"What am I supposed to do? Watch game shows with Grandma and Grandpa?" Ginny pressed her nose to the glass and waved to Ronnie. "If we lived in town, I could have more sleepovers with Lila."

"You girls have enough sleepovers." Although for the life of him, he couldn't remember the last one.

"Dad." His daughter injected the word with sarcasm. "We'd have more sleepovers

if I didn't have to go with you and the crew to the rodeo every weekend. I could go to movies with my friends, too."

He did feel guilty about that.

Wade spared her a glance. "As a kid, I was dragged to rodeos every weekend, and I never complained." Nor had he protested when he'd begun traveling to help manage rodeo stock for the D Double R after his parents died.

Ginny fell back against the seat with an exaggerated sigh. "I don't want to rodeo. I have rights, you know."

"You sound like you've already gone to law school." She was growing up way too fast.

She frowned at him. "Dad, if I was a lawyer, I'd be able to choose my own clothes."

"What's wrong with your clothes?" He glanced at her again, taking in her dress, the one she'd said was too fancy to wear to school.

"The last time you brought home clothes for me, it was a superhero dress."

He fell back against the seat in mock horror. "You love superheroes."

"Dad." There was that heavy sigh again. "I loved them when I was a kid."

You're ten!

Wade washed a hand over his face, all

humor evaporating. "Next thing you'll be telling me is that you want the keys to the truck to drive into town on Saturday night." To go to the Buckboard and dance with no-good cowboys.

"Why wouldn't you let me?" His little girl scoffed. "You don't ever use the truck on Saturday nights."

Wade scoffed back at her. "Lots you know. I'm going to the Buckboard this weekend."

"With Miss Ronnie?" Ginny perked up.

Wade felt a moment of panic. "Yes."

"Nice." Ginny waved at the Halyard twins riding their bikes in the parking lot of their church.

"There's nothing nice about it." Panic morphed into desperation. He needed more separation between himself and Ronnie, not less. "I'm not dating Miss Ronnie. I'm not dating anyone."

"Dad." Ginny turned her big brown eyes his way. She looked nothing like Libby, and he felt guilty about that, too. "I miss Mom. But when I'm a lawyer in Oklahoma City, you'll be lonely. And I like Miss Ronnie."

It was Wade's turn to sigh.

Because there was no use arguing when the world and Miss Ronnie were against him.

"THANKS FOR HELPING me unpack, Izzy." Ronnie set a cookie jar decorated with roses on the kitchen counter, making a mental note to fill it—and cookie plates for the neighbors—soon.

"You're doing me a favor." Izzy sorted Ronnie's collection of cookbooks by size in a cupboard in the corner. "Della is with her dad until supper. It gets lonely when she's gone." Izzy had been a mouse while married to Mike. She was slowly rebuilding her life and her confidence. "Do you think you might find me a date? I mean…" Izzy blushed red down to her white-blond roots. "I'll sign up for your service and pay you, of course."

Ronnie's innards twisted.

One lie begets another.

People were taking her seriously. Even her brother David had asked Ronnie to keep her eye out for someone he'd find interesting. And Ronnie, being a nurturer, wanted everyone to be happy.

"I'll find you a date for Valentine's Day," Ronnie impulsively promised, although she had no idea how. "You don't have to give me money."

"No. I'll pay." Izzy's cheeks were slowly returning to their regular pale color. "What's the fee?"

Ronnie suppressed a groan.

She'd told the five women she'd recruited that their first month was free because she'd been confident that Wade would be snapped up by then.

"What's wrong?" Izzy's expression fell. "It's me, isn't it? I over-stepped the friendship line." She backed toward the living room.

"Oh, Izzy." Ronnie rushed to her friend, taking a gentle hold of her tense arms. "It's me. I started this business without thinking it through."

"That's not like you." Izzy's posture loosened. "When you were rally commissioner in high school, you made a digital presentation for every event. You had columns for profit and loss."

"And yet…" Ronnie raised a finger in the air. "Something always surprised me."

"In this case, it's a fee." Izzy smiled. "You've been matchmaking for free all this time. I bet it's hard to decide what to charge. You'll figure it out."

Everyone had such faith in her.

"I guess I'm really going to do this matchmaking thing." Saying it out loud meant she couldn't waffle anymore.

Izzy laughed. "Yes, I think you are."

CHAPTER FIVE

AFTER WORKING AT the school on Monday, Ronnie made the rounds through town looking for matchmaking prospects. Her efforts were no longer focused on finding a wife for Wade. She needed a pool of candidates, both male and female.

The first stop was Clementine Hardware, where she ordered five gallons of paint and circulated through the aisles, searching for singles while she waited for her order to be completed.

The pickings were almost as slim as her projected profit margin.

Dale Baxter was buying a plunger with a harried look on his cute face.

Ronnie smiled, made a mental note to approach him on another day when he was less stressed, and moved on.

Holly Radcliff was crying softly at the shovel display. She admitted to Ronnie that her cat had crossed over.

Ronnie hugged her, added her to the mental list of possible dates for an as yet undecided man, and moved on.

Nan Ingersoll was working the checkout counter. "How is Hank?" she said after a brief pass at small talk. "He's always too busy to return my… Anyway, I worry about him. Don't tell me," she rushed on. "I shouldn't ask. I'm the one who blew it with him. And wow. I… What an overshare." Nan blushed, unusually out of sorts. She handed Ronnie her receipt. "I just think…maybe it's time to stop dreaming about a life with Hank. And maybe you could help me find someone, so I'll get over him."

"Nan, I'm confused." Ronnie loaded her paint cans in her cart. "How many dates did you have with Hank?"

"Well, just the one." Nan was still blushing, glancing around, seemingly to make sure no one else heard. "But we were best friends in high school. And then one kiss and the man runs for the hills."

Whoa. This was information Ronnie had never heard. "I'm sorry. Of course, I'll keep my eye out for you."

Nan thanked her.

"Best friends," Ronnie muttered, vowing

to ask Hank about that bit of information as she hurried out to her little green Volkswagen Beetle to regroup. There were other places in town to go. The day was still young.

She shifted her efforts to the Buffalo Diner, parking in a slanted spot on Main Street a few doors away. Downtown Clementine could be like taking a step into the past. Amidst the newer buildings were remnants of the old. There was Jeannie's Hair Salon, located in an ancient white clapboard house rumored to have been built by the town's first doctor. Jeannie's was tucked in next to BreeZee's Second Hand Store, located in what used to be the county courthouse. The three-story red brick building was the tallest in downtown. Cooper Brown had started a distillery in what used to be the original jail. And Flicka's Floral was built on the site of the stables.

About twenty years back, the town council had redone the plain gray sidewalks in stained and stamped red concrete such that they now looked as if they were made of brick. They'd added benches for folks to stop and socialize, had planted trees that shaded everything in summer and had encouraged enterprising citizens to open up bars and eateries downtown. That had only annoyed Coronet Blankenship, whose family had run the Buffalo Diner for three generations and served the best pecan pie this side of the Mississippi. Or so Coronet always claimed.

Ronnie poked her head inside the Buffalo Diner, looking to see if anyone single and unattached was grabbing a burger or slice of pecan, but the dinner crowd was comprised of families and retirees. She waved to Coronet and then scurried next door to Clementine Coffee Roasters because Brown's Brewery was closed on Mondays.

"High schoolers," she muttered as she paid for a pound of freshly ground coffee.

Teenagers sat at every table—phones out, laptops open—concentrating on homework or social media despite the loud coffeehouse music that erased all coherent thought from Ronnie's stressed-out brain.

"This is a surprise." Bess appeared beside her, having just received a cup of coffee to go. "Don't tell me you came here looking for the foundation of your team." She glanced around, nose wrinkling before returning her attention to Ronnie. "You won't find your standout in this crowd."

"I'd settle for a utility player," Ronnie said dejectedly. "What are you doing here?"

Bess frowned, pulling Ronnie away from the nearest table. "I just got out of a meeting with school administration, and I needed to decompress before I went home. The school is planning to cut the rodeo team from the program next year."

"Oh, Bess. I'm so sorry." Bess lived for that program. "Why?"

"The town is growing, enrollment is up, and they want to construct a vocational building where our arena and corrals are. They've lined up donations for building a machine shop and computer lab. They also want to construct a 'family and consumer sciences' room where kids can learn to cook and balance a budget, among other things. None of which I can argue with, considering I can't cook or change my truck engine oil or build a website." Bess sipped her coffee. Her red hair was uncharacteristically windblown-looking… Or perhaps she'd tugged on it out of frustration.

Worry for her friend dampened Ronnie's own woes. "The rodeo team is an institution. Why isn't there room for all of these things? You have to fight for the team. What are you going to do?"

"I don't know." And for once, put-together, on-top-of-everything Bess looked at a loss.

She stared blankly at her coffee. "I'm still in the numb stage of grief."

"Do you want to go to the Buckboard and get a drink?" Ronnie checked the time on her phone. "It's still happy hour. You can decompress and I can surf for singles."

"Girl, you need to get out more." Bess smiled weakly. "On Mondays in the winter, the knitting club meets at the Buckboard. Singles avoid their knitting grandmas like the plague, including me."

Ronnie clapped her hand to her forehead. "How did I not know this?"

Bess shrugged. "Because your grandmother moved to Las Vegas after your grandpa died? And because your other grandparents live in Tulsa?"

"I suppose a good matchmaker should be up on this pertinent type of information." Not that Ronnie was happy about it. She'd planned to stop at the honky-tonk next.

"Excuse me." A man in his thirties came up to Ronnie. "Are you the matchmaker? Ronnie Pickett?"

Ronnie nodded.

"I'll leave you to building your team." Bess gave Ronnie a thumbs-up, clearly under the impression that Ronnie was being approached by a potential client.

There were few people Ronnie didn't know in town, but this man seemed one of them. He wasn't tall, didn't wear a cowboy hat or blue jeans, and didn't have the faint drawl of most east Oklahomans. In short, he didn't fit with her vision of matchmaking around rodeo and ranching. "Are you new in town? Looking for love?" Perhaps he liked ducks.

"Actually, I'm looking for a story." He hefted the strap of a laptop bag over his bright blue polo shirt. "I'm Zach Lyon from the *Valley Register*, the county newspaper. I came to do a piece on Clementine High School girls' basketball team. I was just having dinner next door when my waitress mentioned you and…" He paused as he dug into his laptop bag.

"And?"

"I'd like to buy you a cup of coffee." He straightened. "To interview you."

"Why would you want to interview me?"

"Because a modern-day matchmaker is fascinating." He pulled out a chair for her. "How do you like your coffee?"

"YOUR DINNER'S GETTING COLD." Wade's father came into the far corner of the ranch garage where Wade was putting in his daily training time.

"Just a few more minutes." Wade sat on the mechanical bull, practicing his bronc riding form—firm grip on the rigging, shoulders square, free hand high, hips to the ceiling, heels marking the bull at the neck. Every day, he lifted weights and practiced his bronc riding technique. It was vitally important to practice the bronc riding motions and cuing daily to keep his mind-body connection sharp.

The garage was huge—six bays each three car lengths deep. It was full of vehicles—those that ran and those that didn't—housed a workshop, served as storage for spare parts, maintenance supplies and personal items, and was the one place Wade came lately where he was practically guaranteed an hour of uninterrupted time.

"Let me do one last set." Wade dragged his heels back a little and quickly returned them to the start position—*Bang!* His heels pounded the mechanical bull. He drew them back a few inches more and swiftly extended them again—*Bang!* Then he hauled his heels nearly to the rigging, where he held on and returned them once more—*Bang!*

"Looking good, son."

"You know my timing's not been great." Wade hopped down. He'd been practicing riding technique off and on for over twenty minutes. His muscles felt taut and slightly fatigued. "Truth is, my timing has been off for the last two years."

"Grief and worry will destroy a man's concentration." Dad ran his hand over the battered flank of the mechanical bull. "You know, just because we encouraged you boys to take up the sport of rodeo doesn't mean you have to stay at it."

"Honestly? It keeps the memory of my dad alive." Wade couldn't remember the sound of his father's voice anymore. But he could remember the way he rode a bronc. Wade wiped the sweat from his brow with a hand towel. "And it feels like I left things unfinished career-wise." When he'd stopped competing to care for Libby.

"I suppose." Dad spoke slowly, deliberately. He had something on his mind.

Wade shook his head. "You said dinner was on the table."

"Your mother's meatloaf. It'll heat up fine in the microwave." Dad waved a hand absently. "I know you don't want to listen, but you should hear me out."

"No need. This is your retirement speech. You gave it to Chandler five years ago. And Griff two years ago." And countless other fosters before them. Wade bunched up the towel. "Save your breath, Dad. I'm not ready to hang up my spurs."

"There comes a time…" Dad began anyway.

Wade groaned.

"…when a man has to decide what takes priority in his life. You've got a fine little girl who doesn't want the rodeo or the ranch life."

"You and I both know that my ranch pay won't make a dent in law school tuition." Wade had done some searching on the internet last night, and the cost of a law degree was daunting.

Dad paid Wade no mind. "And having worked the stock end of rodeo with me for nearly two decades, you know better than most that when your heart isn't in it, the odds of injury during competition increase."

"My heart is in this." Wade couldn't get the words out fast enough. "I'm in great shape, Dad. I just need to work on my timing is all."

His father studied him a moment and then nodded. "I won't stand in the way of your decision. All I ask you to do is think about Ginny."

"I am." Wade slung his arm over Dad's shoulders. "I made an appointment with Dix to open an account for Ginny's college dreams." He gave the older man a squeeze. "Maybe it's time for you to think about re-evaluating your future. You know, you could foster teens again."

Dad shook his head. "We have Ginny now. She'll be a teenager soon. Raising wayward teenage boys around teenage girls isn't wise."

Although he agreed, Wade knew how important fostering was to his father. "Taking in wayward teens is your passion." Wade drew back. "It's as much your life's work as the rodeo business. Why didn't you tell me we were the reason you stopped? We could have moved into town." He'd be miserable but Ginny would be happy.

"The idea to retire from fostering came to us after Libby got sick." The lines around Dad's face seemed more pronounced, and his shoulders seemed to droop. "At that time and in the two years since she died, you needed us more than we needed to continue fostering. Besides, what does an old man who can barely work a cell phone have to offer a troubled teenage boy nowadays?"

A home. A family. Love.

Wade felt as if a heavy weight had been placed on his shoulders. "We need to talk about this." He didn't want to be the cause of his father's unhappiness.

"You're two years too late on that front, son." Dad cleared his throat. "Life changes. And I've just got to find balance in my life. Libby understood that. She wanted that for you, too."

Libby.

Wade followed Dad out of the garage at a much slower pace.

"I don't...want you...to be alone," Libby said to him in the last days before her passing.

"Libb... Honey..." He'd been too choked up to say more.

"There's a letter...in the nightstand." She'd struggled to fill her lungs with air. "Read it. When you're ready. You have...my blessing."

That letter...

In it, she'd given her blessing, all right.

To marry Ronnie.

"HAVE YOU BAKED something to thank Mary Harrison for the dinner she made you?"

Ronnie chose to ignore her mother while she was using the steamer on the living room wall to remove wallpaper. "Try scraping it again, Mom."

"What about thanking Mary?" Mom took hold of Ronnie's arm instead of using the scraping tool to pry off the steamy wallpaper. "Are you feeling okay? You've been pushing yourself hard since you moved in."

"I've been here two days, Mom. I'm fine." From three rungs up the ladder, Ronnie gestured toward the loose strip of wallpaper. "I have a lot on my mind is all." Like how could she find Wade a wife when it felt like the attraction between them was as hot as a live wire? Like how could she run a matchmaking service while working full-time?

And the worst of it was, Ronnie couldn't admit she'd lied about her plans to begin matchmaking. Not to anyone, including her mother. She'd look like a fool.

Her mother made a half-hearted attempt to scrape the wallpaper off, then gave up altogether. "Do you regret the move to town? You can always move back to the ranch."

"No, I can't. Switch with me, please." Ronnie climbed down from the ladder and handed her mom the steamer. She took the flat scraper, caught the loose corner of wallpaper and ran the scraper two feet beneath it. "Finally. Something's working."

Mom kept the steamer moving over the faded pink rose wallpaper. "What hasn't been working?"

"Other than my bathroom faucet? Matchmaking." Her latest business venture seemed destined to go the way of her jewelry-importing, plasticware-selling and cupcake-making businesses. "In the past two days, I've approached singles and asked them if they need help finding love. And do you know what they say?" Ronnie didn't wait for her mother to answer. "They say no. *No.*" It boggled the mind.

"Asking was your first mistake." Her mother climbed higher on the ladder and steamed the wallpaper nearest the ceiling. "No one wants to admit they need help, especially about something as personal as finding love."

"That makes sense, I suppose. Whenever I set people up before, I just told them who they should ask out without asking permission. I told Wade he needed my help. I didn't ask. But that didn't work, either."

Mom laughed. "You can be so bossy."

Ronnie half-smiled. "But do you know the weird part? Women are coming to me and asking for help. Not the other way around. We'll just be chatting, and they'll mention it in passing. *Oh, and by the way, if you find someone you think is right for me...*"

"Really?"

"Really." Ronnie nodded. "I'm beginning to think I should just hang out in public places more often."

"Ah. You have strong word of mouth, but right now, you're still something of a secret." Mom peeled back a corner of wallpaper and pulled. It tore into a little strip that caused her to groan.

They'd been doing a lot of groaning as they worked their way around the room. Nothing came off in even sheets.

Mom tossed the crumpled strip to the floor. "What you need, besides a stronger steamer, is a sign on a table at the Buckboard that says, 'The love doctor is in.'"

Ronnie chuckled. "That's embarrassing."

"You're starting a business. You need clients. You can't afford to coddle your pride or scare them away by asking."

"I'm starting a business..." The compulsion to admit to her mother that she hadn't exactly planned to start a business was strong. "And you want me to...do what exactly?"

"Advertise!" Mom worked the steamer. "You know what you need? Flyers to spread the word. And then a little poker chip or cute little business card. You give one to each party so they recognize each other."

"Like an invitation." That could work. "I could put the place and time of their arranged date on it, along with the date's first name and maybe a couple of topics of shared interest."

"Icebreaking conversation. Always a plus. You're so smart." Mom steamed her way into the corner. "Do we need to switch? You aren't scraping any wallpaper off."

"Oops. I forgot." Because suddenly, she was excited about matchmaking.

CHAPTER SIX

"THINGS ARE LOOKING up for the rodeo team's future." Bess showed up at Ronnie's house on Thursday night wearing her grubbies and a wide grin.

The wind howled outside, a cold counterpoint to Bess's laughter. February was moving in with a wintery vengeance.

"Bess, not three days ago, the rodeo team's future was grim." Ronnie had just finished cutting paint in the corners in the living room and bedrooms so all they had to do was roll the main walls and ceilings. "What changed?" She removed a paint lid and poured more Hint of Pink paint into a paint tray. The color was a variation of white with a tinge of pink to it in honor of Great Aunt Didi.

"The athletics department got wind of things." Bess picked up a new paint roller and spun it a few times. "Do you know how old the high school gymnasium is?"

"No clue." Her thoughts lately had been on Wade, and it was hard to focus on much else.

"Older than dirt if you believe Coach Thompson. He and his girls' basketball team have a chance to win state this year." Bess covered the roller in paint, sending it back and forth through the pan. She gave a maniacal laugh. "I've never been happier to sit in a staff meeting and listen to angry co-workers."

Ronnie took hold of a roller on a long pole, planning to use it to paint the ceiling. "It could take years to sort out what type of new building is put on your rodeo grounds."

"Yep." Bess made a zigzag pattern across the wall. "So, while I hunker down and let others duke it out on the school yard, what will you be doing?"

While Ronnie covered her roller in paint, she explained how she was changing matchmaking tactics. "As soon as the house is presentable, I'm going to hold a mixer for my clients." She began painting the ceiling.

"Geez. What a mess!"

"My mixer?" Ronnie turned, roller still pressed to the ceiling above her.

"No." Bess had paint on her arm, and her roller dripped on the drop cloth covering the old carpet. "I forgot to warn you that I'm a messy painter."

"Me too." As if to prove it, a drop of paint fell on Ronnie's forehead. She lowered the roller and rubbed the paint away with her forearm. But that only smeared the paint on her arm, which she tried to remedy, but in doing so, she lost her balance and plopped her foot in the paint tray. The tray in turn toppled over as if on cue. With a sigh, she removed her paint-coated shoe, along with the other one. At least, her family wasn't here to witness her clumsiness. "Drip all you like, Bess. That's why I'm painting before I get new flooring. Drips and dunks don't matter."

"Good to know." Bess wiped her arm clean with a cloth. "Have you heard anything from that reporter? I bet his article gets you clients."

"He's going to run something this weekend, I think." Ronnie continued rolling the ceiling.

"Not that I want to throw a wrench in your plan..." Bess pointed to the ceiling. "Did you want to paint it the same white-pink as the walls?"

Ronnie glanced up at the ceiling. "You know, I asked myself that when I bought the paint. But I thought it would be easier to paint it all one color. And it's not like I haven't seen it done in magazines. What do you think?"

Bess shrugged. "Bold choice." And kept on painting.

They made short work of the small living room.

And then the doorbell rang.

"That must be our pizza." Ronnie opened the door.

Griff stood on her porch holding a pizza box. "Surprise."

Bess frowned at him. They had history. And it wasn't the good kind.

"The pizza delivery dude broke down on the corner." The cowboy smiled easily, as if unbothered by the trail of women he'd left in his bad dating wake. "And me, being a Good Samaritan, offered to help him out."

"Dad made him." Ginny snuck past Griff and into the house. "He's next door delivering Miss Izzy's pizza." She glanced around at the walls and paint supplies. "Is that pink? I want to live on this street and paint my walls purple and get pizza on Thursdays."

"Don't forget the ceilings, girlfriend," Ronnie murmured, earning a high five from Bess.

"Ginny, don't tell Grandma Mary about

Pizza Thursdays. She doesn't approve of pizza but once a month." Griff followed Ginny inside without closing the door behind him. He surveyed their work. "You need to put more paint on your rollers, ladies. Your technique is streaky."

Ronnie took a critical look around. She could see the zigzag pattern Bess had made and the lines of her own roller in the ceiling. "You're right. Thanks."

"We're fine. That's what second coats are for," Bess said testily.

"Fair enough." Griff made for the door. "Just because I've got experience doesn't mean you should shoot the messenger."

"Hey, Griff." Ronnie hurried after him, grabbing hold of his shoulder before he could flee. It wasn't often she had someone knowledgeable in home renovations in her realm. "You don't happen to know how to install a bathroom faucet, do you?"

"I do." Griff turned, giving Ronnie his trademark grin. "But my price for doing so is pretty steep. Two slices of pepperoni pizza and a couple of beers."

"Ha!" Bess shook her finger at the man who'd she'd clashed with on their one and only date. "No deal. We ordered cheese pizza and we have no beer."

"Hang on a minute." Ronnie didn't want to turn away skilled labor, especially if it was practically free. "Can we renegotiate?"

"Not today." Wade filled the doorway with those broad shoulders that a woman could lean on. Or maybe it was his no-nonsense expression that said he wouldn't run when times got tough. Or—

"Ronnie?" Wade came to her. "Didn't you hear me?"

"Nope." It pained her to admit it.

Wade stared at her the way he had on Sunday when they'd stood too close in the kitchen.

Ronnie suppressed a shiver, not wanting to interpret what that meant.

Wade lifted her hand, inspecting the paint on her arm. Releasing it, he rubbed at the paint on her forehead with his thumb, reset the tray and then glanced toward her shoes near the paint tray. It was too much to hope that he'd think one of her shoes had been stylishly dipped as a fashion choice.

Wade moved away from her. Breathing easier, Ronnie reminded herself that she was his friend and his matchmaker, not his match.

"We'll give you one slice of pizza and half a beer," Bess was saying, lost in negotiation with Griff.

"Sorry, ladies," Wade said, drawing Ginny away from the wet wall. "We can't help today. We're due home. We just came into town to pick up medicine from the feed store and—"

"Me," Ginny piped up. "But we can come back tomorrow."

"We?" Griff laughed. "Do you know how to change out a faucet, little lawyer?"

"No. But I'm willing to learn." Ginny put her hands on her hips. "When I'm a lawyer for real, I'm gonna need to know about a lot of things."

"It's a date then," Ronnie said.

What did I just say?

"A date?" Wade's eyes widened, turning to look at Griff, who looked similarly shell-shocked.

"One friend helping out another, I mean," Ronnie quickly reassured them, laughing nervously. "I'll expect you both here tomorrow. No one tackles plumbing alone."

"We're coming to town again tomorrow? I'll ask Lila if I can spend the night." Ginny seemed like this plan was preferable to shadowing Griff under the bathroom sink. "I'm so glad the pizza man's truck broke down."

"Me too," Wade said, although not believably or in his usual easygoing voice.

After they left, Bess and Ronnie rolled the paint with a keener eye to detail. With bright walls, clients looking for love, and a working faucet on the horizon, Ronnie could actually believe things were going to work out for her on all fronts.

Bess set her roller in the paint pan and then straightened, pressing her fingers into the small of her back. "When are you going to make flyers for your business? You need to give folks something to think about."

"This week." Ronnie set her roller down next to Bess's and told her about the idea her mother had given her about printing cards. "And speaking of timing... When are you going to forgive Griff?"

"Never." Bess frowned. "That man takes nothing seriously, including relationships."

Ronnie wasn't sure that was true. She'd always thought there was more to Griff—and all of the fosters the Harrisons had taken in over the years—than met the eye. But she knew from experience that Bess felt differently—about Griff, at least.

"Can you spare me another hour to paint the bedrooms?" Ronnie asked instead.

"Sure. I've nothing better to do on a Thursday night." Bess carried their rollers toward the hallway. "Your house is going to look great for the mixer."

Ronnie followed her, juggling the paint tray and a paint can. "We'll be doing your house next."

"Nah. You'll be too busy helping people find love." Trust Bess to drill right to the point. "Just remember that I'm not looking."

"Way to burst my bubble. I had the perfect match for you, too. A tall cowboy with a full-time job who loves the rodeo, gives back to the community and wants a family."

Bess gave a shout of laughter. "Ronnie, you and I both know that man doesn't exist."

"RONNIE PICKETT, you're a woman who knows her way around the hardware store."

Wade rolled his eyes at Griff's schmoozing as he stood outside Ronnie's little bathroom on Friday night, trying hard not to stare at Ronnie and mostly failing. He'd forgotten how easy it was to be with her and how easy she was on the eyes. And if he wasn't careful, he'd forget that his wife—who he'd loved dearly—deserved his loyalty. He appreciated that Libby had wanted him to move on and that she'd wanted him to find happiness again. But a man needed boundaries.

Griff sat on the edge of the bathtub. He surveyed the tools Ronnie had laid out on the bathroom floor as if she was stocking a surgical tray for the operating room. There had to be thirty items spread across a ratty-looking old towel.

"Do you know what all these tools are for?" Wade wasn't sure if he was asking Griff or Ronnie, although he was looking at Ronnie.

"I don't. And that's the exciting part." Griff rubbed his hands together, suddenly gleeful.

"I watched a DIY video on my lunch break." From her position just inside the bathroom door, Ronnie stared at Wade, smiling like she'd just won a barrel racing competition. "And then I bought everything they suggested, thankfully the hardware store was well stocked. I had some time on the way home." Her smile broadened.

Something shifted inside of Wade, something warm and unexpected.

I didn't think I'd be so excited about assisting Griff to change out a bathroom faucet.

But he was. And it was all because of her smile.

Her smile.

Ronnie's smile.

Wade's shoulders stiffened.

Her smile isn't for me.

It hadn't been since she'd told him to look Libby's way, not hers. And his instincts told him no blessing or encouragement from his wife would change that.

But Wade couldn't look away.

Ronnie radiated an optimism that he envied, like she wasn't worried that her match-making business might crash and burn or that Griff would botch up this faucet install. If Wade had her sunny outlook on life, he wouldn't worry about winning purses or paying for Ginny's college education.

Ronnie knelt and picked up a tool with a round attachment, breaking the spell between them. "You know what would be fun at a cocktail party? Guessing what each of these tools is used for. Can you imagine the answers?" She glanced up at Wade, all sass and vinegar.

Wade's mouth went dry.

"I can tell you what most of them are called," Griff surprised Wade by saying. "My biological dad was a plumber by trade until he quit to cowboy. I used to tag along with him on calls sometimes. If he asked for something and I didn't know what it was, it didn't go over well." He sniffed.

Silence descended upon the bathroom. Wade was reminded that there were worse things than being orphaned.

"My great aunt Didi worked for the electric company." Ronnie dove into the void, voice filled with flowers and rainbows. "Back in the day, she climbed up power poles with those spikes on her boots. She fought for that job because it paid more than just being a secretary." Ronnie set the unusual tool back in its place.

Wade was reminded that Ronnie worked as a secretary. He hoped she wouldn't decide to switch careers and become an electric company technician. He'd worry about her more than he already did.

More than I already want to.

"Sounds like ol' Didi could have ridden a bull." Griff had dug into the faucet box. He fit the pieces over the pre-drilled holes in the counter. "How many tools do you think I'll need, Wade? I bet I can install this faucet with four tools."

"Three," Wade said automatically, because he was competitive. "If you can't, you buy the beer tomorrow night."

"That's a bet." Griff turned the faucet upside down, fiddling with the hose connectors. "Of course, if I do it in two, the beer is on your dime."

"I don't care how many tools you use." Ronnie was smiling at them both, not that Griff seemed to notice. "I'll be ecstatic to brush my teeth in here rather than the kitchen sink. I ordered pepperoni pizza. How long do you think this will take?"

"With or without problems?" There were always snags with home improvements. Just like there were always snags with things involving Ronnie. That dare she'd laid down for tomorrow at the Buckboard came to mind.

"Without." Griff rifled through the cardboard faucet box. "If we get into trouble, we can always call Dad. Oops. No, we can't. He took the B team to a rodeo this weekend."

"There is no B team. It's just a small rodeo." Wade, Griff and Tate were staying back this weekend. Wade glanced at Ronnie. He wasn't regretting being in town so far.

"A team. B team. No team." Griff shrugged. "Potato. *Potatoh.*"

Someone knocked on Ronnie's front door.

"I bet that's the pizza." Ronnie hurried down the hall.

"Dude." Griff checked something under the sink. "You and Ronnie have a vibe going on."

"There's no vibe," Wade said, rushing to deny it automatically.

"Oh, there's a vibe."

The front door opened, and Ronnie said, "Oh," as if surprised. "Zach. What are you doing here?"

"Zach?" Griff sent a mischievous look at Wade. "The plot thickens."

It did indeed, and Wade didn't like surprise plot twists. He was down the hallway and in the living room in a handful of steps.

Ronnie stood in the doorway, one hand on the doorknob, one hand on the doorframe. And if there was a clearer way of saying with body language that she wasn't letting whoever was at the door inside, Wade didn't know what it was.

He came up behind her, hoping to provide emotional reinforcement.

"I came by because I wanted to deliver the news to you in person." Zach looked like some random city dude in khakis and a gray polo shirt. What was he doing in Clementine?

"The first article about you has had more on-line reads than any other we've posted in the past year."

"The first article?"

Wade rested a hand on Ronnie's shoulder.

Ronnie gave Wade's hand a look and then Wade a look, and then she shifted around until his hand fell away. She briefly explained how Zach was doing a series of articles on her starting up a matchmaking business.

"Meaning the whole world is watching to see if your business succeeds or not?" Wade blurted without meaning to.

Ronnie nodded. "Isn't that great?" Although the way she said it implied it might not be.

"It's fantastic." Zach didn't catch on to her nuance. He gave Ronnie a smile that said he was going to maybe enjoy this assignment more than he had a right to.

"Hi, Zach. I'm Wade." And if he was feeling more than a little territorial, it was only because Ronnie had been his friend for so long.

"You must be a client of Ronnie's. I'd love to get your thoughts on her matchmaking services."

Wade huffed. "I'm—"

"He's requested privacy." Ronnie grabbed hold of Wade's arm and gave him a tug. "All my work is confidential. I hope you understand, Zach."

"Sure. Yeah. No problem." Zach smiled at Ronnie as if he had a good chance of taking her on a date.

Something akin to contempt gathered in Wade's chest.

Someone ran up the porch steps behind Zach. It was the pizza delivery boy, the same one from last night.

"How's that truck of yours running?" Wade asked him, paying for the pizza despite Ronnie's protests and Zach's curious stare.

"It's not running." The kid gestured to an overly large four-door sedan. "I had to borrow my mom's car. It's more of a gas guzzler than my truck."

"Here's hoping you don't have to drive far with the pizzas tonight." Wade tipped the kid well. And then he took possession of the pizza and stood between Ronnie and Zach. "Ready to eat?"

"I am!" Griff called from the bathroom.

"Who's that?" Zach asked, looking more than a little confused. There were probably more men in Ronnie's house than he'd expected.

"That's…another client. I'm a little busy tonight," Ronnie told Zach. "Why don't you text me, and we'll set up our next interview. I'm really excited about it. And for you, of course."

For you?

How well did Ronnie know this guy? Wade wasn't a matchmaker, but he could tell Zach wasn't the right guy for Ronnie. She needed someone who could stand up to her chutzpah.

Wade carried the pizza to the kitchen while Ronnie walked the reporter out. He went in search of dishes, but all he found were paper plates and napkins.

Ronnie marched into the kitchen. "What was all that posturing about? Zach is a nice guy and—"

"I thought I'd save you some trouble." Wade put a slice of pepperoni on a paper plate and handed it to her. "He wants to ask you out."

Ronnie opened her mouth. Closed it. And then said, "So? Why do you care?"

"Definitely a vibe," Griff whispered, cutting between Wade and Ronnie and reaching for a slice of pizza.

"Between Zach and me? What's the big

deal?" Ronnie rolled her eyes. "I ask again, Wade. Why do you care if Zach asks me out?"

"Why do I…?" Wade closed the pizza box on Griff's hand. "Isn't that crossing the line? He's a reporter. You're his subject."

"I'll handle it." Ronnie passed her plate to Griff, who turned his back to her and mouthed to Wade, *Vibe*.

Wade reached in the refrigerator for a beer, handed it to Griff and pushed him out of the kitchen, leaving him alone with Ronnie.

"What is going on?" Ronnie put her hands on her hips. "You know I work with kids. I can sense when someone is whispering secrets around me."

Wade thrust out his jaw. "We're both worried about you and this reporter. It's random, him showing up like that on a Friday night unannounced. Just doesn't sit well with me. Best keep your eye on him."

"I can take care of myself." The volume of Ronnie's response was out of proportion with the rest of their conversation.

Wade frowned. "You were my wife's best friend. Is it wrong to worry about you or give you some friendly advice?"

"There's advice," she said, still using that

loud voice and poking his chest. "And there's what you did. You gave me an order."

"I didn't." Did he?

Griff appeared in the kitchen doorway, grinning. "Did I come at a bad time for seconds?"

"No," Ronnie said at the same time that Wade said, "Yes."

"Thank you, Ronnie." Griff elbowed Wade aside and filled his plate with two more slices. "I'm not a fan of cold pizza." He returned to the living room, raising his voice so Ronnie could hear. "Or of fights at the dinner table."

"Let's not fight." Ronnie laid a hand on Wade's arm. "We're cranky because we haven't eaten."

Wade knew that wasn't the case. But she was being gracious, so he relented.

Griff had taken up residence on the wingback chair, the pink one that was partially draped in a yellow, flowered sheet. Wade and Ronnie sat on the small love seat, which was covered in the matching flowered sheet.

Vibe, Griff mouthed when Ronnie bent her head over her plate, teasing him the way he had when they were kids, Wade wanting to tackle him and make him take it back.

After they ate, Griff finished up the faucet

install with surprising speed. Wade was astonished that the thing didn't leak.

"It's in my blood," Griff told him, admiring Ronnie's tools one more time before they left. "And it took me three tools, so I guess I'm buying beer this weekend."

"At the Buckboard?" Ronnie pounced on the opportunity. "You know, I dared Wade to dance with someone there tomorrow night."

"I didn't know this." There would be no living with Griff on the drive back to the ranch. His grin practically covered his whole face.

"Are you going to invite that reporter fella?" Wade asked, tamping down his annoyance.

"I might," Ronnie said with more than her usual sass.

Wade tried real hard not to frown. "Why invite him? So you can provide Zach with a photo opportunity of your clients?"

"It's important that he sees me successfully helping people find love." She swatted his arm when he rolled his eyes. "If he writes about my triumphs, it might give hope to someone who's given up on love or tried those online apps and failed."

"Let's leave him out of this tomorrow," Wade said.

Ronnie looked at him funny but nodded.

And even though Wade knew her business was none of his business, when it came to this reporter fella, he wasn't backing down.

CHAPTER SEVEN

"ARE THESE FLYERS for your new business, Ronnie?" Bess picked one up off the table at the Buckboard on Saturday night and read aloud the words Ronnie had memorized, "Hey, all you singles looking for love! Do you work in the rodeo or on a ranch? Are you a fan of rodeo and everything cowboy—or cowgirl—related but too busy to find love? Let Ronnie Pickett save you time and sharpen Cupid's aim. Special pricing and perks for signing up before Valentine's Day."

Ronnie was rather proud of that flyer and of the colorful business cards on order to give to her clients when they were meeting for the first time.

"Your flyer is heavy on the cheese." Allison burst her bubble as she leaned over to peer at the stack of flyers. The ends of her long auburn hair brushed the tabletop. "What are the prices and perks?"

"I'm guessing free." Bess looked like she was trying hard not to smile.

Ronnie snatched the flyer from Bess and returned it to the neat stack on the table in their regular booth. "I'm waiving the sign-up fee and only charging what the popular dating apps charge for the first thirty days. Love is a cutthroat business."

"Maybe that's why your matchmaking worked best when it was free." Jo tousled her short brown hair, which was still damp. She trained horses and had obviously showered before she arrived. "It wasn't a business. It was from your heart. Is Izzy coming tonight?"

"No. She couldn't find a babysitter." Ronnie tried hard to hold on to her optimism. "And about my *hobby*… There's only so much free you can do before you run out of couples wanting you to shepherd them toward the altar." No sooner were the words out of Ronnie's mouth than her friends gave her dubious looks. "I… I don't know where that came from."

Her staunchly single friends stared at her as if they assumed her statement was fact.

Ronnie scrambled ahead, adopting damage control mode. "I don't know why I said it that way." As if she was starting a matchmaking business and ready to charge for the service.

"Ronnie..." Bess began.

"I'm asking my friends for their unwavering support at this challenging time," Ronnie said quickly. "I remember when Jo first started her horse training business and had doubts. We all supported her. I'm just asking the same thing."

The women gave what seemed like reluctant nods.

Ronnie glanced around the Buckboard. Cowboys and cowgirls were starting to enter in increasing numbers, mostly regulars but also a sprinkling of new faces. The bar itself was rumored to have been an old dance hall decades ago. The bar nearly ran the length of the place, from the front to the dance floor in the back. The decor was rustic barnwood and antlers. And the atmosphere was "come as you are."

During the week, the Buckboard served a nice array of burgers and sandwiches garnished with curly sweet potato fries and a tasty garlic dipping sauce. But Saturday nights were made for dancing. Currently, Karen Hartford was teaching line dancing basics to a small group. At seven, there'd be an hour of line dancing, which was what Ronnie and her friends came for. No partner required. At eight, the band would begin to play, and since they always sprinkled their playlist with slow songs, that was when Ronnie and her friends stopped dancing.

Ronnie put on her brightest smile. "This will work. Everyone who comes in here is looking for love."

"Except us." Bess laughed.

True.

"Except cowboys like Evan Thomas." Jo shook her head, pointing to the young man. "He's still besotted with Marjorie Masters, and she and her family moved away seven years back."

Also true.

Allison shrugged, drawing her long auburn hair over one shoulder. "Except for most young ranch hands, who are looking for a stolen kiss, not a potential bride."

Sad but true.

"We can see you've got your work cut out for you." Bess summarized what Ronnie's friends seemed to be feeling—the opposite of optimism.

"I know your hesitation comes from a place of love. I know none of you wants to see me hurt." That was a continued theme in her life—from Ronnie's family to Wade to her besties. "But…are you going to help me or not?" Ronnie gave her friends a stern look. "All I need you to do is circulate and ask people if they're single and looking for love. Then give them my flyer." Because Ronnie couldn't follow her mother's advice.

She needed dates for people. The five women she'd recruited were getting antsy and Ronnie had to have more bodies in the pipeline. So to speak.

Her friends exchanged wary glances but then gave Ronnie a collective thumbs-up.

The group set about working the rapidly filling room.

Ronnie started with a table of what she'd call hard sells. Four women who were younger than Ronnie and far less cordial. "Ladies, you may have heard I'm taking my matchmaking talent to a more formal plane."

"We heard." Evie Grace was the iciest of the four ice queens. She cut Ronnie off before she could get through her pitch. "Do we look like we need help in the love department?"

Ronnie took her time looking over the gals—from Evie Grace's silver highlights with purple tips to Mandy's too-tight bun to

Fern's mile-high teased hair to Annie Sue's thick, fake eyelashes, from their frilly blouses to their brand-new blue jeans. She even leaned back a tad to check out their footwear. Those four- to six-inch boot heels had never seen the working side of a ranch.

I should just move along.

But what she also saw at the table were four women with hope in their eyes. And wasn't that what she was selling? Hope for a happily ever after?

So, Ronnie tried again. "Ladies, how much would you pay for two or three dates a month with some handsome cowboys? Men who meet your discerning standards. Men who you've never dated before. Men who live beyond the small confines of Clementine."

Annie Sue blinked her very thick black semi-circle lashes…and didn't say no.

Fern shifted in her seat.

"Um…" Mandy glanced toward Evie Grace, as if asking for permission to admit she was interested in what Ronnie had to offer.

"Move along." Evie Grace waved Ronnie off.

Ronnie stood her ground. "But—"

"You don't get it." Evie Grace should have gone into the military. She had the kind of demeanor that a drill sergeant envied. "We four... We're *friends*. Nothing—not a job or a man—is going to separate us. We're Clementine folk. Forever."

Her loyal friends may have made sounds of assent, but they were far from boisterous displays of support.

Ronnie backed away, caught Mandy's eye and made the *call me* gesture, earning the wrath of Evie Grace. She scurried on to the next table. And although she didn't meet with exuberant welcome, Ronnie did manage to pass out a few flyers over the next twenty minutes.

Ronnie's matchmaking posse didn't have much more luck than she did.

"I stink at selling love, Ronnie," Bess admitted. "I had two cowboys laugh at me when I asked them if they were interested in romance." She stared longingly at the dance floor where the line dancing was about to begin.

"Likewise. See those ladies over there giving me bad looks?" Jo gestured to a booth in the corner where a trio of cowgirls Ronnie didn't recognize sat devouring a platter of sweet potato fries with their white wine. "Apparently, I gave your flyer to someone's boy-friend at another table."

"Ouch." Ronnie turned to Allison. "How'd you do?"

"Don't ask." Allison set her pile of wrin-kled flyers on the table. "Maybe Izzy can hand out the leftover flyers to feed store cus-tomers?"

"Well…" Ronnie had run into a roadblock with Earl, the feed store owner. "I'm only al-lowed to post a flyer on the bulletin board. I appreciate the effort." She only hoped Hank would come through for her and recruit his friends for possible matchups.

"Enough matchmaking." Bess rolled up her shirt sleeves. "It's been a long week. Can we dance now?"

Ronnie nodded.

The four friends went to stand on the dance floor. Ronnie was hoping for the Electric Slide first. It was her favorite.

Forty-five minutes later, laughing and nearly danced out, the women returned to their booth and ordered drinks, including a non-alcoholic lemonade for Ronnie.

"I'm splurging on sweet potato fries with extra garlic dipping sauce." Bess settled back in the booth. "I wouldn't if there was a possibility of me finding true love tonight, Ronnie. But I see the same cowboys that come every week."

"I could do something about that," Ronnie said, spending a moment daydreaming of a reality where cowboys beat a path to her matchmaking door.

"I value our friendship more than your services," Bess said. "Plus, I'm getting sweet potato fries."

"Hey. Is that Wade at the bar?" Jo pointed. "I can't remember the last time I saw him down here."

Turning, Ronnie's heart skipped a beat, because it was Wade! After last night's bickering about Zach, she'd wondered if he was going to show.

And surely, this compensated for the lack of matchmaking sign-ups, because Wade looked like he'd docked himself at the bar with an anchor. He wasn't going to dance even if his foster brothers were. Tate was already flirting with a redhead sitting at the bar. Griff was exchanging interested looks with a brunette at a table in the middle of the room.

Ronnie carried her lemonade to the bar, taking a seat on the stool to the right of Wade.

Turning his head toward her, Wade cocked his brows. "Still a teetotaler?"

"Alcohol is such a waste of time. It clouds the mind at night and makes you slow in the morning."

"Is that so?" He made a show of sipping his beer. "I always thought it made for slow goodnight kisses and lazy mornings in bed."

Wowzer.

It took effort, but Ronnie ignored his innuendo and kept her game face on. "I can't help but notice that you aren't checking out the available ladies." His back was to the room.

"Slow down. I'm quenching my thirst."

"Griff and Tate are already on the move." Ronnie pointed them out. "Drinks are portable, you know."

His shoulders stiffened. "Doesn't mean I won't find a dance partner later."

Ronnie leaned in, touching her shoulder to his. "I miss Libby, too."

He gave a curt, almost imperceptible nod, swallowing.

Shoulder to shoulder, she could feel his warmth seeping into her. This close, she could smell his woodsy aftershave. She wanted to stay where she was. She wanted him to curl his arm around her. And…and that wouldn't do. She straightened. "Libby wouldn't want you to be lonely."

"I know." Wade stared into the bottom of his half-empty beer glass and said huskily, "We shouldn't be talking about Libby on a Saturday night."

"And especially not if you want someone to date you. Talk of Libby isn't allowed until several dates in." Ronnie glanced around the bar, looking for possible matches for him. She pointed out a woman with softly highlighted brown hair. "How about her? She has a nice smile."

The woman laughed at something another woman said, guffawing so hard she snorted. Twice.

"Pass," Wade said, looking less sad.

Ronnie's gaze traveled around the room once more. "The brunette with the pixie cut seems down-to-earth."

"Griff got there first." Wade nodded toward his foster brother, who slipped into a seat next to the woman.

Ronnie was feeling a little bit desperate, running out of candidates she thought Wade might be attracted to. He needed someone the opposite of Libby—livelier, more outgoing, a woman willing to bring Wade out of the shell he'd hidden himself in when his true love had died.

The drummer onstage began to play a lively tempo, perfect for the Two-Step. His bandmates milled about the stage, strapping on guitars and adjusting microphones.

Wade rested an elbow on the bar and looked at her. "I see someone I can dance with."

"Really? Point her out to me." Ronnie slid off her seat and rose on her toes to look around.

Wade took her hand and pointed her index finger at herself.

"What? No." Ronnie's heart beat a little faster. She tugged her hand free. "The band is starting the couples segment." The energy from the line dancing crowd had been dispelled, and the first round or so of drinks consumed. It was time for people to pair up and dance.

That made her nervous, as did the fact that her hip was touching his thigh.

"You know I don't dance slow." Not with anyone.

"You want to throw me into the deep end of the pool before I've taken off my water wings?" Wade tsked, a mischievous glint in his eyes that wiped away the last of the sadness. "Have pity on me, Ronnie. Or all deals are off."

Deals. She needed to make some. But... Wade was her priority.

"All right. I'll dance with you," she said a bit breathlessly, not sure if it was desperation or attraction making her heart thump so. "But this doesn't count toward our bet."

Wade claimed Ronnie's hand and led her to the dance floor. The closer to the space, the harder her heart pounded. She wasn't just desperate or attracted. She was desperately attracted to him. This was horrible. She wasn't what Wade needed. They were friends and always had been. Love wasn't what she was looking for.

And yet, a part of her was thrilled to be dancing with him.

Wade spun her smoothly into his arms as the rest of the band joined the drummer in the notes of a familiar love song.

Over in her regular booth, Bess, Jo, and Allison watched, jaws hitting the floor.

"You're trembling," Wade said into her left ear.

"I'm not." Ronnie clenched her fingers, trying to stop what he'd noticed but just making it worse, because now she was clinging to him. She forced herself to loosen her grip. "I'm nervous because I'm breaking one of my own rules."

He drew back to look at her with those brown eyes that she just knew took note of everything. "Rules? What rules?"

She gave a little half-shrug and a meek answer, "I don't dance."

Amusement flashed in his eyes. "That's not true. I saw you line dancing when we came in."

"I don't dance *with men*." She looked away, gaze searching for a distraction. And she quickly found one. "Oh, Wade. A blonde just came in. She looks nice."

"Ronnie." Wade brought her closer, spun her faster, all the while speaking in her ear, "I'm not sixteen. You can't distract me like that anymore. Answer my question."

"But she looks really nice." Nicely put together. A nice smile. Was it too much to ask that she be a good dancer? "I wonder where she got those boots." They were a shimmery brown.

"Explain your rules." Wade shifted their joined hands from the dance-rudder position and used their linked fingers to tilt her chin up to face him. "And please look at me when you do."

She didn't want to. But she had no choice now. "I don't think I'm the kind of woman guys want to date."

"What does that mean?" Wade frowned. "Not to mention, isn't that your area of expertise? Your personal dating policy seems hypocritical, or at least detrimental to your success."

Hank had said something similar.

"Oh, I don't date." Not at all. And she was surprised to deduce that this was news to him. "Let's say I meet a man and he wants to get to know me better. And this man is an avid fly fisherman and wants to teach me how to fish in the river. I get waders and a manicure—do not say they are mutually exclusive."

He bit back his smile.

"Anyway, you *know* what would happen next." When he didn't speak, she spelled it out for him. "The fish would catch me instead of the other way around and pull me down the river. I'd lose my footing. My waders would fill with water. And I'd be lucky not to sink to the bottom."

"And be tangled up with his fly," Wade said straight-faced.

"I'm sure you meant the fly on the end of his line." Ronnie thrust her nose in the air. "But you see what I mean. He could end up nearly drowning trying to save me and then try to sue me for pain and suffering."

Wade nodded. "I suppose we each have the same obstacles to a relationship that we had to life when we were in middle school."

She wanted him to expand on that thought, but he didn't give her a chance to ask.

"Enough talk, Ronnie. It's been a long time since I've danced." Wade spun her around the dance floor, ending all conversation. He was a good dancer, knowing how to lead by light pressure over her hip and drawing her arm where he wanted them to go.

They danced two songs in a row without speaking. And since they weren't talking, she could pretend the dance meant nothing. But Ronnie hadn't realized how much she'd missed a man's arms around her.

"When did you become such a good dancer?" Ronnie asked as the second song neared its end. "You never come to the Buckboard."

"There are more places to dance than at the Buckboard." Wade's breath was warm on her ear and brought to mind slow kisses on hot summer nights.

But she couldn't dwell on romantic notions. "Where do you dance?" She drew back in his arms to look into his eyes. "In Tulsa? After a rodeo? Are you dating someone long distance?" Her spirits sank. "You should have told me."

"Obviously, I would have told you if I was, right from the start." He drew her closer.

This attraction between the two of them was inconvenient, because she'd made a promise to Libby to find Wade a new love. And it was more than a little frightening because she'd made a vow to herself not to pursue love for herself.

Think, Ronnie. Think.

She sucked in a slow breath. "I can't stop talking. I was trying to sign you on as a client."

I'M TRYING TO sign you on as a client.

Wade nearly stumbled as the band launched into a third song.

Ronnie's trying to sign me on as a client?

It had been a long time since he'd danced with a woman. He was just getting used to the feel of Ronnie in his arms when she'd dropped that bomb on him again.

Talk about a mood killer. Dancing wasn't a business activity.

"I'm not your client," he said, feeling the need to counter. "And I don't have the patience to date," he added in case she got the wrong idea.

Who was he kidding? *He* had the wrong idea.

Ronnie felt good in his arms, not because she was a woman but because she was Ronnie. He was torn between hanging on to her and walking away.

Ronnie showed no sign of being put off by either comment he'd made. She smiled as bright as a summer sunflower. "Don't you see? Your impatience is all the more reason to let me separate the wheat from the chaff and find prospects for you."

Wade eased her away from him and planted his boots, rooting them in the midst of other couples circling the dance floor. It was time to admit the most logical reason he wasn't going to use her services. "Sorry, Ronnie. But I don't have the money to pay you."

"Really?" Ronnie's dark eyes widened. "But you're Wade Keller. You made a name for yourself by winning and winning big."

"That's mostly gone, along with my sponsors." The last one had dropped him a year ago. "I paid off Frank and Mary's debt, bought them a truck, bought me a new truck, and Libby a new car. We went to Mexico on vacation several times." Where the hot sun and warm sand had done their best to ease his tired, aching muscles, if not the feeling of restlessness. "And then a pair of my horses got sick. Real sick. Vets are expensive."

"You spent it *all*?" She bit her lower lip. *Those lips…*

It took him a moment to form his reply. "I kept thinking I was going to have a better year the next year." It was hard to admit, but she'd been honest with him about why she didn't date, which made him feel better about the overly eager reporter's chances. He owed her the same. "What woman would want an out-of-the-money cowboy like me?"

Someone bumped them. Wade realized he may have stopped dancing with her, but he still held on. He loosened his grip.

"Not so fast." She latched onto his hand and moved her feet, leading for a change. "You need my help in more ways than one."

She wanted to keep dancing? And keep matchmaking?

The two seemed in conflict with each other.

Wade spun her around, trying to keep her off balance. "I know that look you just gave me." She was cheerfully determined to solve all his problems. "And you can forget about it right now."

Her smile blossomed to full wattage in a way that wouldn't let him look away. "Wade Keller, you need a business manager," she told him matter-of-factly. "I can help you there, too. And if you agree to my matchmaking, I won't even take fifteen percent."

Wade didn't want her help. Everyone knew that when Ronnie Pickett applied herself, she left subtlety at the door, not to mention there was risk of the unexpected. He much preferred to rewind a few minutes and go back to the feeling of a fun Ronnie in his arms.

Wrong idea, Wade.

He spun them again, trying to derail the thoughts of Ronnie spinning round his head. She'd rejected him long ago. As a foster teen, he'd wanted to live with his uncle or grandparents, but they'd rejected him, too. Wade took people at their word—from friends to so-called family to sponsors. If they said they wanted no part of him or his life, he accepted that fact and moved on.

Therefore, the unfortunate romantic feelings

he was experiencing toward Ronnie needed to disappear.

He stared at her.

The feelings didn't go away.

Probably because Ronnie's expression was enchantingly blissful. "We'll pay a call on Hollander Saddles this week. And Daily Grind Boots, too."

He shook his head. "You're getting ahead of yourself, Ronnie. Sponsors let me go for a reason."

"Why?" She blinked up at him with eyes so large a man could get lost in them. "Because you've been finishing out of the money? *Pfft.* You were grieving. Everybody understood that. But you're about to turn things around."

"Maybe," he said, glancing away. Winning felt like a lifetime ago. "Either way, I can't go wasting grocery money on chasin' a dream."

The song came to a close and so did his desire to speak to Ronnie about the dead-end situation he'd made for himself.

But instead of letting him go, Ronnie held on to his shoulder. "I want you to be successful again, Wade. But the price for my services is the use of your name in my matchmaking business."

He set her away from him. "You're getting ideas."

She laughed in that easygoing, all-is-right-in-the-world way she had. He would have envied her the carefree feeling… If he hadn't suspected it was all a facade.

CHAPTER EIGHT

RONNIE WAS UP at the crack of dawn on Sunday morning.

Not because she had a lot to do, although she did, but because she'd woken to a languid dream about Wade kissing her.

What was her subconscious thinking? She needed to make Wade a spectacular match with a client of hers. That was the way forward. Not kisses. What would happen if she pursued a relationship with Wade? Given her track record for mishaps, she'd most likely lose his friendship, that's what.

So, rather than risk drifting back to sleep and dreaming of things that she shouldn't let happen with the man whose friendship meant the most to her, Ronnie popped out of bed and started her day.

She'd spent most of yesterday cleaning and sorting through Great Aunt Didi's possessions. She'd dragged all kinds of items she didn't want out to the carport until it looked like she was getting ready for a yard sale. On her to-do list today was putting fresh shelving paper in the kitchen and bathroom cupboards. Next week, the new flooring—her one big splurge—was going to be installed.

But first, she needed to make some matches. Ronnie wrote names of those interested in her services on index cards—one pile for the ladies, one pile for the guys. And then she listed their interests beneath their names and starting pairing the cards. She laid duck-loving Sarah's card next to her brother David's. She moved Nell's card next to Principal Crowder's. Her boss was a few years older than Nell, but he was settled and loved kids.

Ronnie stared at Wade's card for a long time. His interests were varied—bronc riding, horse breeding, single dad, college sports, poker, dancing. Where did he go to dance if not the Buckboard? He'd been so much more straightforward when they were in school and hanging out on the rodeo team.

She picked up a pen and added, "Rodeo coach."

"You're too heavy on the reins," Wade had told Ronnie during her first week on the rodeo team. "You need to direct the horse with your lower body."

Back then, she would have done anything he told her. But this advice had served her well.

She left Wade's card unpaired.

After lunch, she was playing country music full blast, head and torso deep in a low kitchen cupboard and losing a battle with a long sheet of blue flowered shelving paper when a cold canine nose goosed her arm.

"Ay-eee!" Ronnie hit her head on the cabinet shelf and fell on her behind.

A familiar, gray-muzzled face tried to give her kisses.

"Brisket. What are you doing here?" She stroked the chocolate Labrador's sleek coat.

A tall figure filled the space between the kitchen and the living room, sunlight streaming behind him.

Startled, Ronnie gasped. And then she recognized her older brother. "Hank. It's you." She hadn't heard him knock.

He turned off her music and knelt beside her. "You're lucky it's me and not Mom. Brisket and I snuck up on you."

"I shouldn't have been playing my music so loud." What would her neighbors think? Granted, one of her next-door neighbors was Izzy, but still.

"And your front door was unlocked," Hank said, continuing his criticism.

"It's Clementine. No one locks their doors in Clementine."

"Tell that to Mom." He yanked out the creased and folded sheet of contact paper, then crumpled it into a ball. "She thinks you've moved to the crime-laden, big city."

Brisket cocked his ears and ran into the living room, woofed as he climbed on Ronnie's love seat and looked out the front window. He barked once and glanced toward Hank and Ronnie, as if to say, *Come look at this!*

Hank went to see who was outside, patting Brisket and praising him. Then he returned to Ronnie. "Amanda Shea just pushed past with her stroller and her oldest on a scooter."

"The scary locals." Ronnie smiled.

"Hey." Hank pointed at the index cards on the coffee table. He picked up a pink one. "Nell is one of your clients?"

"Yes." Ronnie watched her brother carefully. "Apparently, she's decided to get over you."

Hank slowly returned the card to the table.

And that's when something by the front door caught her eye. "Why is there a bag of dog food here?"

"Mom thinks you need an alarm system. And since Brisket is arthritic and doesn't run around the ranch anymore, he was chosen over Barstow for the job."

Ronnie shook her head. "I'm never home. This isn't fair to Brisket. He's used to the bustle of a ranch."

Hank rolled his eyes. "He's used to sleeping on the front porch and keeping watch over things. Humor Mom, please. Or there'll never be an end to it."

"Fine." She figured Hank would be on his way, but he loitered. Hank never loitered. His cheeks took on a ruddy hue. "I happened to be with Laurie Sue, and she mentioned you had an appointment coming up tomorrow with her boss. The lawyer. Is Tuttle Towbridge still bothering you about getting bitten by fire ants on that date you had?"

Was nothing she did private in this town? "That's my business and none of *your* business." Tuttle was known to be enamored with litigation. Nuisance lawsuits, her lawyer called them and claimed she had nothing to worry about. "*And* don't change the subject. Since when are you dating Laurie Sue? I didn't see you at the Buckboard last night."

"One date doesn't make it dating." Hank

gave her a lofty look. "And there are other places to take a woman than the Buckboard."

His statement only reminded Ronnie of Wade's comment about there being other places to hone one's dancing skills. "If you happen to see Laurie Sue again, remind her that my appointments are private and confidential."

"Even to your brother?" He glanced at the cards on the coffee table before giving her a conciliatory grin.

"*Especially* to my brother."

"Dad, can I have a cell phone?"

"No!" Wade had been pulling on his boots in the mudroom, getting ready to drive Ginny to school Monday morning, wondering if he'd see Ronnie in town and then telling himself to stop wondering. He didn't need a woman in his life. Or a business manager.

"Why not?" Ginny called from somewhere down the hall.

It took Wade a minute to remember what she'd asked for. "You're ten. Talk to me when you're sixteen."

"Dad." Ginny entered the mudroom wearing blue jeans, a superhero T-shirt and an expression too serious for a ten-year-old. She laid a hand on Wade's shoulder. "The world is different than when you were ten. Lots of kids in my class have cell phones"

The world was different now was a good argument. She'd make a good lawyer.

"The answer is still no." He stood, stomping his feet to get his toes settled in his boots.

Ginny sighed like the put-upon teenager she'd be one day. She was growing up too fast, especially this winter. She turned her back on him. "Check my braid, please."

There was another thing that had changed recently. Wade used to plait Ginny's smooth brown hair. Suddenly, she was too old for his help and wanted to do it on her own.

"You're crooked here at the end." He glanced at the clock on the wall. They had an extra fifteen minutes before they had to leave. He loosened the decorative hair band at the end and was unraveling the last two inches of her braid before he realized the blue bow in his hand had once been Libby's.

His throat didn't close. His chest didn't tighten. His heart didn't ache with loss. And his fingers didn't fumble over reworking his daughter's braid or twisting the band and bow back in place. That was progress. "All good, sunshine. Get your shoes on and grab your backpack."

She lunged for her shoes. "And then can we talk about a cell phone?"

"No." He slid into his thick work jacket and put on his dingy cowboy hat.

"Can I take my bike to school? Lila, Piper and me want to ride to Lila's house after school." The house that was down the street from Ronnie's.

"Did you clear this with Lila's mom?"

"Yes." Ginny rolled her eyes. "Can you put my bike in the back of the truck? Please?"

"I will if you hurry." Wade left her to get ready and went outside. The crisp morning air and clear blue sky were bracing. He headed toward the large garage that housed the ranch's workout space and everything from an old car Chandler was restoring to a couple of tractors to quads to baseball bats and bicycles.

The D Double R sat on over one hundred acres and was a large stock operation. On the original ranch proper, there were many buildings. Tall cottonwoods and broad oaks towered over rooftops and lined Lolly Creek as it wound its way through the property.

In addition to the garage, there was the old

original farmhouse Wade and Ginny lived in, the huge rambling ranch that was Frank and Mary's home, the tiny ranch foreman's bungalow, a bunkhouse, a big barn and stable, several training paddocks and an extended arena.

There were noises and voices coming from the stable. His brothers were up and moving, feeding stock and saddling horses for the day's work. They'd be checking livestock that had been to rodeos over the weekend for injuries and health. Discussions would begin about which stock to send out next weekend. The animals in outlying pastures would be fed and checked on, including the large pasture where bucking broncs came to retire.

Wade entered the garage through a small side entrance. Each of the six bays could store three cars bumper to bumper. The far back corner was devoted to the weight lifting and training area with the mechanical bull. Sunlight gleamed through windows, the closest of which was near Libby's blue dust-covered car. It was parked behind a muddy quad and next to his father's workbench.

Wade moved closer to the little blue coup, recalling Libby's soft smile at his surprise gift and her gentle protest, "You shouldn't have."

She'd been right. He should have been smarter with his money. He should have known that no one stays at the top forever. He needed to be smart with his money and resources now. Maybe he should sell her car to start Ginny's college fund.

The door behind Wade opened and his mother stepped inside. She wore blue jeans and a black peacoat buttoned all the way up. Her straw-straight silver hair stuck out from beneath a black beanie. A red dish towel hung out of one coat pocket, as if she'd been in the kitchen when she'd decided to come outside.

"Shouldn't you be headed into town?" The question should have been a casual one, but there was nothing casual in his mother's gaze. She searched Wade's face the way she had when he'd first arrived on the D Double R, broken-hearted and bitter, trying to hide his raw emotions. "School starts soon."

"I came in for Ginny's bicycle." Wade turned, weaving his way through the assortment of items that filled this garage bay. "She wants to ride bikes with her friends after school."

"Bikes…" His mother followed him at a slower pace. "Soon she'll be old enough to drive Libby's car. You were looking at it just now. Are you planning on saving it for her?"

"I haven't decided." But now that Mom had planted the idea in his head of saving it for Ginny, he felt guilty. It was hard to draw the line between practicality and sentimentality. And Ginny might be sentimental about the car.

He located Ginny's purple bike and safety gear. Helmet and pads in one hand, he hefted the bike above his shoulders with the other, turning back around and confronting the idea of Ginny driving head-on. "Don't you think Ginny should drive the old work truck at first like the rest of us did?"

"Old work trucks are cool to drive." Mom still had that inquisitive look in her eye. "Ginny might be entirely different though and fancy something else."

"Not my girl." He retraced his steps until he reached her, the woman who'd been his mother for more than half his life. She wasn't getting out of the way. "Something on your mind?"

"Many things." She reached up, softly touching his cheek. "The boys tell me you were dancing on Saturday night with Ronnie Pickett."

Wade sighed. "It's no big deal. She wants me to help advertise her matchmaking service." *And find me some sponsors.* He refused to hope she'd succeed in the latter.

"And you feel uncomfortable dating again," Mom surmised, still studying him. "Can't you see yourself making a new life with another woman?"

"I can. And that's the problem," Wade said gruffly, recalling the feel of Ronnie in his arms, a feeling that had kept him awake two nights in a row. "I feel like it's cheating." It was part of the reason why he'd ignored Libby's letter.

"Ah." Mom took her red dish towel out of her pocket and playfully swatted him with it. "You've forgotten what it was like to come here and move on."

"I haven't forgotten." Wade could remember very clearly the feeling of isolation and grief when he'd arrived at the D Double R. He set the bike down, needing to ground himself. "But that was different than believing I can love someone again."

The words tasted sour, coming and going. Libby and Ronnie. One here. One not.

"Is it? You lost your parents, and you once

told Frank that he'd never replace your father." Her point was mildly made but landed with a significant thud in Wade's chest. "And now, you call him Dad."

"And I call you Mom." He ran a hand over the back of his neck, reminding himself that whatever bumps were ahead for himself and Ginny, they were nothing like the bumps he, Mary and Frank had gone over.

The question was: *Did he want to make the bumpy journey to love again? And could he withstand the pain if he lost someone a third time?*

Mary took Ginny's bike helmet and pads from him. "And now, you're mature enough to realize that there was room in your heart for two fathers and two mothers, all of whom loved you differently."

Wade nodded. "I see where this is going, but it's a bit premature."

"I just wanted you to acknowledge it." Her gently lined face and understanding smile still had the power to calm Wade. "Libby wouldn't fault you for moving on. Ginny won't put up a fuss, either. And neither will anyone here."

"I know," he said in a small voice.

"We want you to be happy in whatever you decide. We always have."

But the problem was that he'd made no decisions and was unclear about what would make him happy.

"GOOD MORNING, RONNIE." Leo Nabidian led Ronnie into his office early Monday morning to review where they stood on the small claims case Tuttle had brought against her for pain and suffering. Leo sat behind his large walnut desk. "And thank you for bringing me a coffee." He raised the Clementine Coffee Roasters cup she'd given him.

Ronnie settled into a seat on the other side of his desk. It was a small office with little on the plain white walls other than Leo's law school diploma. And yet, she felt as if she sat a long, long way away from him, especially when he opened her folder.

She swallowed. "Coffee is the least I can do, considering you agreed to see me at seven," Ronnie said graciously. He was leaving her plenty of time to get out before Laurie Sue started at the reception desk and to get to work by seven thirty.

Leo cleared his throat. "I'm going to cut right to the chase. Tuttle's lawyer found a judge in the next county over where the incident occurred who's willing to hear the case."

"But... It was an accident." Ronnie's heart sank. "This is Oklahoma. Anyone could lay down a blanket on an ant hill."

"Yes, I know, but your history speaks for itself, I'm afraid. We just need to let this play out. Can you imagine if this made the papers? A judge would have no choice but to laugh it out of the courtroom."

Ronnie wasn't laughing. "To be fair, Tuttle did get bitten over fifty times, but that's only because he jumped to his feet and one foot sunk into the nest."

Leo cocked his head. "If my mama was alive, she'd say this is why you should only date cowboys. A cowboy would have had his boots on."

Ronnie tried to smile at his joke. The news was just so crushing. Just one more reason not to date. She'd make a mess of things for sure and not only get hurt but hurt someone else in the bargain.

"Things will all work out in the end." Leo's normally reassuring smile wasn't working its magic today. "Now, don't you worry. His suit has very little merit."

"Thank you," Ronnie got to her feet. "Here's hoping good news is just around the corner."

But Tuttle had refused to let this go for over six months. She wasn't optimistic.

A few minutes later, she'd traveled the few blocks from Leo's office to the school, smiling stiffly to the occasional greetings tossed her way. She continued along the sidewalk next to the parking lot and the drop-off line.

"Miss Ronnie!" Ginny hopped out of Wade's truck, carrying a bike helmet and a bright yellow backpack. "I'm riding bikes with Piper and Lila today. See?" She smiled at Wade as he lifted the girl's pretty purple bicycle from his truck bed.

Wade was looking as handsome today as he had in her dream Sunday morning. She drank him in from his black cowboy boots to his dark blue jeans to his blue jacket and straw cowboy hat. His warm gaze settled on her, and she immediately wanted to walk into his comforting embrace… Had he offered it. Why couldn't he look like just another cowboy? Why couldn't he affect her like other cowboys? Other cowboys didn't plague her with tempting images of hot kisses or drift into her dreams with passionate embraces.

Kisses? Strong arms around her?

Strike those thoughts.

Look what happened the last time she'd dated. *Tuttle and his lawsuit!*

But it was too late. Thoughts of kisses and hugs heated her cheeks.

Wade set the bike on the sidewalk beside Ronnie, glancing at her sharply. "Are you okay?"

Ginny pushed her bicycle toward the racks.

"This is my Monday face," Ronnie told Wade in a tight voice. She raised her coffee cup in half-hearted cheer. "Have fun riding after school, Ginny."

Wade paused and then sidled up close to peer into her face. "You're not fine. What's wrong? How can I help?"

"Some things can't be fixed by you, Wade."

He brushed a lock of hair behind her ear in a touch that was so tender, it stole her breath.

Ronnie nodded toward the line of vehicles waiting to drop off their kids. "You should get going before—"

Someone farther down the drop-off line honked, reminding Ronnie to keep moving.

As long as she kept moving, the reality of her situation wouldn't sink in. Thanks to Tuttle, soon everyone would know she was a disastrous date.

If they didn't already.

CHAPTER NINE

"CAN YOU REPEAT THAT?" Norma asked into the phone.

Ronnie looked up from the staff meeting agenda she was typing during the upper grade's afternoon recess.

"I…" Norma, the elderly school assistant who'd been working there since before Ronnie was a student, was shouting into the landline, "I can't hear you. *Say that again!*"

Ronnie rushed to Norma's side. "Let me help."

"No!" Norma cried in a frustrated voice. "I've got this. Please, Mrs. Headtoover—"

"Who?" Ronnie asked.

"—don't mumble," Norma said louder. "I can't hear you when you mumble." She covered the phone speaker and said to Ronnie, "She must be calling from a dead cell phone zone. She keeps dropping out."

Principal Crowder came to stand in his office doorway, looking like he wasn't going to take no for an answer the next time he offered Norma a retirement package.

Ronnie hated to see anyone fail, including her co-worker of a decade, Norma.

Ronnie pointed at the phone receiver. "Let me try, Norma." She claimed the phone from her co-worker and held it to her left ear, shouting just as loud, if not louder, than Norma. "Hi, Mrs. Headtoover. What can I do for you?"

"It's *Mrs. Hightower.*" The poor woman sounded frustrated, as the phone connection kept cutting out. "I need to pick up Elana for a dentist appointment. I'll be there in ten minutes."

"Of course. I'm sorry we had problems hearing." Ronnie rushed to apologize. "I'll call Elana to the office. She'll be ready when you get here." She hung up the phone and patted Norma's back consolingly. "We've got this."

Norma wilted over the top of her desk.

Ronnie hugged her. "It's okay, Norma. That phone connection was awful."

Principal Crowder returned to his desk, shaking his head. "Nothing we can do about cell phone service, ladies."

"Hey, Miss Ronnie."

The greeting was echoed by other soft, indistinct voices behind her.

Ronnie turned toward the long counter separating the office desks from the main reception area. "Well, if it isn't my three favorite fourth graders." Wade's daughter Ginny, Izzy's niece Lila and Allison's daughter Piper. "What trouble are you up to today?"

She was only half-teasing. The girls were gems, but they were increasingly entering the age where they tested the waters. And they had a secretive look about them.

"No trouble, Miss Ronnie. We're changing our afternoon bike plans to horseback riding." Ginny nodded slowly. "Can we call our parents?"

"You know I have to dial the phone for you." Ronnie looked them over with a decade of experience at sussing out signs of mischief. "And if I hear anything different while you're talking to your parents…"

"Don't worry, Miss Ronnie." Allison's daughter Piper had inherited her mother's auburn hair, blue eyes and her ability to look innocent at all times. "We don't have anything up our sleeves. In fact, we don't even have sleeves." Feeling the need to prove it, the girl peeled back her jacket to show Ronnie she wore a sleeveless sweater.

Ronnie turned her scrutiny to the third member of the group.

It was Lila who let the cat out of the bag. Her pale cheeks were flushed a brighter hue than the white-blond hair streaming down her back, perhaps because now that Ronnie lived on her block, there was less chance of her getting away with anything at school.

"What are you girls up to?" Ronnie set the old black push-button phone on the counter.

"Nothing," Ginny said too quickly. "Do you know my dad's phone number?"

"I have all your numbers on file." And she'd been thinking about calling Wade later to discuss the strides she'd made during her lunch break to get him some sponsors. She punched in his phone number. "Hi, Wade. It's Ronnie from school. It's not an emergency." She always let parents know up front that there was no reason to panic when she called.

"Ronnie?" Wade's strong voice communicated more to her in two syllables than Principal Crowder said in his annual Welcome Back to School address.

Wade's tone said, *Are you okay? I'm here*

for you if anything is wrong. You can count on me.

Admittedly, that was all embellishment on Ronnie's part. He was probably just curious as to why she'd called.

Ginny took the phone receiver from her. "Hey, Dad. Can I go over to Piper's house after school to ride horses?"

Her two friends gathered closer, leaning in and trying to hear. Outside the office, two boys peered in the window—Max and Dean, Jo's twin boys. They were also fourth graders.

A light bulb went off in Ronnie's head. Jo's ranchette butted up to Allison's ranch.

"Yes, I was invited… No, we haven't asked Miss Allison yet, but you know that Miss Allison always says yes… Oh, okay." Ginny handed the phone back to Ronnie. "Dad wants to talk to you again."

"What are those girls up to?" Wade asked when Ronnie was back on the line.

"I'm sure I have no idea."

"Ronnie…"

She eyed the suspected co-conspirators, both inside the office and out. "Okay, I have an idea, but I'll only tell you if you pick me up at four thirty today." She was holding out because kids riding together was innocent.

And if it wasn't, Jo and Allison were more than qualified to deal with it.

Ginny gasped, draping her torso over the counter. "Miss Ronnie, are you asking my dad out?"

"Don't get any ideas, Virginia Keller." Ronnie held up a hand. "Your daddy is my client."

Wade may or may not have groaned.

Sometimes it was better to ignore such noises.

"You're finding Dad a wife? Cool, but…" Ginny shook her finger at Ronnie. "Don't forget that I get a say."

"Stop leading my daughter on," Wade practically shouted through the phone. "I'm not your client. You always ask me to support your new businesses, and I always agree. But not this time."

"I don't know what you mean." Ronnie sniffed. It wasn't only school children who feigned innocence. "I don't always ask you—"

"I ordered imported jewelry from you when you started that online jewelry store."

"I hardly think—"

"I bought a set of plastic kitchen storage containers from you when you were going to be the midwestern sales leader of plastic containers."

Ronnie's jaw dropped. "That was over three years ago."

"And I put a standing order in for weekly cupcakes when you started that cupcake-making business last year. I was your best customer."

"And I appreciate it, but—"

"And now you want to find me *a life partner*? Couldn't you locate some other good friend to support your latest business venture?"

No, because you're perfect.

And on top of that, he was something of a pushover where she was concerned. Why hadn't she realized this sooner?

"Don't read too much into today, Wade. This meeting is about getting you signed up with new sponsors." The first one, anyway. "Now, if you'd rather sit at home and feel sorry for yourself, I understand. But if you want to ride the spring circuit, you're going to need those sponsorships." She almost hung up on him.

Almost.

She'd been lucky to make two appointments for him on such short notice—one with a sponsor, and one for drinks with a sweet blonde she'd met at the rodeo over a week ago. Setting up those appointments had lifted her spirits. Lawsuit be darned. Life went on. And so did Ronnie.

"Fine," Wade grumbled. "What time did you say?"

She told him again, then hung up and faced the group of girls. "Ginny, your father isn't going to be home for dinner. So, Piper, you're going to have to ask your mother if Ginny can stay for supper at your house or if she can give her a ride back to the D Double R."

Ronnie smiled as she dialed Allison's number.

She was moving ahead with her plans for Wade.

With leaps and bounds.

"WHY DOES WADE get first ride?" Griff countered his grumbling with a sly grin. He sat on a fence rail in the paddock where a hired transport had just dropped off three bucking horses Dad had purchased.

"Boo-hoo." Wade wasn't entirely satisfied after his call with Ronnie and was more than happy to release his frustration on someone else. He was suspicious about Ginny changing her plans. And he didn't trust the plans Ronnie was most likely making. He set his cell phone on the hood of a ranch truck and began putting on his bronc riding gear, starting with tape on his wrist. "These are horses, not bulls, Griff. Otherwise, I'd be happy to give you the first ride."

The D Double R didn't buy outside stock very often. They had their own breeding program for horses and bulls, building lines of animals that enjoyed a bit of fun in the arena.

Still winding athletic tape around his wrist, Wade scanned the trio of horses that nervously trotted about the paddock. "Let's see what the bay can do." The mare was compact with sturdy legs. "Where'd she come from, Dad?"

"That's Jelly Genius." Dad was in his element, and it showed. His white hat tipped back, forearms leaning on a paddock rail. "A nice lady up Tulsa way bought her mama as a trail riding horse. Nobody realized her mare was pregnant. Jelly was kept in a pasture without gentling or training. When she did get around to hiring someone to help her train the filly, they couldn't break her of bucking."

Wade watched Tate rope her from horseback.

As the lariat settled around her neck, the mare reared, pawing the air.

"She has attitude." Wade felt the familiar adrenaline rush. He tore the tape to make a seal and reached for his elbow brace.

"She might not take a chute," Griff noted, less amused now that there was danger in the air.

It was another sunny winter day. Little wind. Brisk but not chilly. Ideal for bronc riding.

In the saddle on his favorite black gelding, Ryan dropped another lasso over the bay's head, trotting a good twenty feet. The mare was now held on both sides. She stopped rearing and bucked a little.

"Makes me wonder how they got her in the transport trailer." Wade glanced back, but the rig that had delivered the horses was long gone.

"I've seen worse." Dad gestured toward the fidgeting mare. "Look at her. She doesn't charge. Might be she's less mean than independent. You boys know a lot about that."

They did, indeed. Wade continued putting on his gear. "If you're riding, Griff, shouldn't you put on some safety gear, at least?"

"Nah." Griff hopped down from the rail, strutting a little. "I prefer it just be me and the horse. I'll borrow your glove and rigging though."

"And this would be why you're retired," Wade quipped.

Griff gave Wade a friendly shove. "I retired because I got smart. 'Bout time you did, too."

Wade rolled his eyes.

Tate and Ryan guided the bay mare into the chute, working as considerately as they could. They all knew the horses were nervous. And the D Double R prided themselves on providing stock that was biddable when it came to handling in the chutes. And that meant training. And training for these animals started now.

"If you get the bay, I call dibs on the leggy gray stallion." Griff drew back as the horse he'd identified trotted past, tossing his head and whinnying.

"That's A Walk in the Park." Dad looked happier than he had in ages. The lines around his face were less pronounced, and he was as fidgety as a boy on his first day of school awaiting recess. "He's a thoroughbred with solid racing lines. But he has no interest in racing."

"He looks a bit delicate." Wade strapped on his spurs.

"They've got him at racing weight. We can fatten him up some." Dad grinned. "He's got great length with those legs. He'll cover a lot of ground in the arena in eight seconds."

Wade began warming up—squats, leg lifts, good-mornings and so on. Griff wasn't as glib about riding as he pretended to be. He joined him, although his warm-ups were half-heartedly performed. It was his mouth that was getting the greater workout.

"I hear you're cutting out early today to meet Ronnie." Griff spoke with a slight smile. "Our boy is going to get his groove back. Not just on the dance floor but in the arena."

Wade gave his brother a more than friendly shove. "Mind your own business."

"You are my business." Griff grinned. "My family business."

Wade couldn't argue with that.

"What's with the strawberry roan?" Wade asked. The gelding stood with his back to them, never a good sign in a horse.

"I'm not sure. An auction house outside of Oklahoma City gave me a call. Nobody could ride him. Not to mention, he's a biter."

Wade and Griff exchanged glances.

Griff made a mock bow. "I'll leave the nipper to you."

"You'd only leave a bad taste in the roan's

mouth." Wade stopped his warm-up routine to get his riding chaps. But he was smiling.

It felt like a long time since he'd been excited about a ride.

CHAPTER TEN

"YOU LOOK AWFULLY fancy for a regular school day," Wade said when Ronnie got into his truck that afternoon. In fact, she looked beautiful. It was all he could do not to reach for her hand or touch a lock of her black silky hair. "Did you change clothes since this morning?"

"I did. I asked to leave early." She wore a long frilly dark blue skirt, a white fisherman's sweater, and a bright red leather jacket with playful fringe. Instead of sparring with him the way she usually did, Ronnie looked him up and down. "Did you get thrown by a bronc today? You're covered in dirt."

He bristled. "Are you complaining? I'm here on time. And yes, I've been working on my bronc riding technique. We bought a few new buckers, and it's my job to test them out."

Her dark eyes flared with unwarranted annoyance. "Well, we need to stop by the feed store before we go. We have ten minutes to spare if you drive fast."

"The feed store? Why? Do you need to pick up some of your matchmaking flyers?" He chuckled at his own joke. He'd seen them tacked on the community bulletin board this morning. "You haven't told me where we're going, anyway." And he was curious if he was headed for a date.

"I told you what my plan for you was on Saturday night." She huffed. "I'm taking your career in hand. We're having a meeting with Gary Hollander of Hollander Saddles. Don't you listen?"

"Gary Hollander?" He quelled the urge to laugh hopelessly. "That's a waste of gas."

"You can judge all you want when we get back. Now, time's a wastin'. We need to make it over to the feed store." She pulled a lipstick from her purse.

He waited to see what color she'd chosen—pale pink—before he obliged, pointing the truck in the feed store's direction. But he held no hope for the meeting she'd arranged. Gary Hollander wasn't going to change his mind about Wade being one of his posse of spokespeople, not until Wade started winning again. "You owe me an explanation as to what Ginny and the girls are up to."

"They're hoping to ride with Jo's boys."

"Boys?" Wade practically gagged.

"What's gotten into you today?" She tried to slap him on the back, as if he'd been choking. "They're just kids."

He shook his head. "Since Christmas, Ginny's been like a pendulum, swinging from superhero worship to wanting to wear more dresses and now conspiring to hang out with boys. What's next? Makeup?"

Ronnie laid a hand on his shoulder. "Save the upset dad speeches for another two years or so. Trust me when I say she's still your little girl. I see this all the time at school."

Trust her?

Wade had mixed feelings about that.

He pulled into the feed store lot a few minutes later.

Almost before he'd shut off the truck engine, Ronnie and her pink lips were hopping out and power walking up to the feed store. "Izzy? Izzy, we have an emergency."

Wade ambled after Ronnie, assuming he was a spectator.

"What do you need?" Izzy came around from behind the cash register. She was a sweet white-blonde whose reserved nature reminded him a little of Libby.

"I need jeans and a shirt, please, Izzy.

Pronto." Ronnie waded into the circular racks of men's clothing. "In Wade's size. And we'll need some cologne."

"Okay." Izzy retreated behind the counter where some products were displayed.

"Whoa, whoa." Wade made as if to back out of the store. "We're here for me? I did *not* agree to this."

"Which part?" Izzy asked. "The clothes or the cologne?"

"Ignore him, Izzy. We need the works. We've got an important meeting." Ronnie moved hangers quickly out of the way. "Wade doesn't realize sponsors want him to live the winner's circle look, not appear down on his luck."

He hated that Ronnie had a point. He caught her eye before relenting. "Okay. But I draw the line at smelling pretty."

"I have a sampler." Izzy came forward, holding a small bottle. "It's for spritzing." And without waiting for permission, she spritzed him.

"Hey." He stepped out of a cloud of citrus fragrance and joined Ronnie at the racks, because he was afraid if she had her way, she'd dress him in hot pink, her favorite shade.

"Sorry," Izzy said. "Ronnie told me to."

And wasn't that the trouble? Too many people did what Ronnie told them to.

Soon, Wade emerged from the dressing room in stiff jeans and a plain, scratchy black shirt with pearly buttons.

Izzy spritzed him with cologne once more before he leaped out of the way and told her to stop.

Ronnie moved in, tugging his shirt down and smoothing the starched material over his shoulders. And just like the other night at the Buckboard, he was tempted to draw her close.

But before he acted on the impulse, she stepped back and gave him a critical once-over. "It'll have to do."

While he grabbed his dirty clothes and jacket, Izzy handed Wade's hat to Ronnie.

She put it back on him at a jaunty angle, nodding approvingly. "Looking good. Don't wear your jacket when we get there. Let's get going."

"Did you clean my hat?" Wade removed it and gave it a gander. There was no dirt in the white straw. It looked almost brand new.

"Of course, we cleaned it. What do you think the steamer is for? Just rolling the hat brim?" Ronnie towed him toward the exit.

He dragged the heels of his dirty work

boots and pulled Ronnie back, making sure he spoke in her good ear. "Hey, I didn't pay."

"I put it on my tab." Ronnie smiled, all pink lips and pearly whites, pushing him toward the door.

"I can pay my own way." He tried to hit reverse, but Ronnie was having none of it.

"It's not charity. I'm investing in my business." She stomped her blue suede booties a little. "Can we argue while you drive?"

"I guess. But Ronnie, my pride is taking a hit today." He opened the door for her.

"As long as we get positive results from your potential new sponsors, you can live with your wounded pride."

He supposed she was right.

Argument forgotten, they were then on their way toward Friar's Creek, hardly speaking, which was fine with Wade.

He snuck a glance at her. She stared out the passenger window, worrying on her pink lower lip.

Wade touched her arm softly, speaking when she turned his way. "How's your house coming? Get anything else done?"

His interest earned him one of Ronnie's trademark smiles, as bold and beautiful as her fashion choices, including that fringed red leather jacket. "I boxed up Great Aunt Didi's clothes. But first, I went through all her pockets. I found ninety-eight dollars and forty-two cents, one of her fanciest watches and her old flip phone. Isn't that funny? She must have lost her phone at some point. When I go, they're going to pry my cell phone out of my cold dead fingers." She gasped, angling toward him. "Given that you've lost your parents and Libby, dead jokes are insensitive. I'm sorry."

"Don't apologize. People pass on, one way or another. And it's funny that Didi didn't ask anyone to look for her phone or mention it was lost."

"It is." Her smile reappeared. "Great Aunt Didi was a character, wasn't she? She used to tell me she was leaving me more than a house." Ronnie's smile faded once more. "And speaking of leaving… Libby told me she left you a letter. Did you ever find it?"

Wade opened his mouth to admit he had and then caught himself. If he did, Ronnie would want to know what Libby had written. He shook his head.

"Really? That's odd that you haven't found it." Ronnie tapped her fingers on the center console. "Have you gone through her things?"

"Kind of." He cleared a throat suddenly thick with emotion. "You know, she had her own closet." There'd been no need to clear her things out. And every once in a while, he'd open her closet doors and breathe in the faint scent of Libby, of lavender and comfort.

"I'll come over and help you," Ronnie said staunchly.

He shook his head again.

"Don't you think it's time, Wade?" Ronnie leaned on the console. "How will her things look to someone you're dating?"

She was right. But still, he didn't agree.

Ronnie sighed, digging in her purse. "Why is your first response always no?"

"Because." No was safer. Yes was risky. About the only thing he said yes to anymore was riding rough stock. And agreeing to Ronnie's schemes.

Eventually, when he boxed up Libby's things, he'd put his willingness to say yes to Ronnie away, as well.

Before he knew it, she'd applied another coat of pink lipstick. He turned into a long driveway. Eventually, he parked in front of the large barn where Gary Hollander made his custom saddles.

"Let me do the talking," Ronnie told Wade before getting out.

His pride protested, but all he said was "Be my guest." Last time he'd spoken to Gary, he'd been given his walking papers.

Gary Hollander made his world-renowned saddles out of a large barn on his ranch. His wasn't a big operation. Gary was more interested in quality than quantity. And his limited quantity tack commanded luxury prices.

The older cowboy ambled out of the barn wearing rumpled jeans, a shearling coat and no cowboy hat. He had silver hair, a grizzled chin and shoulders bent from years of hard work. Surprisingly, Gary's expression was as close to welcome as Wade had ever seen.

Or perhaps all that warmth was directed at Ronnie.

Gary greeted Ronnie with a kiss to her cheek. "It's always great to see you. And you look good enough to put in a sales campaign. Can I call my photographer?"

Hardy-har.

Wade's shoulders tensed.

"Is that an offer?" Ronnie preened a little, but in a nice way, as if she appreciated the compliment rather than her accepting what was her due.

"It might be." Gary studied Wade with a curious expression in his faded blue eyes. "What brings you by?"

"Wade." Ronnie took Wade's arm and executed one of those shoulder hunching gushes she'd mastered when they were kids. "Isn't he just the greatest?" Her long skirt brushed against Wade's legs, and the scent of roses tickled his senses.

Gary continued to give Wade a once-over, holding back his assessment, perhaps waiting for Ronnie's sales pitch.

She gave Wade's arm a gentle shake. "Wade's coming out of his slump, Gary. And you'll be wanting him on your endorsement roster again. In fact, we're here to offer Wade at a special price." She batted her thick black eyelashes. "It's a limited time offer."

Gary blinked slowly as if calculating figures in his head.

Meanwhile, Wade prepared himself for a serious lowball offer or—*more likely*—a rejection.

Ronnie might have doubted her pitch, as well. Her grip on his arm tightened.

Wade covered her cold hand with his own, rubbing it a little. Sunny winter days on the plains were deceptively cold, and he wished he hadn't left his coat in the truck.

A smile spread slowly across Gary's weathered face. "I'd be willing to bring Wade back on if you came along as a package deal, Ronnie."

"What?" Wade would have wrested his arm from Ronnie if she hadn't held on.

"That's a novel idea." Ronnie continued to smile, but Wade would have sworn he could see the wheels spinning in her head.

Gary nodded, as if he, too, were still putting things together. "You two sure look good as a pair. Loads of people know who you two are. Ronnie's in a lot of magazines for those cowgirl duds. And Wade was somebody once."

Wade bristled.

Not that Gary noticed. "Plus, I hear Wade's been fostering retired broncs." His smile returned. "Throw in a photo session with Jouster, once one of the scariest broncs on the circuit, and we've got a deal." He named a sum.

A five-figure sum.

And Wade, who was in need of five-figure sums, had to work up saliva to swallow past his suddenly dry throat, because even split two ways between himself and Ronnie, it was still five figures to each of them. He could plan out the spring circuit entries with his share *and* start a college fund for Ginny.

"I don't know, Gary. I'm awfully busy." Ronnie finger-combed a lock of long hair over her shoulder.

It was all Wade could do not to shout, *"She'll make time. We accept!"*

Ronnie rubbed a hand over the small of Wade's back as if they truly were a couple. The pressure to make the deal eased somewhat.

Almost of its own accord, Wade's arm looped around her waist.

Ronnie was back to fluttering those eyelashes at Gary. "What if you just take Wade and Jouster?"

"Uh… Picture this. I can see the ad now." Gary's expression turned distant. "Wade carrying one of my saddles away from a grazing Jouster and walking toward you to share a romantic picnic." He looked pleased with his creativity. "My wife just loves celebrity couples. Can't get enough of them. And we don't have hardly any of them in rodeo."

A couple?

There was a red flag.

The way they were hanging on to each

other... He could see how Gary would get the wrong impression.

Is it wrong?

It took him longer than usual to tell himself it was.

Meanwhile, Wade kept his arm where it was around Ronnie. He'd come this far following her lead. He glanced down at her, waiting to hear if she was going to refute Gary's assumption of romance or let it stand.

She laid a hand on Wade's chest. It was a warm hand, having been kept that way by his fingers, and Wade was tempted to cover it with his to keep it against him and the chill.

"Gary, just so we're up front," she said as friendly as all get-out, tapping her hand lightly on Wade's chest, "this here isn't officially anything other than a lifelong friendship. In fact, I'm trying to fix Wade up with someone else."

Gary scoffed. "You should take a longer look in the mirror. I think my idea is brilliant."

"If you want us as a package deal, I'll have to wear Cowgirl Pearl fashions, which means another sponsor will need to get involved." Her hand fell away from Wade, leaving him oddly bereft.

"A tricky negotiation? No problem. That's

what I have a lawyer for." Gary grinned. "He's the best. And he happens to be my brother-in-law."

Wade was compelled to tell them that Jouster wasn't going to like this idea. The gelding liked people just fine until they came into his pasture. "But—"

Ronnie pressed that warm hand to Wade's shirt once more, this time over his abdomen, not his heart.

It might have been his imagination, but her fingers moved a bit more than was necessary.

He swallowed.

"You won't regret this, Gary." Ronnie shook the older man's hand and indicated Wade do the same. "We'll be looking for your paperwork in a week or so."

They got back in the truck and headed down the long drive toward the two-lane highway.

"Did that just happen?" Wade laughed, shell-shocked that Gary was willing to take him back.

"It's not funny. A package deal isn't what I had planned." Ronnie's shoulders sagged. "I don't want this to distract me from my matchmaking...business. We can pretend to be a couple in a photo shoot, but I want to be clear that you're on the market." She noticed Wade staring at her. "What?"

"You're a serious businesswoman," he said with pride.

She rolled her eyes. "I have been for some time."

"I mean… I don't remember you taking any of those courses in school." And she hadn't gone to college.

Her features tensed, pale pink lips drawn tight in annoyance. "What I learned about business, I learned after high school, and I learned because of sponsorship opportunities and business attempts."

"Point taken." He smiled apologetically.

"If you want something, you have to ask for it," she added, still prickly.

"Noted." He smiled harder.

At the end of the driveway, when Wade would have headed toward Clementine, Ronnie directed him in the other direction toward downtown Friar's Creek.

"Don't tell me you made another meeting?" He played it gruff, but the reality was that he was grateful to her for the opportunity with Gary and was excited about other ideas she might have up her delicate sleeves.

"You have a drinks meeting." Ronnie

checked her phone. "Looks like we'll be on time. How's that pride of yours doing?"

"Just fine." And he meant it. "Thank you."

"What can I say? I have a knack for putting things together, including couples." She pointed ahead. "Take the next turn right."

"Into the historic district?"

"Yes. Silver Springs Bar & Grill." She leaned across the truck and sniffed. "You smell nice."

"You had to check? You were close enough to notice at Gary's." It was time for a little payback for being kept in the dark, in the form of a tease. "Along with other things."

"What do you mean?" Her cheeks bloomed bright red, a better color for her than that pale pink.

"You were checking out the goods at Gary's." He patted his abdomen.

"I was nervous." She crossed her arms over her chest, closing herself off.

"You were nervous, and you just grabbed onto the nearest safety bar. My six-pack." He grinned.

"Stop it."

"Sorry." He'd let the proximity of a woman carry him away. This was Ronnie. She wasn't supposed to do that to him.

He parked in front of the restaurant, and they got out. She came around and met him on the sidewalk, fussing with his shirt and adjusting his hat. Her blush hadn't faded much.

Because she's still thinking about my six-pack.

He grinned again. Whatever was happening between them was new and not entirely unwelcome, especially after the last two years. But perhaps it only meant that he needed to date, not that he needed to date Ronnie. "Who are we meeting with? Daily Grind Boots?" That was the other company she'd mentioned Saturday night.

"Not *we. You.*" Ronnie headed toward the restaurant in that swaying gait of hers. "You agreed to my deal. This is your first date."

Wade dug in his boot heels. It was one thing to think about dating. And another to actually take the plunge.

Ronnie reached for the door handle, finally noticing that Wade wasn't behind her. "Come along. Helene doesn't bite. Or if she does, you might enjoy it." She chuckled. "Get it? A little nibble on the ear. A little nip on the—"

"Stop." He had no idea who Helene was, nor did he have any interest in her. But Ronnie's talk about nipping was making him think about the slender column of her throat in a way that was taboo.

"Sorry. That was matchmaker humor." Ronnie came back to him, hooking her left arm through his right. "Too much?"

He nodded.

It didn't escape him that Ronnie didn't want him. Somewhere deep inside, a voice whispered, *Yes, but you're too late. She wants to pass you off again.*

The way she had with Libby.

He didn't like the chaos rolling through him. The unexpected—and unwanted—attraction to Ronnie. The feeling that the reins of his life were being taken from his hands— for sponsorship opportunities, for his love life, for his future.

"I apologize for springing this on you," Ronnie was saying. "Let me get you up to speed. There will be no dinner. No dancing either. It's just a drink. Helene texted me. She's sitting in a corner booth." Ronnie took a step forward. For being such a slight woman, she had a strength he couldn't deny, because he slowly followed her lead. "You're looking for that zing of attraction."

He'd already found it with Ronnie, but if

she felt the same, she was fighting it just like he was.

"And also, look for things you have in common—a love of ranching or rodeo, perhaps a television show or basketball. You like basketball, especially college."

Ronnie liked college basketball, too. And rodeo. And pink. And roses. And his kid.

Wade washed a hand over his face.

"A shared sense of humor would be nice. Listen for her laugh. A laugh should give you a sense of joy when you hear it." Ronnie laughed a little.

And it was joyful.

Wade frowned. He must have hit his head when he'd been thrown by that roan earlier.

"Now, I want you to strut in there like you are Wade Keller, champion bronc rider." She released him at the door, opened it and gestured he enter.

Wade rolled his eyes. He held the door and indicated she ought to go in first. "You should have told me about this."

"Why would I tell you? You'd just give me an excuse not to come." She flounced in ahead of him, smelling of roses and rosy futures. She brushed off the hostess and pointed out his date in a corner booth. She handed him a small business card covered in teal and pink flowers. On the back, she'd written: *Helene, Silver Springs Bar & Grill, sports & rodeo enthusiast, owns a horse.*

He held up the card. "What is this?"

"Those are topics of conversation to get the ball rolling." And then Ronnie headed to the opposite side of the bar, where she'd probably order a glass of non-alcoholic lemonade and a plate of nachos, the way she had when they'd gone somewhere with Libby.

Libby. Ronnie had set them up. Right after she'd rejected him.

Wade set his shoulders back and approached his date.

CHAPTER ELEVEN

Ronnie kept her gaze firmly on the television screen in the bar, currently playing an Oklahoma State basketball game. She refused to look in Wade's direction.

Because if he was hitting it off with someone else, she was afraid she wouldn't like the way it would make her feel.

What is happening to me?

This was Wade. Libby's Wade. She'd been the maid of honor at their wedding.

But I fell for him first.

Ronnie chewed on her bottom lip, trying to nip that thought in the bud. She'd been a kid when she had a crush on Wade. A sixth grader. Young crushes took a back seat to confessions of love by one's BFF later in life. And now, she didn't need to fall for Wade all over again. She needed to help him fall for someone else. Her matchmaking business depended upon it.

How good would it feel to say, "Wade was

one of those confirmed rodeo bachelors, but with my help, he found true love. And you can, too."

It would feel darn good.

Self-lecture complete, Ronnie sipped her lemonade.

Wade claimed a barstool next to Ronnie. "If it wasn't for the contract with Gary, I'd think this adventure of yours today was a waste."

Ronnie glanced from him to the empty corner booth. "How can you be done?" Her nachos had yet to arrive. "Did you even give Helene a chance?"

"I did." Wade set his barely drank beer on the counter. "I told her I was a widowed single dad. And do you know what Helene asked me first? Not anything about Ginny. She wanted to know if it was true that successful bronc riders make six figures."

"Oh." With sinking spirits, Ronnie removed Helene from her mental matchmaking pool. "Oh, I'm so sorry."

"And before you ask, Helene may be a rodeo fan, but she doesn't watch TV—or read the news—and she inserted *um* before every sentence." Wade sipped his beer. "That grated on my nerves. But more importantly, it got me thinking."

"I'm afraid to hear what comes next," Ronnie said weakly.

He leaned closer, capturing her gaze. "Are you sure being a professional matchmaker is really your calling?"

How dare he ask me that with a twinkle in his eyes!

Ronnie eased away from him, trying to sell mock affront. "Do not consider this a failure on my part. This is a learning experience for both of us."

"How so?" Wade picked up his beer and gave her an odd look over the rim of his glass. "Did we learn your knack for matchmaking ended in high school?"

"No." Ronnie frowned. Hadn't he followed her matchmaking successes over the past fifteen years? "I assure you that this is part of the process." *Ooh, good one.* "Haven't you ever watched those TV shows where people shop for a house? The real estate agent always shows them a variety of options, always trying to narrow down what kind of house will be exactly right for them based on their reactions to each showing."

Wade smirked, clearly not buying it. "If you were my real estate agent, you'd be fired."

"Ha!" Ronnie sipped her lemonade, trying

to act calm while searching for a silver lining in the rubble. "It wasn't a total bust. Admit it. You found her attractive. And you liked that she recognized you as Wade Keller, rodeo champion."

He scowled. "You don't know that."

"I do. I saw you give her that smile you used to flash to all the girls in high school." Pre-Libby days. She tried her hand at impersonating his playboy expression but was afraid she didn't come close. "And then when you shook hands, Helene gushed and held on to you a little too long. Oh, and your eyes twinkled."

He slowly spun his beer glass on the counter. "I don't twinkle."

He did and it was adorable.

"Cowboys don't twinkle," he added.

"Maybe not, but you did glow." Ronnie was certain of it. That's when she'd stopped looking.

"Regardless." Wade drummed his fingers on the bar top. "Don't spring a date on me again without warning."

"How can I?" She tossed her hands. "From now on, every time I ask to see you, you'll be suspicious of my intentions."

"As I should be." And there it was. His twinkling eyes and supercharged smile.

Be still, my heart.

Before she had time to comment on it, her nachos arrived.

Ronnie generously moved the plate between them, willing to share. "Set aside the disappointment that Helene was a bust and admit it. You aren't happy being alone. It's why you haven't been winning. You try to put up a brave front for Ginny and the family, but I know you."

It was true. Back when they were on the high school rodeo team together, she'd known when he was going to have a good ride. There'd been a swagger to his step and that light in his eyes. He looked happy, which was a change from the expression he gave her since Libby died—distant and grumpy.

She selected a chip from the top with cheese and tomatoes. "Do you still have fun bronc riding? Or is it the money that you miss?"

"I…" Wade seemed taken aback by her question. His dark brows quirked, and he gazed at a spot across the bar instead of at her or the nachos. "I had fun riding today. It felt like old times." He seemed to breathe easier with that answer out in the open. He picked up a chip loaded with meat and cheese. "What about you? Why did you quit barrel racing?

And don't tell me it was because Yanni pulled up lame that one time. You could have ridden another horse."

"I…uh…" It was Ronnie's turn to hesitate. She shoved a loaded chip in her mouth, stalling.

Of course, Wade kept quiet and waited for her to answer.

"I was late out of the gate," she blurted, never one to hold back a secret when he pressed, even back in school. "It had happened once before when I wasn't collected enough at the start, and because of that, Yanni pulled up lame."

Wade scoffed. "Everybody's mind wanders."

"Did you miss the part where I said it wasn't the first time?" Ronnie drew another chip from the platter. "The instructions people were giving me were getting lost in the crowd noise. You can't stay on top of the leader board if you aren't confident and competent."

He gave her a quick perusal as if to say she was both, shaking his head. "You quit, Ronnie Pickett. That's not like you."

"Why do you have the impression that I've got every aspect of my life together? My family certainly doesn't." She told him about Brisket coming to live with her as her mother's security alarm. "I admit, my life can get messy. But I'm old enough to veer away from most trouble and clean up what trouble I do find myself in…myself. I don't want to live in the bubble my family's made for me."

"That's not… They wouldn't. Okay, they might. But they *shouldn't*." Wade looked unhappy with all options. "And, maybe you have a point. You sometimes get overzealous without thinking things through, but I've never thought that should hold you back from trying. Or trying again. I just think you're brave all around, mayhem resulting or not."

Something inside her chest softened a little. Something that shouldn't.

"Although…" Wearing a sly smile, he turned the nacho plate so that he had access to the most loaded chips. A test was coming. "I wasn't buying your case of the Mondays this morning. You had on a brave front face."

"*Pfft*. As if." How did he read her so well?

Wade nudged her with his elbow. "Wanna tell me about it?"

Discuss her lawsuit? "Nope." She directed his attention to the television overhead. "Last two minutes of the fourth quarter and our star player just fouled out."

He followed the direction of her gaze. "You say that like he's been carrying the team. Have faith that the others will step up and pull the extra weight."

"Like family…" she murmured.

"Exactly. Like family." He turned in his seat to face her, angling his knees on either side of her.

It would have been romantic if they'd been on a date. It would have expressed his openness to what she was saying, conveyed his interest in her. He had a direct gaze that didn't flinch from hers.

"Ronnie. Hello?" He leaned closer, peering into her eyes, a playful grin on his face. "What happened this morning?"

"Don't pretend like the doctor is in." She gave his shoulder a gentle push, desperate for a little space and a little privacy. This was too intimate, not aligning with her goals.

"*The doctor is in*," he parroted, taking hold of his beer. "If you're the love doctor, what does that make me?"

"You've always been more like the camp counselor, a calm and steady presence when chaos roils around you." At least, he had been for her.

"That's an odd thing to say." And it drew another searching gaze from him.

"Why do you think Griff gravitated toward you when you were younger?" Ronnie turned the plate back around, putting the chips with the most cheese in front of her once more. "You didn't fly off the handle the way some boys from the D Double R did."

"I flew off the handle enough." Wade heaved a weary sigh. "Of course, I reserved those outbursts for my parents. They took the brunt of everything a grieving boy had to go through."

"My mother and Mary have always been good friends," Ronnie admitted. "I remember Mary telling my mom that I was handling my awkward growth spurts well. Given the chaos I could leave in my wake, those few words meant a lot to me."

"My mom is a wise woman." Wade stroked the dark stubble on his strong chin, considering her. "But I'm afraid we've come full circle. You haven't answered my question about what was bothering you this morning."

And here Ronnie had thought she'd dodged his curiosity. "Have you always been this persistent with unanswered questions? Or is this a new thing?" She inelegantly stuffed another chip in her mouth.

Wade rested his elbow on the bar and his chin in his hand. The spark in his eyes seemed to dim. "I'll let you get by without answering if you do me a favor tonight."

"Anything…" His request thrilled her for too many reasons. "*Er…* Not anything. What's the favor?"

Wade faced forward in his seat, but kept his face turned toward hers. "I need help buying Ginny a dress. One that doesn't look like a toddler would wear and one that doesn't look like a teenage girl would wear." He drained his beer and checked the time on his cell phone. "And then you can remove me from your dating pool."

"I would be more than happy to dress shop with you." Ronnie signaled the bartender for the check. "But I'm going to set you up on another date."

He rolled his eyes.

"You know that you can't say no to me."

"Yeah." He stared at her for a moment, mouth pulled to one side. "But for the life of me, I have no idea why."

"NOT THAT WAY." Ronnie grabbed onto Wade's arm when he would have gone into the little girl section of the department store. "I see the tween section farther down."

"Tween? She's ten, remember?" Wade got a whiff of Ronnie's sweet perfume and allowed himself to be led past racks of little girl clothes.

"Tweens are the few years before they officially become teens." Ronnie stopped in front of a display of skirts. "Here we are."

Wade placed a hand over his heart, as if he were having a heart attack. "You're supposed to be helping me. I bet all the skirts here are way too short for Ginny. Not to mention, it's barely February, and she'd freeze her tush off. Isn't there a dress code at school? Shouldn't you be enforcing it?"

"Calm down." Ronnie removed his hand from his chest, giving it a squeeze before letting go. "Don't panic. I meant, this is the section for Ginny. It looks like they have their first shipment of Easter dresses on the next rack." She dove right in, the same way she'd done earlier at the feed store when picking out a shirt for him.

Wade hung back and let her work. Admittedly, there was something hypnotic about watching Ronnie shop. She was quick and ruthless but also charming, biting her lower lip when she considered an item, wrinkling her nose when rejecting one.

"How about this?" Ronnie held up a bright orange dress with a big yellow sash. That dress said, *"Look at me!"*

"Can you see Ginny running around the playground in that?" Wade shook his head. "That's something you would have worn as a kid."

"You're right." Ronnie gave it another critical look, smiling a little. "In fact, if it was in my size, I might wear it today." She returned it to the rack and continued sorting. "What about this?" She held up a pastel blue dress with a busy pattern of...

"Are those sheep?" Wade held up his hand in the universal gesture for stop. "I don't think Ginny's gonna like that. She wants to feel adult."

"You're right. There's a definite kindergarten vibe here." Ronnie resumed sifting through options. "And by the way, do you see how much I'm learning about what you and Ginny are looking for? It's the same as me trying to find you the perfect woman."

"There is no perfect woman."

She paused her search, gaze connecting with his. "How right you are."

There was approval in her tone. He smiled. "I'm a wise man, just like my momma."

"But you're metaphorically sitting on a rocking chair in the shade watching life pass you by." Ronnie tsked. "If there's one constant in life, it's change." She paused, perhaps caught by the depth of her own words. "Anyway, you need to be moving forward, not sitting in your rocking chair."

"Never knock a good rocking chair, just like you never knock a good horse."

They'd been friends for so long that their banter felt comfortable, like climbing into a much-used broken-in saddle. Conversation with a woman had been missing from his life for too long. He was enjoying himself. He hadn't thought once about Libby's passing.

"This one is *the* one, I think." Ronnie held up a pale yellow dress that had no frills and would nearly cover Ginny's knees.

"Agreed." He was almost sorry she'd found an acceptable choice. It meant their time together was going to end.

They walked toward the checkout.

Ronnie's stomach growled, reminding him that they hadn't eaten anything beyond nachos. She walked on, skirt swaying at her ankles, as if assuming he hadn't heard.

Wade touched her arm, waiting until she looked at him. "I'll buy dinner."

"Oh, I'm not hungry." It was a bald-faced lie. Her stomach growled again, louder this time. That woman operated at full throttle all day long. Of course, a few nachos weren't going to fill her up.

Wade shrugged. "No sense denying it. Everybody in the store heard your stomach just now."

Her hand flew to her waist, and she blushed. "It was that loud?"

He could just kick himself. "I was only joking. I'm betting nobody heard a thing."

She grinned as if she'd gotten one over on him. "My stomach wouldn't be growling if you hadn't eaten half my nachos," she teased.

"I DON'T WANT to be a burden." Ronnie sat at the kitchen table in Frank and Mary Harrison's house on the D Double R Ranch.

"Reheating dinner is no problem," Mary reassured her. Wade's foster mother wore faded blue jeans and a soft chambray shirt, as comfortable as her demeanor. Her short, gray hair was in a small ponytail, but strands had fallen out to soften the lines around her face.

When he'd invited her home for leftovers,

Ronnie had assumed he meant food at the house he shared with Ginny, not his parents' house. Mary flew around the kitchen, switching glass dishes in and out of the microwave and filling plates with steaming hot food. She'd been glowing since Wade had brought Ronnie home for leftovers. "It's only pork roast and potatoes, not Barnaby's Steakhouse."

"It's perfect, Mom. Thanks." Wade slid into a seat across from Ronnie, although he didn't look at her. He put his arm over the back of Ginny's chair. "How was horseback riding today?"

"It was fun." Ginny picked at a plate of rhubarb pie, staring at Ronnie with a glazed look in her eye, as if she'd long since passed *tired* and was drifting into *exhausted* territory. "Piper is going to compete in barrel racing at a junior rodeo soon. We rode around barrels a lot."

"You know," Wade began with what seemed like the utmost care. "We have barrels here if you're interested in seeing if you like it. Your horse Pepper has experience as a barrel racing horse."

"Dad." Ginny lowered her head to her plate and offered a weak smile.

Wade glanced at Ronnie. "I wasn't saying that I can teach you. We've got plenty of friends around Clementine who've competed at barrels, including Miss Ronnie."

Without lifting her head, Ginny looked up at Ronnie.

How odd that the girl's expression and the conversation said so much to Ronnie. Ginny's big brown eyes conveyed reluctance, longing and a sense of hope. But such a slim thread of hope.

"I grew up on a ranch with boys," Ronnie said impulsively. "Hank put me on his speedy pinto when I was six or seven. That horse gamboled all over the course, and I very nearly tumbled out of the saddle. Scared the daylights out of me. Took me a long time to get back on anything." Despite her brothers trying.

"That sounds like what happened with you and Holly." Wade ruffled Ginny's hair.

"My mom asked a friend of hers to give me barrel racing pointers." Ronnie leaned forward, lowering her voice as if imparting an important secret. "She'd won a lot of competitions. The first thing she did was ban me from riding Hank's horse. She said I had to learn to walk before I learned to run. Or I'd end up getting hurt."

Ginny lifted her head and sat back in her seat, interested. "What a smart lady."

Ronnie nodded. "I can show you some exercises you can start out with if you like. I usually ride barrels Sunday mornings. Do you want to come over to my family ranch?"

"Can I, Dad?" Ginny squirmed in her seat.

"Sure." Wade's smile was directed at Ginny, but it warmed Ronnie's heart.

Libby, you'd be so proud of him. Of them.

Ginny loaded her fork with pie, settled now that there was a potential solution to her riding dilemma. She'd always been a resilient child. She sent Ronnie a grin much like Wade's. "Are you guys dating?"

"No," Ronnie said evenly, because in her experience, betraying any emotion would be seized on by any inquisitive girl as a yes. "Your dad had a date earlier."

"Oh, really?" This seemed of interest to Mary, who'd been puttering behind Ronnie at the sink. "When can we meet your girlfriend, Wade?"

"I don't have a girlfriend." Wade frowned at Ronnie, in what looked like a return to the withdrawn, grieving man of the past two years. "And I can't count what happened tonight as a date. It was a blind date and it lasted less than fifteen minutes."

"Speed dates last less than five minutes," Ronnie countered softly, earning a chuckle from Mary.

"It wasn't so much a speed date as a drive-by." Wade buttered a slice of bread, all trace of upset covered behind the basic action. "And just like that, I drove on by."

Ginny wiped at a smudge of rhubarb on her cheek, only making it worse. "Was she pretty?"

"Yes." Ronnie folded her arms over her chest and smirked at Wade, daring him to agree.

Wade scowled at his bread.

"Was she as pretty as Miss Ronnie?" Ginny was nothing if not persistent.

Ronnie hesitated to answer, not wanting to appear vain. She and Helene were two different kinds of pretty.

"Miss Ronnie is prettier." Wade had no qualms. He shoved a chunk of bread in his mouth and gave Ronnie the kind of teasing look that dared her to argue.

Why would she want to argue? She hugged his assessment close to her heart.

"If Miss Ronnie is prettier, then you should

date Miss Ronnie." Mary set plates in front of Wade and Ronnie. "Don't fill up on bread, Wade." She changed topics easier than a runway model changed her ensemble. It was a good trait for a woman who lived with a ranch full of men.

"Do this. Do that." Wade reached for his water glass. "Make up your mind, Ma."

Ronnie stifled a laugh.

Griff entered the kitchen from the living room. "Dad's asleep in his chair. Should I wake him? He's missing out on Wade bringing a lady home. That never happens."

Standing at the sink, Mary glanced at Griff over her shoulder. "Let him sleep. And get a slice of pie before you head to the bunkhouse."

"Yes, ma'am," Griff said. He cut himself a slice of rhubarb pie and then took a seat next to Wade, grinning at Ronnie.

Ronnie had never approached Griff about her services. Now was the perfect time. "Griff, I'm running a special before Valentine's Day. I bet I could find you several interesting dates."

"I have no trouble finding companionship." Griff used his fork to point at himself. "I'm the sociable bachelor at the table. You should stick to helping Wade."

Wade gave Griff a sideways glance.

Griff laughed.

Ginny smiled.

There was a private joke here. "What's so funny?"

"You aren't the only one in Clementine, or in this house, who thinks I need to date," Wade admitted.

"I'm in good company, then." Ronnie looked around. She'd only been in the main ranch house a few times, mostly in the living room for gatherings.

Everyone was eating, except Mary, who was putting dishes away. A sign on the wall caught her eye.

"Rodeo Academy." Beneath the sign was a bulletin board with pictures of the foster boys the Harrisons had taken in. Some of the photos were of teens competing in rodeo events. A few of the pictures were of boys holding trophies or standing with prizes won—a saddle, a pair of silver tipped boots, a big straw hat. The latter was held by Wade and looked to be the hat he wore every day. "Your ranch used to supply the high school rodeo team with stock."

"That was back when we had kids in school." Mary sat down next to Ronnie, turning slightly to face her. "Other parents wanted a chance to chip in after our last son graduated. Folks like to be involved."

"I hope they still have a chance." Ronnie told them about the uncertainty of the rodeo team's future and that it hinged on how quickly certain departments at school and their administration sorted out their priorities.

"That rodeo team helped so many kids stay out of trouble." Mary's hand covered her mouth. "We can't let this happen."

"If they ever decide who gets the building on the current high school rodeo grounds, we might offer the D Double R as its new home. It would give Dad something to do." Wade looked thoughtful.

"There's just one problem with that." Griff pushed his empty pie plate away. "Bess is bad at delegating. That's why her volunteers have given up volunteering."

"We're not looking for drama," it sounded like Mary said.

Ronnie couldn't bring herself to disagree. Bess was a bit of a control freak—a one-woman show. Still, this was her best friend they were talking about. She had to say something. "Bess runs a tight ship. I'll give you that. But she's not looking for drama, either. Quite the opposite. Like you, she wants to continue giving kids something that stretches their wings and builds their confidence. It'd be a shame if that went away in a town like Clementine, where there aren't a lot of things kids can do in their spare time."

Her statement received nods, even from Griff.

After she'd eaten dinner and a small slice of pie, Wade drove Ronnie home.

When he parked at her curb, Ronnie could see Brisket peering at them from the front window. He'd taken the love seat as his personal doggy bed. "You don't have to walk me up."

"Tell that to Mary." Wade got out when Ronnie did and fell into step beside her going up the front porch steps.

Someone had taped a note on the front door. Brisket banged his nose against the front window, eager to get to the humans or outside to relieve himself.

"Just a second, Brisket." Ronnie took the note and opened it. "It's from Zach. He wants to do an interview about my matchmaking progress. Too bad you and Helene didn't hit it off."

"Are you sure that guy isn't a stalker? Shouldn't he be calling or texting?" Wade took the note and crumpled it up.

"Maybe he just likes to deal with his subjects in person." Ronnie considered herself a good judge of character. Zach didn't strike her as a creep. She unlocked the door.

Brisket charged out, barreling between them, and racing down the porch steps to the front yard.

Wade turned to watch him go. "You're going to need a doggy door in back."

"I'll add that to my ever-growing list of projects." Ronnie set her purse and keys down on the table just inside the door. "Before that, I'm going to help you find love, Wade." She turned and found herself in Wade's embrace.

How did this happen?

Pulse racing, Ronnie raised her questioning gaze to Wade's face. Had he been about to follow her inside and caught her before they collided? Or had he purposefully taken her into his arms to kiss her?

There was heat in his gaze.

She may not have dated much over the

years, but she recognized intent in those eyes of his.

He wants to kiss me.

She drew a sharp breath.

I shouldn't.

She released it.

We shouldn't.

The Ronnie of yesteryear, the girl who'd begun a crush on Wade at age twelve, wanted to argue those shouldn'ts. She'd always wondered what kissing him would be like.

And even though Ronnie was older and should have known better, she didn't argue with her younger self. In fact, she didn't move a muscle as his lips lowered toward hers.

She didn't stiffen when those same lips touched down and brushed across her, teasing her mouth to open.

Oh yes.

Ronnie wound her arms around him and accepted what he offered. She didn't think. She didn't judge. She didn't evaluate right or wrong or anything but his warmth and strength as he deepened the kiss.

Oh yes.

She melted against him, hands gripping the crisp material of the new shirt she'd bought him hours ago at the feed store. His big hands settled into the small of her back, drawing her closer. And it felt so right. So good.

Brisket pounded up the porch steps and jumped at their legs, knocking them apart.

Knocking some sense into Ronnie.

Too little, too late.

But still…

She was breathing heavy, staring up at Wade, not quite sure if she'd stop him from another kiss if he was of a mind to try that again.

Oh my.

Brisket wiggled between them, settling on her feet, and staring up at them, begging for attention.

Here's my out.

She didn't want it.

Standing across from her, Wade's hands had come to rest on Ronnie's shoulders. He wasn't fidgeting, like Brisket, but that heated look in his eyes said he was more than willing to pull Ronnie close once more.

She started to smile because kissing Wade had been on her bucket list.

A truck turned down her street, deep engine rumbling like it was looking for trouble.

The driver would find it. Here they were, standing in her well-lit porch.

What a time to remember that kissing Wade flew in the face of everything she wanted for her future. For *his* future.

This would be a heck of a lot easier if she hadn't kissed him back.

"Oh, Wade…" Ronnie scrambled for a defense. "I'm… I'm so sorry. That shouldn't have happened."

That's right. She was taking the blame.

Brisket stared up at her adoringly, approvingly.

Ronnie needed his encouragement because Wade's expression was nowhere near accepting as the truck came closer. She reached for the hands he had resting on her shoulders and tried to gently extricate herself.

If anything, he held on tighter. "Are you… Are you trying to apologize for kissing me?"

Ronnie forced her dry throat to cough out a too-fake laugh. "Yes."

Wade's laugh had much more emotion behind it, but humor wasn't one of them. "Unless I'm missing something, *I'm* the one who opened the chute on that kiss."

Ronnie experienced a moment of panic. It wasn't just her matchmaking business she was thinking of; it was the direction for her whole life. She'd finally found a little freedom, and she wasn't about to let it go for anyone. At least, not yet. "No, no. It was me. All me. I fell into you and—"

"My lips happened to be in your way?" Oh, she didn't need a sign to recognize the sarcasm in Wade's voice. And that look in his dark brown eyes…

"That's it exactly," she said quickly, pushing onward. "You should watch where you leave your—" her gaze landed on his mouth "—lips."

The truck rumbled past, slowly. It was Charlie John's truck. His ex-wife lived around the corner. Charlie was a mechanic at Luddy's Garage, which was gossip central for men in town. There were even wooden rockers on the front porch of the office where old Luddy sat on slow days.

Wade smirked. He knew people would be talking about their kiss.

Brisket whined, trembling impatiently as he waited for affection and one of the dog treats in the kitchen.

"You should watch *where you step*, Wade," Ronnie amended her last statement. Too late, she realized she still had her fingers wrapped around his hands on her shoulders.

She let her hands drop.

Wade stared at her. And stared.

She didn't know whether to stay or go, reach for Wade or turn tail and run into the house. All she could do was stand there in front of him and wait for him to decide.

What's wrong with me?

She didn't know. All she knew was that she couldn't make up her mind. Ronnie's cheeks heated until they felt hot enough to sizzle bacon.

Finally, Wade's hands dropped away, and his deep, taunting laughter filled the air. "I never thought I'd see the day."

"What day?" Ronnie slid her boot from beneath Brisket, which he took as permission to leap up at her. She caught his large front paws before he tackled her, and she fell back in the foyer.

"The mighty Ronnie Pickett is afraid." Wade shook his head.

"That's… You're…" Ronnie wrestled Brisket back to all fours.

A smile was building on Wade's face, but it wasn't a happy smile. If anything, that smile said he was disappointed in Ronnie. "All this time… All the bold talk… All your matchmaking *and* meddling. It's all because you're afraid to grab hold of love for yourself."

The truth of his words registered, not because she hadn't suspected it herself but because he knew it.

"Afraid," she scoffed anyway, quaking in her pretty boots. "I don't know where you get your ideas."

"It came to me. From your lips to mine." Wade leaned forward and repeated his assessment in a gentler tone. "Afraid."

And then he left her on the front porch. He left her, Brisket and the cold, harsh truth.

CHAPTER TWELVE

"YOU LOOK LIKE a coyote stole your breakfast," Griff said to Wade the morning after he'd kissed Ronnie. He drove with his brother along a ranch road cutting through their outer pastures.

The heater on the old truck was blasting to counter the winter cold, and yet they both only wore jean jackets over their T-shirts. Hard work kept them warm outside.

"And I know you, Wade. If you skip breakfast, you get cranky."

Wade bit his tongue and kept silent…for about two seconds, because that was how sharp his frustration over the situation with Ronnie cut through his normally thick-skinned patience. "Have you ever imagined what it would be like to do something, and then the reality was spot-on while simultaneously—" *immediately afterward* "—being completely different?"

Kissing Ronnie had been heaven. It was the aftermath that had gone deep south.

Griff stopped the truck at the pasture where the retired broncs Wade saved were kept. He parked very close to the fence and the feeders. The small herd of twelve was grazing at the far end of the pasture. A few, including Jouster, lifted their heads and took notice of the truck.

Griff turned to Wade. "I take it you kissed Ronnie. What did she do? Develop a case of amnesia?"

"No." How had Griff known? Wade cleared his throat and tried again. "No. I was talking in hypotheticals about…" His brain stalled, most likely due to lack of sleep.

The herd ambled toward them, led by Jouster, the dapple gray stud that only a couple of cowboys had ridden for a full eight seconds. The bronc was a legend. It was no wonder Gary had wanted him in his ad campaign.

"You kissed Ronnie?" Griff fished for the truth. "Has she given up on finding you a wife? Or did you dynamite your friendship?"

"I have no idea what you're talking about." Wade hopped out of the truck.

Griff did the same on the other side. "I'm

talking about the vibe between you two. There is a promise of sparks and fireworks whenever you look at each other."

"You have an overactive imagination." Wade used the rear bumper to climb into the truck bed, wondering if what Griff said about noticing sparks was true. He'd felt them but had attributed it to a general attraction to a woman, not the combustible chemistry the kiss had promised for him and Ronnie.

Wade hefted a hay bale over the fence and into one end of the feeding trough.

"I should have gone to Hollywood and written rom-coms." Griff reached through the rails with the wire cutters and nipped the bale's bindings. He pulled them free and spread the flakes. "Is that what you're saying?"

"Yep." Wade tossed another bale in the middle trough.

At the sight of the food, the horses broke into a trot.

Griff snipped and spread the second hay bale across the trough. "So, which was it? A rejection? A broken friendship? Or…" He shook his head. "It can't be that Ronnie is a rotten kisser."

She for sure wasn't that.

Wade tossed a third bale over the fence and into the feeder.

Jouster broke into a gallop.

Griff snipped, pulled the baling wire free and spread flakes of hay. "I get it." He gathered all the cut wire and stowed it in the truck bed. "You're a gentleman."

Which was why Wade wasn't taking the bait. Griff had no secure lock when it came to confidential information, and Clementine was a small town. They'd already been seen by Charlie.

Wade climbed down and got back into the cab.

Griff turned the key in the ignition. "But just so you know, our Miss Ronnie has always loved you."

Wade didn't like the direction Griff was taking. Because *always* implied since they'd met, since he'd been with Libby. And why would she say they didn't suit all those years ago if she'd loved him? Truly loved him, not just a girlish crush...

He turned to check on the retired horses, looking for any sign of lameness, abnormal eye color that signified infection, or abrasions. But they all seemed the same as they had the day before. Poky white whiskers, old scars on their hides, sway backs and bony withers. And despite it all, they looked happy.

If only he'd been able to look at Ronnie last night after they kissed and seen nothing had changed. Or that something had changed for the better. Instead, she'd panicked. And then she'd tried to take the blame for the kiss and classify it as a mistake.

I bet you didn't expect that, did you, Libby?

"Back in high school, girls liked talking to me." Griff chuckled as he put the old truck in gear. "Who am I kidding? They like talking to me today, too. Never question my intel, bro. Ronnie was into you back then. And the fire has just been banked until now."

Wade kept his questions and opinions to himself. But those same thoughts whirled around his head like a spring tornado. He couldn't shake the impression that Ronnie's loud, colorful, confident presentation to the world was a front. He'd seen fear in her eyes. And it wasn't fear that she was betraying her best friend by kissing him. This was different.

Ronnie had kissed him back enthusiastically. And that kiss would have gone on longer if not for Charlie and his truck. He wasn't misreading the attraction between them and neither was Griff.

But now…

He didn't know what to do about it. Let Ronnie make the next move? If she thought this was a mistake, he'd be waiting a long time.

"I'll tell you what you need to do," Griff said, as if reading his mind. "Act like nothing happened. That'll throw her off. You know she likes to be in control, and you having short-term memory loss will force her hand."

Wade let the idea settle over him. It wasn't a bad plan.

He glanced over at his brother from another mother. "Sometimes you surprise me."

"I'll let you in on a secret." Griff grinned, tipping his hat back. "Sometimes I surprise myself."

WADE, I APOLOGIZE for overstepping the friendship line. I don't want what happened to distract from helping you find a wife.

Ronnie paused, having lost her place in the computerized school attendance report because she was mentally polishing what needed to be said to Wade.

She was determined to stick with the misconception that she'd initiated that kiss.

You're afraid.

His words echoed in her head.

I'm not afraid of anything but losing our friendship.

Would he laugh in her face if she said that? Ronnie hoped not.

"For the last time, I can't hear. Your voice is breaking up. Please call back on a landline!" Norma shouted into the phone. And then she hung up.

Ronnie spun in her chair, assessing the situation and her need to step in.

Principal Crowder stood in the doorway to his office. "Are you okay, Norma?"

"I'll take a turn at the phones," Ronnie said.

"Ronnie…" Her elderly co-worker pushed her thick glasses up her nose. "Has everyone in Clementine turned in their landline? Don't they realize cell phone coverage is spotty on the rolling plains?"

The phone rang.

Ronnie snatched up the receiver, holding it to her left ear. "Clementine Elementary and Middle Schools. This is Miss Ronnie." She loaded her greeting with sweetness, fully expected a caller who was upset over a bad connection.

"Hey, Miss Ronnie."

Wade.

Ronnie gulped. Her mouth was drier than the Oklahoma prairie in August. And her thoughts...

Had she practiced what to say to Wade Keller, champion kisser? She knew she had. But she couldn't remember a word.

Well, she remembered one word: *kiss.*

Or perhaps two: *sizzling.*

Ronnie panicked and hung up the phone.

"Who was that?" Norma demanded. "Another bad connection?"

Ginny skipped into the office. She carried her yellow backpack and yellow coat. Her cheeks were pink, most likely a result of her skipping in the brisk winter wind.

But right now, Ronnie imagined her own cheeks to be a deeper color of the pink her Great Aunt Didi had loved so much.

"I'm supposed to go to the dentist today." Ginny laid a crumpled note on the counter. "My dad said he'd call the office before he came, but we were just doing art, so I checked myself out."

Ronnie was beginning to understand Wade's concern that Ginny was testing the limits too soon. She was bending the rules like a high schooler. Ronnie should know. She sometimes covered for the high school office secretaries.

"Ginny, you can't excuse yourself from class like that." Ronnie tried to look stern. "Please return to class until your father—"

Wade walked in the door looking cheery and kissable.

Ronnie was confused. Where was the scowl? The contemptuous lowered brows? The scorn because he knew she was afraid?

He smiled at her. "Miss Ronnie, you hung up on me."

"My finger slipped on the hold button?" Did she just end her excuse with a question mark? *Ugh.*

"That's not like you," Wade said smoothly. There wasn't a stain on his jeans or a tear on his jacket. He didn't look like a working cowboy. He looked like a successful rodeo champion on his day off.

And I'm into it.

Wade smiled the way he used to smile at her before she'd announced her decision to find him a wife. "Anything bothering you?"

Yes, I kissed my childhood crush.

And I liked it!

She'd hardly slept last night, alternatively

reveling in the experience and hating that it happened.

He quirked a brow. "Miss Ronnie…"

"No. Nothing is wrong." Ronnie smiled, trying not to remember what it felt like to be in his arms. "Not at all."

Ginny stared from her father to Ronnie and back again, finally shrugging. "Hey, Dad. Am I still going to the dentist?"

"You are, sunshine." Wade never took his eyes off Ronnie. "We still have things to discuss."

"We do?" But he'd been the one to walk off after that kiss.

Wade nodded. "Sponsorships… Contracts… *Dates*…"

Dates? With me?

No.

No-no-no.

"Are you setting Mr. Keller up?" Norma came to stand next to Ronnie at the counter. "Ain't love grand. I fell in love with my first crush. He swept me off my feet when he gave me the last unbroken red crayon in kindergarten. People like us—widows and widowers—shouldn't be alone, Mr. Keller."

"That's what Miss Ronnie tells me." Wade took Ginny by the hand and turned to go.

"Dad, can you take me and Piper and Lila to the movies on Friday night?"

"Sure, sunshine."

And then they were gone.

Wade, I apologize for overstepping the friendship line. I don't want what happened to distract from helping you find a wife. And by the way, I'm not afraid of anything but losing our friendship.

Ronnie sat at her desk and laid her forehead on the blotter.

Why couldn't she remember those words sooner?

"Dad, why was Miss Ronnie acting weird?" Ginny held on to his hand, swinging their arms between them as they walked to the parking lot.

"Huh." Wade worked to contain a smile. "She did hang up on me when I called the office, but she said it was an accident."

"And you asked her if she was okay." Ginny started to skip, acting like the little girl he wanted her to be awhile longer and making his heart light. "I know what it is."

"You do?"

"She's finally in love." Ginny ran the last few feet to the truck, lifting the handle.

"You think so?" Wade dug in his pocket for the keys, unable to contain a smile any longer.

"Yep. Ned Himper said she had a coffee date with his dad."

"Ned…" Oliver Himper's kid? Wade unlocked the door and helped her inside.

"And Michael said Miss Ronnie came to his ranch the other day and mostly talked to his dad." Ginny was in chatter mode, not taking note of Wade's reaction. She buckled in.

And Wade's reaction was grim.

"Lila said she saw Miss Ronnie going into Principal Crowder's office and closing the door."

Wade shut Ginny's door and walked around to get behind the wheel, hoping that Ginny's diatribe was over.

"And Piper said that Irma said that someone saw Miss Ronnie going into the house next door to talk to a man." Ginny paused and looked at Wade with innocent eyes. "Miss Ronnie could be in love with anyone."

Wade started the truck and backed out, clouds forming over his head.

"Who do you think it is, Dad?"

"I couldn't hazard a guess, sunshine." Not a one.

"Ronnie."

Ronnie lifted her head from her desk because it sounded like Principal Crowder was calling her.

He was. He sat behind his desk and gestured for her to enter. "And shut the door."

Ronnie grabbed a pen and notepad and hurried into Gerry's office, closing the door behind her. She sat in one of the green padded barrel chairs across from him. It was a comfortable chair, and she'd always thought it was considerate of whoever had purchased them long ago. If you were sitting in the principal's office, you needed some comfort, and the guest chairs were like a warm hug. "I'm sorry about all the bad calls coming in."

"There's nothing you can do about that." Gerry straightened the pens on his desk, a nervous habit.

"Oh." Ronnie waited to be told why she'd been called into Gerry's office.

"I was wondering…" he trailed off. "This never gets any easier for me."

He wanted to have an uncomfortable conversation? Was she being let go? Maybe the school district was re-organizing budgets to free up money for construction of the new building on the rodeo grounds. There'd been rumors...

Ronnie's pulse pounded in her temples.

"You know..." Gerry leaned forward as if about to whisper.

She fought off a grimace, reaching for her confidence. "You can tell me the bad news. We'll get through this like it's just another day."

"No bad news." He opened his desk drawer—the one where he kept all his official paperwork—and took something out.

It was smaller than she expected. More colorful than she expected. It was her business card, the one she'd given him this morning with information about his date on it.

Understanding dawned. "You're nervous about your date tonight?" She'd set him up with Daisy, a part-time cowgirl who worked at Flicka's Floral. He was looking at Ronnie funny, so she rushed on to explain, "I mean, of course, I knew you were nervous. But you shouldn't be. Daisy is a lovely woman. You share many of the same interests—gardening, love of the outdoors." *Incredible organizational skills.*

Gerry's expression eased.

Ronnie reassured him some more and then escaped to her desk and the incomplete attendance records.

"What are you and the big man up to?" Norma asked conspiratorially.

"Love," Ronnie said, knowing that Norma was aware of her matchmaking. "It makes people nervous."

Falling in love or paving the way to love…

If that's what was happening between her and Wade, it made her lose focus. And for the next few weeks—at least until Valentine's Day—Ronnie needed to stay the course.

CHAPTER THIRTEEN

FRIDAY NIGHT, Wade took Ginny and her friends to the movies in town. There was a new family-friendly animated film playing, and the theater was really full.

That didn't stop his mind from wandering.

He hadn't seen or heard from Ronnie since Tuesday when he'd picked Ginny up to go to the dentist. He looked for her and that cheerful green Volkswagen Beetle of hers on his trips into town. He'd almost texted her several times to ask if she'd heard from Gary about the contract. But something held him back. Maybe it was the fact that he didn't want to go on any more dates unless they were with her. Because he was certain that she'd give him a well-rehearsed speech about her rules and her business goals if he didn't pretend that kiss never happened.

Wade dodged a pair of kids racing up the movie theater aisle.

Ginny darted in front of him. "Dad, don't sit with us. Please."

Ouch.

"Okay." Wade gave Ginny the bucket of popcorn and the drink he'd planned on sharing with her and watched his little girl walk away from him. And then he turned, surveying the theater for a place to sit. No way did he want to spend the next ninety minutes sitting next to someone else's kids. Adults. That's who he was looking for.

A flash of color caught his eye.

Ronnie sat on the far side. She was wearing a hot pink wool jacket. And instead of all that color feeling like it added to the chaos in the movie theater, the sight was like a tall drink of refreshing water. *And bonus!* There was an empty seat next to her.

He ambled over to her and sat down, placing his hat on his knee. It was all he could do not to lean over and plant a kiss on those rosy-painted lips of hers.

"Hey." Ronnie didn't look at him. "You should ask if a seat's taken before you plunk down."

"Is this seat taken?" He stole some of her popcorn.

"I could have a date," she said, continuing

her half-hearted protests as if he hadn't said a word. "I could be saving this seat for him."

She didn't date. She'd told him so last week at the Buckboard. He touched her forearm, waiting for her to look at him. "You wouldn't be here if you were on a date. You'd be fly fishing down by the lake, waiting to admire the sunset or doing something equally romantic or adventurous. Were you saving this seat for a friend?" He hoped not.

Wade took some more popcorn.

"No. I'm here alone." She still sounded out of sorts. And the look on her pretty face was worried. "A teacher gave me a movie ticket package that expires today." And there was only one movie screen in town. "You know, that's my popcorn."

"You came alone *and* bought a popcorn bucket?" There was something about teasing Ronnie that made him smile, even when things were uncertain between them.

"It was part of my ticket package. Do not take pity on me," she rushed on. "I go to the movies by myself a lot." She gave her head a little shake, still carefully not looking at him. "Not a lot, but you know what I mean."

Wade had no clue what she meant. "Pity? I'm not sitting with you out of pity." He put his elbow on the armrest and set his chin on his hand. "Ronnie, can we sit together and share popcorn? Ginny ditched me for her friends." He pulled a sad face.

She closed her eyes and shook her head slowly. "You are incorrigible."

"Yeah, but we're friends, so it's okay." He ate some popcorn and thought about kissing her. "Did you hear from Gary?"

"No." Ronnie shook the popcorn bucket. "I'm having a housewarming party on Sunday. You'll be there."

Annoyance landed with a thud between his shoulders. "That sounds more like a command than an invitation."

She smiled sweetly. "Your presence is requested."

"This isn't a surprise date, is it?" He grabbed a handful of popcorn, taking his time eating it and not bothering to give her grief when she vehemently denied she was setting him up.

He knew Ronnie too well. She was arranging another date for him. The housewarming party may or may not have been a ruse. The question was: *How was he going to outsmart her?*

The lights dimmed and the young crowd

grew only slightly less boisterous. Listening to the movie was going to be a problem.

Ronnie didn't appear worried, or at least no more worried than she had been when he sat down.

Wade continued to help Ronnie eat her popcorn, looking for clues to her mood. She gave nothing away.

Now he had a new problem. With each movie trailer, he was getting thirstier and thirstier. If he stopped eating popcorn, he'd lose the excuse to invade her space. People were still coming in, filling up the theater. If he got up to get a drink, he might lose his seat. He wouldn't put it past Ronnie to give it away.

He swiped her drink and took a sip.

"Hey." She nudged him with her elbow.

Since he didn't want to raise his voice to give her some glib excuse for mooching off her beverage, he just smiled and set the cup back in the holder.

The animated feature began with a big chase scene, emphasized with loud crashes and louder music, all of which drowned out most of what any of the characters had to say to each other. He realized this was going to be a long ninety minutes.

Beside him, Ronnie sunk lower in her seat, hugging her tub of popcorn.

He leaned forward and mouthed, "Can you hear?" He pointed to his ear.

She shook her head.

"Me either."

The poor sound quality persisted, and Ronnie slumped about as far into her seat as she could without falling to the floor. Clearly, she was getting the same low level of enjoyment out of the show that he was.

Finally, she got up, handed him the bucket of popcorn and left.

Without a second thought, Wade put his hat on, grabbed the drink, and followed her out.

"Hey." He caught Ronnie before she pushed through the lobby exit doors. "Wait."

She turned. "Sorry, I… I have a headache. You can tell me how the movie plays out next week."

"You'll have to ask Ginny." He gestured toward a bench against the wall because he couldn't follow her out and leave Ginny and the girls. "I'm not going back in. I could barely make out what they were saying."

"You too?" Ronnie let the door close, slowly following him toward the bench.

"It's the sound system," one of the teenage workers behind the counter told them. "We blew a speaker with that slasher movie last weekend. All that screaming." He rolled his eyes. "My manager expects most of the audience to suffer through it since everyone wants to see the show. I can comp you tickets if you want, Miss Ronnie."

"That'd be nice. Make it two." He'd take her on a movie date someday soon. Wade planted himself on the narrow bench and patted the spot next to him. "You want to wait with me for the movie to end? Otherwise, I'll be twiddling my thumbs alone for another hour."

"Sure." Ronnie sat down. "What else am I going to do on a Friday night? Clean the oven?"

He handed her the soda. "Don't tell me Miss Didi was ninety and didn't manage to keep her oven spotless. I can't believe it. The next thing you'll tell me is that she left a tangle of knitting in the hall closet."

Ronnie laughed, looking more at ease than she had in the theater or on her porch after he'd kissed her. "Worse. She kept every grocery receipt for the past ten years."

"That's not so bad," Wade said. "I keep

every entry fee receipt. I file them with my taxes."

She bobbed her head. "Are you competing in the rodeo in Tulsa tomorrow?"

"Yeah. Most of the crew drove the stock out there today." But he'd promised Ginny a night at the movies with her friends.

"Good. I made a tentative meeting with Daily Grind Boots. They'll be at the rodeo, too." She gave him one of her bright smiles. "I'll confirm it first thing. It's at ten thirty. Can you make it?"

"There you go again. Trampling a man's pride by making him business meetings he should be getting on his own." Oh, what a show Wade was putting on. He could barely contain his excitement for both the sponsorship meeting and the fact that Ronnie seemed to have forgotten her determination to put distance between them. "You should take pride into account more often."

"Yours or mine?" she said.

"Why, Ronnie Pickett." He grinned. "Are you telling me with all the risks you take and the number of times you've face-planted with failed businesses, that you have any pride left?"

She drew back, blinking wide eyes as if she hadn't expected him to tease her.

He tsked. "You're taking yourself far too seriously, honey."

Honey?

Wade jerked his gaze away from her lips and shoved popcorn in his mouth, knowing he'd crossed a line but wanted to divert her attention from that fact.

No such luck.

Ronnie laid a hand on his arm. "We're just friends, Wade. Not to mention that you're my client. Our course is set."

"Our course isn't set in stone. I'm not paying you for services, you know." What was going on here? He'd kissed her. And it had been a doozy of a kiss.

Hadn't it?

He began to doubt.

"You shouldn't be calling me honey," she said gently.

"It's just a figure of speech." He hung his head, looking away. *Libby, if you're up there, help me out, darlin'.*

Ronnie poked him in the ribs. "Well, if you aren't able to give up your honeys and so forth, you can head back into the theater."

And watch a film with a flimsy plot and bad sound by himself? No way.

If he was going to explore this budding attraction with Ronnie, he was going to have to be the best friend she ever had.

CHAPTER FOURTEEN

"WADE, YOU LOOK PERFECT." Even so, Ronnie took her time smoothing his tan competition button-down over his shoulders, using the excuse that, "You have a lot of real estate space on this shirt for sponsor logos."

It was Saturday morning and they were at a rodeo in Tulsa. What a difference a day made.

She and Wade were back on solid ground—that kiss was far behind them.

They were about to meet with Daily Grind Boots. And there was a new crowd of rodeo competitors and fans just waiting for Ronnie Pickett's help finding love. She may have fallen into matchmaking for money, but with a few bumps behind her and fewer standing in her way, things were looking up.

"Are you nervous?" Wade stared at her, an unfathomable expression in his eyes.

"No. Why?" She led him toward the Daily Grind Boots vendor tent.

"Because you have a lock of hair out of

place." Wade took Ronnie gently by the arm and smoothed her hair over her shoulder.

And just like that, Ronnie's pulse raced, and her gaze veered from Wade's eyes to those kissable lips.

Get a grip, girl!

She drew a deep breath, thanked Wade and charged ahead.

"Hang on." Wade caught her arm again. "Only desperate people show up at a business meeting sweaty and out of breath."

"You're right." Ronnie took another fortifying breath, reminding herself not to lose her cool. This was just a meeting. This was just her familiar friend Wade at her side.

"Here." Wade tucked her hand in the crook of his elbow and then said something she didn't catch as the crowd roared over whatever was happening in the arena.

I should ask him to repeat himself.

But his touch threw her off.

Ronnie stared at her hand and then at his handsome face, taking in his reassuring smile, the warmth of his brown eyes. What had he said?

But there was a rhythm to asking someone to repeat their words, an interval that avoided awkwardness. Those seconds had passed, the gap ever-widening. And now, she had no recourse but to tell herself that whatever he'd said had nothing to do with attraction or kisses, although she might have unwisely wished otherwise.

"Together," Wade said the word in a tone that implied the emphasis of words previously spoken.

Together?

Ronnie's pulse kicked up as nerves kicked in.

Together on another sponsorship deal? Or together-together?

His smile lost some of its shine, and his eyebrows quirked with unspoken questions.

The last thing Ronnie needed were Wade's questions.

"Together," she agreed, anyway, and with false cheer. "Shall we skip toward our goal across the yellow brick road?"

"There will be no skipping or rushing. No sweating by me. No glowing by you." His wry humor settled her nerves.

Nothing here to see, folks. Just two people who are fond of each other headed toward a business meeting.

She gave a curt nod and tossed a lock of hair over her shoulder. A strand tangled in her fingers and came free. She scattered it to the wind, but not before she realized it was *a gray hair*!

Ronnie practically stumbled, twisting to double-check. But the strand was gone, and her heart was pumping as if she'd received a scare.

Wade paused and turned to face her. "I said, 'Do we need to slow down?'"

She shook her head. "No. It's nothing."

Just the visible aging of Ronnie Pickett.

Ronnie mustered a smile and tugged him forward.

This isn't my week.

Using her free hand, she fiddled with the hair draped over one shoulder, trying to inconspicuously check if there was more gray.

Please, no. I need this to be my week.

Only seven more days until Valentine's, and there were plenty of people to pair up, successfully so.

Ronnie hit the speed button on her walking pace.

"Slow down, honey."

Honey.

He'd called her that last night at the movies. Ronnie liked it. She liked it too much. She'd told him not to call her that, anyway. He'd countered that it was a cowboy idiom.

And yet, it wasn't the endearment he'd used with Libby. Libby had been *darling*.

The distinction circled through her head, twining with memories of heated kisses and tender touches and…

Keep your focus, Ronnie Pickett.

She couldn't get mired in her feelings for Wade, not when she wanted to show the world—or at least Clementine and the single folk on the Prairie Circuit—that she was a skilled matchmaker. If people saw her with stars in her eyes over Wade, she'd be fending off advances from full-of-themselves cowboys, like Cord.

I am so full of myself.

And off her game. She blamed it on Wade. Once he started dating someone, everything in her life would go back to normal. Except she'd have the memory of that kiss and the pleasure of hearing him use a term of endearment in reference to her.

They reached the boot vendor tent. The marketing director stood at the back talking to…

Cord.

Holy crab apples! Now isn't the time to be off my game.

"Looks like we have competition." Ronnie held on to Wade's strong arm with one hand and fiddled with her skirt with the other. "Cord hasn't made a clean ride on a bull since last summer." She glanced at Wade, thinking what she didn't want to say since it felt spiteful. *Cord wasn't sponsor material.*

"Maybe Cord deserves a second chance, same as me." Wade drew Ronnie to a stop and said, "I know how it feels to lose everything."

And Ronnie knew how much Wade needed those sponsorships to pay his entry fees. She moved in front of him and placed her hands on his muscular biceps. "I have a plan for you. Maybe someday I'll have a plan for Cord. But for now, you need to have the mindset that any opportunity deserves to be yours. Yours first and foremost."

Cord ambled past, exchanging a head nod with Wade.

"We're here," Wade said to someone behind Ronnie.

Great. She hadn't heard a thing.

Ronnie turned anyway, a smile on her face and her hand extended for a traditional shake. "Lance?"

"Yes." Lance had a strong grip and a show-man's smile that rivaled her own.

Worry skittered up her spine.

Everything that had gone wrong this week pressed in on her and made her doubt—Leo's semi-hopeful update on her case, the botched date for Wade, that surprise kiss of his, her inability to enjoy the movie last night, *her first gray hair*!

Lance moved things right along. "Wade, I've followed your career. Glad to hear you're staging a comeback. I know you also work for the rodeo stock company."

"Yes, sir." Wade was in his element and shining—shoulders back, head high—and Ronnie might have been happy for him had she not missed whatever Lance said when he turned around just then and rifled through some boot boxes.

Darn crowd noise.

"I'm a size thirteen," Wade said, face turned toward Ronnie. "And it's too bad you don't make boots for women. Ronnie makes any-thing look good."

This man...

She'd forgotten what a charmer he could be. He was so kind and considerate. It warmed her heart.

Lance turned back around, handing Wade a large Daily Grind Boot box. "You have a story to tell about your daily grind. I like that. If you wear our boots today and like them, we can talk about sponsorships next week. My business card is in the box."

Wade thanked him.

The two men shook hands. Lance smiled at Ronnie and turned away, dismissively.

Ronnie's stare felt hot enough to bore a hole in Lance's back.

"See you around." Wade looped his arm around Ronnie's waist and guided her out of the tent. "If you wanted that limp fella's handshake so bad, you shoulda stepped forward and taken it," Wade said when they'd put a good distance between themselves and the Daily Grind Boot booth. "I got what we wanted. It seemed too easy, but facts are facts."

"Not everyone likes their boots." Ronnie glanced over her shoulder, still steaming about Lance's snub. "That's why they give out so many freebies. You're lucky you got a pair. Cord didn't."

"He didn't have Ronnie Pickett as his good luck charm." Wade stopped at the access door to the men's dressing room. "Wish me luck, honey."

And there it was again. Ronnie held back from swooning. "Best of luck, Wade. I have a good feeling about today." He had a bit of swagger in his step and a look in his eye she hadn't seen at the rodeo in too long.

"I have a good feeling about a lot of things," he said with the beginnings of a knowing grin.

They stood staring at each other, and Ronnie had the oddest feeling that she should add to his luck by giving him a kiss.

Instead, she gave him a smile and a wave.

And regretted it all the way to the stands.

"Square hole. Round peg," Griff said to Wade as they sat their horses waiting for the next bull rider to take a spin.

"What's that supposed to mean?" Wade had been staring Ronnie's way, having spotted her in the crowd. Her red-and-black buffalo jacket was hard to miss. He could almost imagine he'd heard her screaming for him in the crowd when he lasted eight seconds on Coffee Hangover. "Are you back to talking about Ronnie?"

"Not even. I'm referencing those boots

you're wearing." Griff nodded toward Wade's foot in the stirrup. "The Daily Grind brand is known for their square toe. It's not my style. Admit it. You don't like them, either. It's hard to fit that big square toe into a stirrup with ease."

"You're just jealous because you never got a free pair or were considered as a sponsor." Wade couldn't remember if he'd had trouble getting his boots in the stirrup, which had to mean they'd slipped in just fine. And if it was a disconnect to look down and not see a pointed boot in the stirrup, he'd get used to it if it earned him money for entry fees.

"I had plenty of sponsors when I was winning." Griff sniffed, looking away.

In a nearby chute, a cowboy lowered himself on the back of Hustle Train, a beefy Brama mix who delighted in turning on a dime to rid himself of pesky cowboys with dreams of grandeur.

"I remember those sponsors of yours." Wade grinned. "Chicken fertilizer and a regional brand of popcorn, nothing as prestigious as Hollander Saddles or Daily Grind Boots."

"Don't count your chickens before they've hatched." Griff tugged his cowboy hat low on his forehead and rode out to the middle of the arena, ready to shadow the bull in case the rider lasted eight seconds and needed a pickup.

Ryan brought his horse closer to Wade's. "Do you think I could hire Ronnie?"

"To find you a woman?" Wade was shocked that his good-looking younger brother would be interested in such a thing.

"No. To be my business manager the way she is for you." Ryan gestured toward Wade's stirrup. "It's a sweet deal to be paid to wear homely boots they gave you for free. Even better because if they hurt your feet, you'd never know while you were in the saddle. And it's not like they're going to do a home inspection to see if you're wearing them on the regular."

"These boots aren't homely." Wade looked down at the square toes. "They're just different."

"I'll agree with you if Ronnie says they're in fashion. Otherwise, that's a no." Ryan adjusted the coiled lariat in his hand, ready to do more than herd Hustle Train back to the stock area if need be. "But back to my original question. Do you think Ronnie would represent me?"

Something akin to jealousy reared its ugly head inside him. He didn't want to share Ronnie with anyone for any reason.

Wade drew a deep breath. "I think you'd have a better chance of her agreeing to find you a great match."

"I think I'd prefer her to find me a sponsor." Ryan laughed. "I live and breathe for the rodeo. I'll have plenty of time for romance later." Ryan rode off toward his position on the opposite side of the arena just as the chute opened and Hustle Train lunged a good five feet sideways.

The tall cowboy on the bull's back didn't hang on long past the bull's first big spin.

While Ryan and Wade drove the bull out of the arena, Wade's brain was miles away, thinking about Ryan's sentiments regarding the life he'd chosen to live and wondering...

What did he have to offer Ronnie besides a second-hand heart?

"THIRTY OFFICIAL CLIENTS in just a few weeks." Zach tapped notes into his cell phone. "You've got to be happy with your momentum."

"Happy?" Ronnie chuckled, watching the flow of rodeo goers from her position beneath the main stands early Saturday afternoon. "I'm too busy to reflect on my own feelings. But yes, things seem good. And in some cases, first dates have led to a second." Take that of her principal, who'd hit it off with Daisy. They were going on their second date tonight.

Zach reached into his pocket, withdrawing one of the flowery business-size cards Ronnie had given him, the ones she handed out to clients to remind them of their date's name, their meeting place, and suggested topics of conversation. "These cards have the Ronnie Pickett stamp all over them. Colorful, cheerful, and more discrete than walking into a coffee shop carrying a red rose." The hallmark of dates of old.

There was something wistful about the way he spoke that tickled Ronnie's matchmaking senses. "I could fix you up with someone, Zach."

He quickly shook his head. "That wouldn't be right. People would think I'd only gone on the date for the article."

"You need someone understanding of your schedule," Ronnie told him. "You cover news all over the county. I bet that makes for irregular hours."

His eyes widened.

"And I bet you have ambitions beyond this remote corner of Oklahoma," she continued. "You don't want to put down roots here. You're someone of a mind to move closer to a hub of activity, like Tulsa or Oklahoma City."

"Or Dallas," he said absently, gaze drifting aimlessly the way folks did when they were considering what was being said. "Big news happens in places like Dallas."

Ronnie smiled, letting his mind wrap around the idea. She'd found over the course of the week that she didn't need a sales pitch with a pricing discount as much as the ability to pinpoint what someone was looking for in a significant other.

Zach drew a deep breath, bringing his attention back to Ronnie. "But don't you put time on finding someone for me. You say your housewarming mixer is late tomorrow afternoon?"

"Yes, four to six. You're more than welcome to swing by." She'd invited plenty of clients and potential clients, but she'd made sure when she invited Wade and his family that she only mentioned the housewarming part. He'd dig in his heels at showing up to a mixer.

"I just might drop in, if only to see you in action. You're good reading material, Ronnie.

See you later." And with that, Zach tucked his phone in his pocket and moved along.

Ronnie smiled as she began circulating through the crowd behind the main stands on the lookout for potential matches.

She had a lot to be happy about. Wade had finished third on his bronc ride today, earning a little money for the first time since he'd found out Libby was sick. Ronnie had been right about Wade needing a boost to both his ego and his wallet in order to get back in the money. Just wait until he met the next woman she had in mind for him.

She was also smiling because more people were seeking her out today—cowboys who were intimidated by dating apps, cowgirls who hadn't found *the one* and were tired of the dating scene. She'd handed out a lot of flyers for her mixer tomorrow, dropping Wade's name as one of her most celebrated guests, along with Tuf Patterson and John Garner. Wade would be surprised when he found out he was among the most asked about bachelors on the rodeo circuit. Having so many charming cowgirls interested in him was going to be the best boost to his ego. Why, next weekend he was sure to win first prize!

A tall brunette cowgirl stopped in Ronnie's path. "Where did you get that jacket? It's fabulous."

Ronnie held out the ends of the red-and-black patterned buffalo jacket and struck a pose. "This is part of Cowgirl Pearl's winter collection, which you can order at our booth or buy online. And where did you get those boots? They're divine." Not to mention, the warm brown boots with flowered embroidery complemented the cowgirl's flowery button-down.

"I found this great bootmaker in Fort Worth last Christmas." The cowgirl gathered her hair over one shoulder until it tumbled in soft, pretty waves. She looked to be Cord's age, maybe a year or two out of high school. "Half boots are in right now. And I can even wear these to a nightclub."

"Those boots can go anywhere," Ronnie agreed. She introduced herself and learned the woman's name was Violet.

"Oh, you're the matchmaker. Everyone's talking about you," Violet gushed in a way that made Ronnie happy. "I thought you'd be older, from what people were saying."

The glow of happiness shattered inside her because...hello, gray hair. "And what exactly are they saying?" Had she misinterpreted the interest in her business?

"Oh, you know." Violet plucked a hair from Ronnie's shoulder.

Was that a gray hair?

Violet whisked the hair away before Ronnie could identify its color. "That there's a matchmaker, and she has this old-fashioned approach to finding love for you."

"That's true." Ronnie just didn't want the word *old* applied to her. She tried to scan the asphalt at their feet.

Was that a gray hair?

She saw nothing.

"Are you single?" Ronnie spotted a familiar face in the crowd behind the woman and cut Violet off before she could answer. "And look. There's Odelette now, the creator of Cowgirl Pearl. I'll introduce you, and you can ask about this coat." Ronnie waved to her boss at Cowgirl Pearl.

Odelette was in her forties, with curly blond hair and a tall, sleek figure that made Ronnie envious because everything looked good on her. Today, she wore a patchwork velveteen jacket in various shades of black over a silver turtleneck sweater and slate-gray jeans.

Introductions were made. Violet explained that she was from Oklahoma City, a former junior rodeo queen who was now looking to make a name for herself as a model. They had to shout because competition announcements were being made.

"Do you mind if we move away from the speaker?" At Odelette's nod, Ronnie led the women away, feeling a bit left out, as they seemed to be chattering non-stop behind her without her participation. And she had the distinct impression that she was missing more than just idle chitchat.

In fact, when they circled up a good distance away, Odelette gave Violet her business card and said, "I'll set up a meeting."

A meeting? What meeting? But the younger woman had already left and was weaving through folk toward the grandstand.

"Ronnie..." Odelette fiddled with the lay of Ronnie's coat collar. "I was wondering if you could talk to Violet about your experiences being one of our models and spokespeople. Violet has a look that's going to be great for our fall collection."

Ronnie experienced a moment of panic. "Am I being let go?"

Odelette smiled and said something, but the roar from the arena stole her words away. And then she waved, moving on.

Ronnie didn't move for a long time, letting

the crowd flow around her. A lawsuit. Gray hair. One-limit kisses. And now a potential loss of the sponsor she'd had for nearly a decade.

She had the feeling that Wade's star was on the rise while her star was starting to flare out.

CHAPTER FIFTEEN

RONNIE RODE YANNI around the barrels on Sunday morning as if she were chasing a championship.

What a waste. Those days are long gone.

As were the days of her youth. She'd found another gray hair this morning, right before she'd opened an email from Odelette with a meeting request. One that included Violet and was to be held by video conference.

Wade, Ginny, Ronnie's mother and Hank stood at the gate with Brisket when Ronnie crossed the finish line she'd drawn in the dirt earlier.

Ronnie slowed Yanni to a walk and tried not to get her gaze caught on Wade, which was hard, considering he looked good in a red flannel checked shirt and blue jeans. His straw cowboy hat was tilted back, and he smiled as if he were happy to see her.

Truth be told, Ronnie was happy to see him, too. She smiled without meaning to, and her heart pounded out a joyful rhythm in her chest. "Hey, guys."

"Hey." Wade nodded by way of greeting. It didn't matter that he was reserved. Her heart thumped faster because she recalled the firm pressure of his lips against hers and...

Hold your horses, girl.

Ronnie drew a deep, calming breath and forced herself to look elsewhere.

Hank stood silently apart from Wade and his daughter, arms crossed. Her brother looked less disapproving than simply hungover and in need of caffeine. His eyes seemed squinty behind his sunglasses.

"Ronnie, you have visitors." Mom beamed at the assembled, although her smile wobbled when it passed over Hank for some reason. "How about if I pop into the kitchen and make some cookies."

"That won't be necessary, Mom," Ronnie assured her.

"It is," Mom said adamantly. "It's not often that a kind and caring man shows up at the ranch asking for you."

"He brought Ginny to see me," Ronnie called after her mother's retreating back.

Wade chuckled. "Now I see where you got your matchmaking skills."

Ronnie forced a laugh and then gave Wade's daughter a genuine smile.

"Hi, Miss Ronnie." Ginny wore jeans instead of the dresses she'd been favoring lately at school. She also had on a cowboy hat that looked new, tan cowboy boots that had nary a scuff and a jean jacket that was crisply pressed, all of which said she spent little time on a horse at the D Double R. Or that those were her good "visiting" clothes. But Wade didn't seem the type to stomach buying duds that got next to no use, especially for a growing child.

Ronnie dismounted and slipped Yanni's reins over his head. "Ginny, you came. Are you ready for those barrel racing pointers?" The morning was sunny with the warm promise of spring around the corner. Perfect for riding.

"I'm not going to ride him, am I?" Ginny took a step back, staring at Yanni as if he had a mean streak and wasn't to be trusted.

"You're not," Ronnie was quick to reassure her, dispensing a series of loving strokes over his nose. "Yanni is too much horse for a beginner. You're going to ride Santa." An elderly piebald that had been Ronnie's first horse when she'd been competing. "He's good-natured and knows what to do on the barrels, but he's about twenty. His knees pop and he can only manage a slow trot. Does that sound okay?"

Ginny nodded, smiling bravely and making Ronnie wonder what had happened in her past to make her so hesitant about riding.

Ronnie led Yanni toward the barn, noticing in passing that Wade wasn't wearing his Daily Grind Boots. She stopped, pointing at his feet. "Those aren't the new boots you were given yesterday."

"Yeah. Well." Wade grimaced. "Turns out… My toes might not be used to the style. I tripped over my own two feet all morning until I put my regular work boots on."

"Does that mean you aren't interested in their sponsorship?" *Does this mean I need to find him another sponsor?*

"Should I be endorsing a product I don't use?" He looked down for a moment and then back at her. "That's a serious question, by the way. I'm torn."

"You should decide based on whatever helps you sleep at night," she told him.

"Then it's a no." Wade's warm gaze landed on Ronnie.

Oh my.

Was this the state of their friendship now? A slow simmer?

Ronnie forced herself to look away and ask her brother, "Hank, can you saddle Santa for me? Use my old saddle." The one she'd started using when she was about Ginny's age. The one Mom had wanted to keep for future grandchildren.

"Yes, ma'am," Hank said curtly and headed toward the barn.

"I'll do it, Hank." Wade turned to follow.

"Bring her a helmet, too. And a lariat, just in case that interests her," Ronnie called after them before smiling at Ginny. "How would you like to ride the barrels once with me on Yanni?"

Ginny took another step back, hands raised as if her gut instinct was no, nah-uh, never. "Miss Ronnie, I only came because you said we'd go slow."

Ronnie was swift to reassure her. "I only plan on walking Yanni through the clover leaf and giving you some tips for when you ride Santa. And if that doesn't work out, maybe Hank will show us how to rope. There's more than one way to compete at a rodeo."

"Oh. Okay." Ginny swallowed, raising her

chin as if holding her nose in the air would bolster her spirits.

"You can sit behind me." Ronnie swung into the saddle, removed her boot from the stirrup and extended a hand down toward Ginny.

"My dad used to do this." The little girl grabbed hold of Ronnie, tucked her boot in the stirrup and levered herself behind the cantle like a pro. She tucked her fingers in Ronnie's back jean pockets, which made Ronnie smile, reminding her of childhood rides with her parents.

"Listen up." Ronnie turned Yanni around until they faced the barrels. She let Yanni walk toward the first one. "There's more to a barrel race than just riding fast."

"Piper says you have to do tight turns," Ginny said in a tone more like her confident self.

"Yep. And tight turns are made by practicing cuing your horse." Ronnie guided Yanni toward the first barrel, keeping a close rein on him because he was tossing his head and trying to break into a run, more than ready to take another pass at full speed. "Have you ever tried to run in a circle? On your own two feet, I mean."

"When I was a baby, I played Duck, Duck, Goose."

"I bet you did in Miss Windley's first grade class." She'd probably had twenty-five students in the Duck, Duck, Goose circle. "And when you run around the circle, if you didn't keep your feet under you, you might have slipped and fallen."

"And got tagged." Ginny sounded a bit dejected, as if that had happened more times than she'd have liked. She was competitive, like her father.

So why was she uncomfortable in the saddle? Ronnie made a mental note to ask Wade.

"A horse has to keep their feet under them around each barrel. And the way you do that is practice doing small circles around the barrel. A lot." She guided Yanni around the first barrel, pointing down. "You see how close our feet are to the barrel."

"Piper knocked the barrel over before. Lots of times." Oh, the confidence. Ginny made it sound as if she'd never make that mistake were she to go at it for real.

They completed the first turn and walked toward the second barrel. Yanni tossed his head, eager to put on a show. Ronnie continued to hold him back, sparing him a couple pats on the neck to let him know walking was what she wanted from him right now.

"And every time your horse does the turn properly during practice, you tell him what a good boy he is."

"With words and actions." Ginny patted Yanni's rump. Ronnie had felt her shift and caught the movement out of the corner of her eye.

The gelding swished his tail.

"Hey!" Ginny protested, wrapping her arms around Ronnie and leaning forward.

"We're okay. He's ticklish back there. Every horse is different." Ronnie kept Yanni close on the turn around the second barrel. "When you're polishing your technique, you need to go slow around the barrel, even if you galloped over to it."

"I'm not galloping. You promised." There was panic in her high-pitched voice.

"Not today," Ronnie repeated. "And probably not tomorrow. But if you want to compete, even if it's only with Piper when you visit her ranch, you'll need to go faster, but safely."

Yanni tried to break into a trot as they headed for the final barrel.

Ginny released a little squeal even as Ronnie brought him back in check.

"Have you ever fallen off a horse, Ginny?" Ronnie didn't want to wait any longer to ask Wade.

Ginny leaned forward until her chin brushed Ronnie's shoulder to say, "I almost have a couple of times. When we trot, I bounce. And when I bounce, I scream. Uncle Griff says that just makes a horse go faster."

"Sometimes." But almost falling didn't leave the level of fear Ginny seemed to have. "If you haven't fallen, why scream?"

Yanni tossed his head, prancing as they approached the last barrel.

"Because..." Ginny rested her chin on Ronnie's shoulder. "My dad gets thrown all the time. Same with Uncle Griff when he rode bulls. They get all scraped up. There's blood and bruises."

"I'm not talking about competitive bronc or bull riding. I'm asking you about riding a horse in general. You seem afraid." Ronnie glanced over her shoulder, trying to get a good look at Ginny's face.

There was no fear there. No panic. "Mom didn't like to ride. She didn't want me to ride when I was younger."

"Your mama was a townie." Someone who hadn't grown up on a ranch or ever owned a horse. "But I've been on trail rides with you. You did just fine."

"Maybe." Ginny's arms were still wrapped around Ronnie's waist. She felt the girl shrug. "Piper told me she was riding before she learned to walk."

"That's an exaggeration. Piper didn't ride alone until she was older, I'm sure. You shouldn't judge yourself by anyone else's yardstick."

Another shrug. The sprite was determined to use any excuse to say she couldn't ride when it seemed she longed for the talent of a true horsewoman. "My grandma Mary says not everyone is cut out for the saddle. Just look at my Uncle Dix. He doesn't like to ride. He runs the bank."

"He works in the bank."

Ginny made a non-committal noise.

"And no one should make you do something you don't like. It's just that growing up on a ranch, most kids like to ride. And the practice, including falls and near falls, makes us stronger riders. Just like how you got better at bike riding, by practicing."

They crossed the finish line. Yanni snorted, plodding toward the barn.

"Look at us," Ronnie said. "We made it

through one time. Walking and no falls. Do you want to go again?"

"Yes, please, Miss Ronnie." Wade's confident little girl was back.

Ronnie hoped she could continue encouraging her. She herself had gained so much from barrel racing. The sense of achievement that came from doing something well. How to get over the sting of loss and the humility to congratulate the winner. So many life lessons.

But none of them had prepared her for the jolt of attraction she felt when Wade came into her line of sight lately.

"YOU WERE RIGHT about Santa." Wade leaned on a fence rail inside the arena near Ronnie, trying to keep a friendly distance and alternatively wishing he didn't have to. "That piebald's joints pop with every movement."

"It's hard to be all that nervous when your mount is as rickety and slow as he is." Ronnie nodded and then shouted a word of encouragement to Ginny, "Slow is how you learn."

Panting, Brisket ambled over to them, navigating around a mud puddle created by the water trough that was outside the arena behind Wade. The Labrador plopped down in the dirt by Ronnie next to the lariat Hank had left them. Brisket wanted to be near Ronnie, same as Wade.

But much as Wade wanted to be close enough to touch Ronnie and run his fingers through her soft, thick hair, he'd often sensed over the past week that something weighed heavily on her mind. And he wanted to know what it was, admittedly, because he hoped the attraction between them wasn't what was bothering her.

Hank was in the barn behind them, but for how long? And if Wade knew his daughter, Ginny wouldn't last much longer walking through the clover leaf. If he wanted to talk to Ronnie about a sensitive topic, it was now or never.

"Something's been troubling you all week." Unable to resist touching her any longer, Wade brushed her hair over her shoulder, letting his fingers linger a moment longer in those velvety tresses.

"Would you believe me if I told you I found some gray hairs?" She gathered her hair behind her, lifted her hat, and tucked it all underneath.

Out of his reach.

Wade sighed, tipping his hat back. "You're

too stubborn to get discouraged by something like a gray hair or two."

"That's it, Ginny. Tight turns." Ronnie looked to Wade. "It's not just gray hairs but I can handle it." When he opened his mouth to protest that sentiment, she added, "If I need you, I'll ask." She tugged the hem of her teal chambray shirt down over her slender hips. "Are you coming to my housewarming party this afternoon? It's adults only."

"I was told to be there. I'll be there," he said darkly.

She glanced at him.

Ginny glanced over, too. At their feet, Brisket lifted his broad head, looked up.

"You're upsetting everyone," Ronnie told Wade. She picked up the lariat.

"You know what else is upsetting? That you won't tell me what's bothering you." He lowered his voice and moved closer, "Much less talk about that kiss the other night."

Ronnie took a step and stumbled over Brisket as he jumped to his feet and in her way. Wade grabbed for her hand but ended up with the loose end of the lariat, pulling without finding any tension.

Ronnie fell backward as Brisket barreled forward and into Wade's legs, sweeping them out from under him and knocking him face-first into the mud puddle.

It was a cold and wintery mud puddle. The wet seeped into his jeans, his hands, and the front of his shirt.

"Dad?" Ginny called from the center of the arena. "What happened?"

Hurricane Ronnie.

"Wade, are you okay?" Ronnie clambered to his side and took hold of his arm, giving it a tug. "I'm sorry. I'm so, so sorry."

Wade knew he should laugh it off. It was just mud. But there was too much exasperation bottled inside of him, and the ineffectual tugs Ronnie was making on his arm weren't helping him to his feet or to keep the lid on his temper. And the mud...

"Dad, what happened?" Ginny asked again as Wade stood up.

He shrugged off Ronnie's hold on his arm. "Ronnie happened."

The moment the words left his mouth, Wade regretted them.

He was reminded of something his father used to say: "The easiest way to hurt someone is to voice the truth they've been telling themselves."

He was probing her sore spot—her ability to create a vortex in an otherwise calm moment.

Brisket trotted off. Forty feet away, Santa's joints popped as he plodded toward a barrel away from the fence with Ginny twisted around to look back at Wade.

Heedless of the mud, Wade drew Ronnie closer. "I'm sorry. That was insensitive. I know this was an accident."

She stared at him with huge, watery eyes. "But accidents have a way of following me around."

"That's not true." But they both knew it was. He shook his head. "Even if it was true, I don't care about that."

"You did a moment ago." Ronnie closed her eyes but didn't move away. If anything, her arms tensed beneath his hands. She opened her eyes and stared into his. "I don't date because things like this frequently happen to me, and when they do, it's upsetting. To everyone involved. I understand that. And I…" She moved her hands to brush at the mud on the front of his jacket. It was a futile effort. "I realize there's a dose of kismet about my life. I don't know if I was born under an unlucky star or what." Her hands fell away.

"Dad?" Ginny had rounded a barrel and was heading back their way.

"Keep going Ginny, I'm okay." He needed more time to talk to Ronnie. "Yeah, life is unfair. But it's unfair to all of us in different ways. And no matter the hand we're dealt, we work with it. We find our strength. We look for silver linings. And we count our blessings." Ronnie was one of his.

She chewed on her bottom lip, shoulders rising toward her ears. "My life is unpredictable in that I don't know how serious the havoc my little missteps cause is going to be." The way she looked at him…as if he should understand there was more to what she was saying…

He couldn't see it.

"The other night at the Buckboard, I told you about a make-believe, fly fishing date." Again, Ronnie's tone implied he should be having an aha moment. Her eyes were huge, staring up at him and begging for him to fill in the blanks. "I did, in fact, go on a disastrous date like that, not fly fishing per se. And I am, in fact, being sued."

"Tell me who's doing this." Wade had a sudden urge to teach the man some manners.

"I know you don't really mean to threaten

someone with bodily harm." Ronnie exhaled, shoulders coming down. "But that lawsuit and the visceral reaction you just had to landing in a mud puddle are why I don't dance with guys at the Buckboard. It's why I can't kiss you anymore. I value our friendship too much."

"Because you think I'll break a leg and hire a lawyer?"

"Keep working those turns, Ginny," Ronnie called in a thick voice that didn't quite reach cheerful, as if they weren't suddenly in the middle of an argument about relationships.

About our relationship.

"Because I think you'll get frustrated, Wade, when something happens." Ronnie took a step back from Wade. "Then I'll get upset. Then we'll have a falling out. Maybe I'm wrong. Maybe you won't break a limb and blame me for the accident. Perhaps you'll try to wrap me in a bubble the way my family does, and I'll end up resenting you. However it happens, I know where following a road paved with your kisses will lead us. Our friendship will dead-end. And I… I like our friendship too much to let that happen."

Wade pondered Ronnie's words and attitude, trying to find an argument to sway her. She was afraid, but not in the way he'd expected. Those rules of hers…

"Ronnie Pickett, you're afraid you'll bring your bad luck to a relationship?"

Ronnie nodded. "That's right."

Wade couldn't hide his disappointment. He disagreed with her. Heck, for all Ronnie knew, he could be her forever. But she wasn't willing to try him out and see. "You think whoever marries you will grow weary of the accidents and leave you?" He wanted to be very clear about things, even if it meant restating what she'd said. "Whether it's me or someone else?" Because she had rules for all men, not just him.

She nodded again.

He wished she was teasing now, testing him like she usually did, like she always had. But he knew that wasn't the case. He lifted her hat, freeing all those dark, silky curls. "Ronnie Pickett, you're a fool who doesn't know the first thing about love. Love isn't a gentle trail ride where you know where you're headed. Love doesn't care if you have good luck or bad. Love accepts foibles and forgives the fallout from bumps in the road." He gestured toward his muddy clothing. "Love cares about who you are inside, about what your values are and how you make someone feel when you're together. Why would you deny that for yourself?"

Ronnie shook her head. "You don't get it."

He pushed her hat into her hands, wanting to make her see the fallacy of her thinking. "Then explain it to me. Explain how falling in the mud or in a river makes you less deserving of love."

Instead of arguing, she ran away, grabbing onto a gate rail and using it to pivot toward the barn. The entire portion of fencing between the gate and Wade vibrated, like Wade's equilibrium.

He couldn't even find the words to calm Ginny when she sent a questioning look his way.

Because he believed there could be something important between him and Ronnie. And Ronnie only saw stop signs ahead.

Chest heaving, Wade would have followed Ronnie, desperation in his veins and heart in his hands, but a strong grip caught his arm.

"Let her go," Hank said, having reached for him between the arena rails. "You've got Ginny to watch."

And much as Wade wanted to go after Ronnie, he knew where his responsibility lay.

"COME DOWN FROM the hay loft, Ronnie," Hank called not long after Ronnie had fled up the ladder. "Wade is taking off with Ginny."

A truck engine started nearby. Gears shifting before it drove away.

Wade.

"Ronnie, don't make me come up there," Hank said in a good imitation of their mother's voice.

When she didn't show herself or answer, her brother appeared at the top of the ladder and spotted her. He came over to sit in front of Ronnie on the wooden loft floor, nudging her knee with one hand. "You've always been a thorn in my side, hanging out in the hay loft where there are no safety rails. What would Mom say?"

Ronnie wiped her eyes, declining to comment. Wade couldn't see the favor she was doing him by ending things before they started. And her brother was being glib?

"So what if your life is sprinkled with unexpected mishaps? So what if someone has to get used to taking a tumble in the mud every once in a while? Quit acting like you are less deserving of happiness."

He'd heard.

Ronnie wanted to shrivel up and play possum. But that had never worked for her, so she wiped her nose. "Why can't you or Wade see? I'd need to marry someone with the patience of a saint to be guaranteed a lasting relationship."

"Man, would you listen to yourself?" Hank's brows lowered, along with his tone. "You sound like Mom."

I do. And wasn't that upsetting.

Ronnie folded her fists against her thighs. "Because she's right."

"She's not." Hank had dark circles under his eyes and a grim set to his mouth. "I refuse to let you label yourself as a burden or a risk to a relationship. And if you'd listen to Wade, he's refusing, too."

Her shoulders sank. "I know everything you say is true. I know it in here." She tapped her chest over her heart. "But then the enormity of it all rises up, and it's like I'm drowning. It's so frustrating."

"Why? Because you have hardship?" Hank scoffed, gaze casting about the space between them, searching for something only he understood. "No one is perfect, Ronnie. Do you want to know why I haven't settled down yet? The real reason?"

She nodded, more than happy to turn the spotlight on him.

"Because I want to build this ranch into something more than Dad ever dreamed of. And to do that takes sacrifice financially. My truck is ten years old. I can't tell you the last time I bought a pair of blue jeans." He removed his hat and ran a hand over his thick, black hair. "I never go out with my friends. And yet, I went out last night and drank too much. But do you want to know why I have dark circles under my eyes? And why I've been cranky all morning?"

She nodded again.

"Because I bought a couple of rounds for everyone. I spent hard-earned cash that I'm supposed to have been saving to buy a prize bull." He mashed his hat back on his head. "So what if I fall in love? If I can't provide or contribute to the partnership, it won't work. In fact, we'll just end up divorced. And that's why I avoid love. Not because I have you to take care of; you can take care of yourself, although you are a pain in the butt sometimes."

"Hey!" Ronnie grabbed hold of Hank's

hands, having caught the most important statement in his diatribe. "Who are you in love with?"

He jerked his hands free. "You and that matchmaking... Don't you get it? This isn't about me. This is about you and your happiness. You have to attack this with the same verve you approach any problem or dream you've ever had." Hank made as if to get up but then sat back down and took hold of her hands. "You've had your eye on Wade Keller since I don't know when. But you're nice and so you stepped aside. And Libby and Wade found happiness. This time, it's your turn. Don't let your penchant for finding trouble stand in the way of what you've always wanted."

Ronnie didn't know what to say. She was still clinging to the argument that Wade deserved more than she could offer. So she said nothing.

Not even when Hank left her.

She sank back in the hay, knowing she'd be itchy for hours afterward.

Wade is right. Hank is right.

But she couldn't kick the feeling in her heart that they were wrong, no matter how many times she told herself otherwise.

CHAPTER SIXTEEN

"Now that's what I call a housewarming party." Griff drove slowly past Ronnie's house.

"And you say nothing ever happens in Clementine," Ryan teased his brother Tate from where both were sitting in the back seat.

Wade frowned.

Cars and trucks lined the normally quiet street. Music pounded out the open front door. Cowboys and cowgirls filled the porch, the walkway and, from what Wade could see, the living room.

"She said it was a housewarming party?" Wade clutched the bouquet of flowers in his lap. "Somebody got their wires crossed." And he didn't think it was him.

He hadn't talked to Ronnie since she'd run off this morning at the Pickett Ranch. He'd brought her flowers and planned to stay long after the party was over to talk in more depth. At least, that's what he intended until he'd seen the type of party she was hosting.

"Dude, look at all those red plastic cups. This is a kegger." Griff practically crowed with enthusiasm. "I shouldn't have gotten out my Sunday boots for this. I'll be worrying the whole time about some yahoo spilling brewski on me."

"Don't get ahead of yourself," Wade cautioned even though he suspected Griff was right both about the type of party that was going on and the risk to a good pair of boots, his included.

What was going on?

Wade began to worry. And his worry only increased as they had to park three blocks away and walk back to Ronnie's. It may have been February, but the sun was already setting. And the music carried to them as the four men rounded the corner on the far end of King Street.

"Is that Tuf Patterson?" Ryan pushed his way ahead of Wade on the sidewalk. "It is."

"What's a bull rider from Kansas doing here?" Increasingly, Wade was getting a bad feeling.

"That's John Garner across the street," Ryan's twin Tate said. John was the saddle bronc leader from last year. "Since when does rodeo royalty come to Clementine?"

"Since Ronnie Pickett decided they all needed to fall in love," Wade griped. He spotted a splash of color through the living room window, Ronnie's black hair and red dress heading toward the back of the house. He left his brothers outside and pushed his way through the front door.

"There's the man I came to meet." A sturdy brunette with a wide smile and a cup of beer in each hand greeted Wade at the door. "I'm DeeDee Reynolds. If you haven't heard, I ride bulls and I'm single." She tried to give Wade one of her red beer cups. "Ronnie wants to fix me up with a roper, but I know what I want, and it's a seasoned man with a good head on his shoulders."

Someone behind Wade squawked with laughter. Since it sounded like Griff, Wade didn't turn around to see if his brother was laughing at his expense. Wade tipped his hat to DeeDee and pushed forward. But it was a crush, and he only made it to the next circle of cowgirls.

"Wade. Wade, hi." A short-haired blonde wearing a black wool gambler hat, chunky turquoise jewelry and a long flowing white dress stepped in his path. She glanced over her shoulder at the women she'd been talking to. "I call dibs. He's the one for me!"

Wade clenched his jaw, gaze drifting over the crowd searching for Ronnie. He took a step around her.

The blonde moved to block him, the same way a cutting horse moved to keep a cow from rejoining the herd. "I'm Sara, no H. Barrel racer. Single." She fluffed the hair that barely touched the back of her neck. "And I own my own ranchette up by the Kansas border. I can't eat shellfish or tomatoes—allergic. And I like kids."

Wade was a bit taken aback by the info dump. Was he supposed to respond in kind? He didn't think so. "Did Ronnie tell you to say that?"

Sara with no H did a little shoulder roll, smiling slyly. "Not exactly."

Wade kept walking. At least he'd figured out that this shindig was less a housewarming and more a calling card for Ronnie's new business. Whenever women stepped in his path or caught his eye, he gave them an apologetic "Not interested."

He reached the hallway and neared the kitchen opening. A quick scan revealed what looked like a line for the bathroom but no Ronnie. He continued into the kitchen.

There appeared to be couples taking up space on the salmon-colored linoleum. The cowboys sent him wary glances, as if their competition had unexpectedly shown up at a bronc riding event. The cowgirls waved and smiled and went back to their conversations.

Wade took a time-out to find a vase in a cupboard above the sink, fill it with water. He stuck his bouquet inside without removing the purple cellophane wrapper. And then he turned and asked no one in particular, "Where's Ronnie?"

"On the patio," someone said.

He wormed his way out back. The evening still retained some of the day's unseasonal warmth. Ronnie had strung lights from the patio overhang, laid a colorful rose-patterned rug on the deck, and cut back the ivy in the large pots such that they no longer looked overgrown. There was a crowd here, as well, mingling around the keg.

Ronnie stood at the far end of the patio wearing a cute red dress with her favorite red boots, seemingly making an introduction between a young cowgirl and an equally wet-behind-the-ears cowboy. The handful of cowboys and cowgirls watched Ronnie in a way that made Wade nervous, like they were just waiting for an opportunity to make a run at her.

What was going on here?

Movement behind Ronnie caught his eye.

Zach, the pompous reporter.

The man held up his phone as if he was recording every word being said. Wade gritted his teeth. But he bided his time, waiting for Ronnie to finish speaking with the couple before he approached.

"Excuse me." Someone grabbed hold of his arm. "But I'm next."

Reason for the edgy watchfulness is now clear. Not that it made Wade feel any better.

"I'm not in line for matchmaking." Wade shrugged his arm free. "I need to talk to Ronnie about something else." Misleading him about parties and excuses for not wanting to date him.

When Wade turned back around, Ronnie and Zach were speaking.

Heat steamed in Wade's veins.

That man is too close.

He stomped over, uncaring about the queue. *"Ronnie."* It was all he could do to keep from taking her hand and leading her away, although the question was: *Away where?* People were everywhere. Private, this gathering was not.

"Wade, thanks for coming." Ronnie's smile lacked its usual glow.

It was just another reason he wanted to rescue her.

She looped her hand through the crook of his arm, which he quickly decided was a good sign. "I just finished launching a match and answering some questions from Zach. Isn't the party wild?"

"Too wild, I'd say." His comment earned him a flash of her dark eyes. "Can you spare me a minute?" Wade stared at Zach the way Tornado Bill stared at riders he'd thrown and planned to stomp. *"Alone."*

"Of course." Ronnie thanked Zach and told him he should circulate. "There's a cowgirl inside with short red hair and a pink fringed leather jacket. I think you should talk to her. She's looking to go places."

Zach tucked his phone into his back khakis pocket. "Is she one of your matchmaking successes?"

"No, Zach," Ronnie said in a patient way Wade recognized. "Her name is Willa and I'm betting you two might hit it off."

Rejection! Wade stifled a cackle.

Meanwhile, Zach looked crestfallen. He spared Wade a mulish look before heading inside.

"You've crushed him," Wade told Ronnie. "He's sweet on you."

Ronnie laughed self-consciously, eyes on the patio cue of lonely hearts. "I'm not his type."

"That's what you said about the two of us in high school." How could he still love Libby and feel this measure of frustration over something Ronnie had said to him in the past? As if he were angry over time lost with Ronnie.

Ronnie didn't respond how Wade expected—with that brash fire of hers. In fact, for once, she looked at a loss for words.

"How much longer will this be?" An earnest cowgirl with a blue leather jacket smiled hopefully at Ronnie. "It's getting cold out here."

"What?" Ronnie seemed to blink back to the present. "Oh, Candace. I wanted you to meet Lars. You share a love of rescue animals and superhero movies." She made hand gestures like those airport workers who parked planes on the tarmac, guiding Candace and—apparently—Lars closer. "You live in the same county. And, if nothing else, I think you'd work well together establishing a charity for animal rescues. Candace, tell Lars about the significance of that coat you have on. It has quite a story, Lars." She waved to someone in the back. "Sam? Monica?" Ronnie moved away from Wade and repeated a similar spiel to another couple, this time urging them to talk about a love of international travel.

And moved on to repeat…

And moved on to repeat…

Until the patio was full of couples, including Ronnie and Wade.

Now was his chance. Wade steered Ronnie toward the narrow side yard.

"What are you doing?" She dragged her feet. "I've got to check on people inside."

"Even busy entrepreneurs need a breather." Wade stopped near a large vine draped over the fence that looked as if it couldn't decide if it was going to make it through the winter. He faced her. "What's going on here?"

Ronnie tried to play innocent, shrugging. "I'm having a housewarming party."

"Emphasis on party." Wade gave in to impulse and softened his stance. "When I imagined your housewarming, I pictured a few friends gathering for a beer or a glass of wine. I hoped to be able to have a few private words with you." After what she'd told him this morning, he had a lot to say. "But the reality is…" Frustration welled inside of him again, spilling out into his words despite the best of intentions. "You decided to throw a real crowd-pleaser, complete with name-dropping rodeo stars. As soon as I entered, I was stared at, flirted with and propositioned." Okay, he might have made that last part up.

"I'm sorry I wasn't up front about the invite. But the event's going great." Ronnie pointed at the house. "Admittedly, things are bigger—and louder—than I expected. I only invited a select few cowboys and cowgirls, thinking it'd be a quiet gathering where folks could really get to know one another."

"Word probably spread," Wade said, wishing she'd reach out to take his hand.

"I even had a wonderful woman picked out to meet you." She grabbed hold of Wade's elbows. "She's a horse breeder currently located up in Kansas and—"

"By the border?" Wade frowned, thinking of Sara, no H.

Ronnie tilted her head. "Yes, how did you know?"

"We met. She's not my type." *She's not you.*

A siren chirped out front, the way cops hit the button when they wanted to catch someone's attention. It did the trick.

"Oh my goodness." Ronnie hurried toward the side gate. "The sheriff is here. I hope no one is hurt."

"I hope none of your neighbors called the cops on you," he said, following her to the front yard.

"SHERIFF UNDERWOOD, what can I do for you?" Ronnie had never been caught so much as jaywalking. But she feared only two weeks after moving in that she was breaking a law.

Normally, Sheriff Underwood was easygoing, even mellow. He had a middle-age paunch and a friendly round face. When she saw him around town or on school grounds, he always had a kind word for her.

Tonight, he looked at Ronnie as if they'd never met. And his voice…

"Do you know how many laws you're breaking, Veronica?" There was an expectation in his tone that she'd respond with a correct answer. Or at least a very good guess.

"Let's see…noise…" Although she'd scheduled her mixer for late afternoon, that probably didn't preclude her from breaking a noise ordinance. She hadn't been out front since people began arriving. Someone's truck was parked on the sidewalk in front of Izzy's house. Shoot. What was wrong with people? "…parking…" She followed the direction of the sheriff's cool gaze. "…fire code…" There had to be too many people in her house for safety reasons. "And that's just about it," she finished hopefully, wondering where Wade had gone.

"That's not just about it. I'm just getting started." Sheriff Underwood pressed the button on the handset strapped to his shoulder and requested backup.

Ronnie hoped that was because Clementine was a sleepy town and the sheriff wanted to share this unique event with others in his department. Because the alternative was that he planned on handing out multiple citations and perhaps even arrests.

"But…" Ronnie took her cell phone out of her dress pocket, glancing at the time. "We were just wrapping up. My little soiree was listed from four to six p.m." It was almost six now. "Give me a few minutes to shoo folks out the door." Ronnie turned, surprised that Wade, Griff, Ryan and Tate were already on it.

Someone shut the music off. The living room and porch lights flashed off and on over and over, just like they would at a club.

She faced the hard truth then, about how her "intimate mixer" had turned into something resembling a college frat party.

"Is there anyone you suspect needs a designated driver?" Sheriff Underwood asked her sternly.

"No." He didn't like Ronnie's answer, so she hurried on: "But I was out in the back for at least an hour..." She stopped, realizing she was only digging her hole deeper.

"Hey, Sheriff." Wade came to stand beside her, placing a hand on the small of her back and not so much as raising an eyebrow when she inched closer. "Looks like Ronnie invited some friends over for a housewarming party, and each friend invited a half-dozen more. It could happen to anyone."

"But it happened to Ronnie, who's new to town." There was an edge to Sheriff Underwood's voice, one that promised a ticket was forthcoming.

"I'm not new," Ronnie protested, albeit weakly.

"You've never lived in town," the sheriff pointed out. "We do things differently here.

There are more rules than you'll find on a remote ranch. Here you need to worry about how your actions impact your neighbors." He turned, watching a pair of cowboys saunter down the middle of the street, and she lost whatever he said next.

She was happy to see there were several couples walking together as they left her house. Happier still that no one seemed to be weaving as they walked.

A trio of cowboys came out of the side gate carrying the keg. She had no idea who they were, but they must have been the ones who supplied the beer and the red plastic cups.

Truck engines fired up, and she waved back to the cowboys as they left. The sheriff moseyed after them. If he said anything more, it wasn't to her.

Another sheriff's SUV pulled up, lights strobing red and blue, lighting up the street. Wade said something about checking on the house and went inside, leaving Ronnie alone.

Only then did she notice her neighbors had come out on their front porches and lawns. She waved and shouted, "Sorry," several times. She was going to have to bake cupcakes and distribute them with profuse apologies this week.

Apparently dismissed by the sheriff for now, Ronnie went into the house, where Wade and his brothers were cleaning up. Wade had a trash bag, and the men were picking up beer cups, discarded napkins and such.

"You don't need to help. I've got this," she told them, although she didn't immediately leap into action. Her ears were ringing, probably from all that noise, and her legs felt unsteady.

It was probably a good thing that the cowboys from the D Double R ignored her.

"Okay, then." She went to her bedroom and let Brisket out. He raced around, bouncing off the cowboy cleanup crew, and then scampered out front to do his business.

Wade and his brothers went about their tasks efficiently and without interacting with Ronnie or Brisket when he returned to her.

"Okay, then," Ronnie said again, going into the kitchen. There were no more cupcakes. The hors d'oeuvres plate was scattered with crumbs and discarded toothpicks. Her punch bowl was empty. And someone had brought her flowers.

Wade.

She unwrapped the brightly colored bouquet before wiping down her serving plates, certain that Wade and the sheriff would want to talk once her guests had safely left the neighborhood. "I don't know whether to feel elated or crushed at these results."

"Both." Wade appeared at her side, took her hand and suggested they move out to the front porch where the sheriff awaited her.

Wade's brothers were nowhere to be seen.

"You scraped through this one, Miss Ronnie," the sheriff scolded. "I never would have expected something like this from you. And on a Sunday, too."

"It won't happen again," Wade assured him. He was taking charge the way Hank always did, not listening to Ronnie or letting her make decisions.

Or in this case, excuses.

A twinge of anger put a kink in her neck.

"That's my line, Wade." And although she was gently scolding him, Ronnie tried to look repentant for the sheriff's sake. "It won't happen again." She'd learned her lesson. Mixers would no longer be held at her home.

The sheriff and his deputy got into their vehicles and left.

Wade turned to Ronnie, brushing a lock of hair away from her face. "Are you all right?"

"Yes." She sighed. It was hard to stay mad

at him when he was only trying to be helpful. She called Brisket, who was once more on sniff patrol, and then went inside, assuming that Wade would follow. Now that the sun was down and the excitement over, she was cold. "I didn't see Zach leave, did you? I hope he went before the sheriff arrived. That wouldn't look good in the article."

Wade closed the door behind him. "You mean, you hope Zach hit it off with the redhead you steered him toward instead of you. And you hope he doesn't write that your party drew the attention of the police."

"It was a success, though." She pointed toward the street, anger trying to work its way back to her neck. "Did you see how many couples walked out of here?" Sure, most of them were freebies, but didn't she have to give away free samples to generate more business?

Wade nodded. "The sheriff was right about one thing. This isn't like you. The Ronnie I know wouldn't consider a bunch of rowdy cowboys taking over her party a success. She'd have the gumption to keep control." It was amazing how she knew he was right but resented him telling the truth to her face.

Wade closed the distance between them

and wrapped his arms around her. His warm breath so close to her skin gave her a delicious shiver. "You've been in situations where tempers flare. That could have happened here given the drinking. Someone could have been hurt. What if that someone was you? Or Brisket?

"I know you want to prove yourself and your independence…" He stared at her thoughtfully before he spoke again. "But you've proven to a lot of people, including me, that you can do anything you set your mind to, look at that matchmaking business, for instance."

"Oh, but—" She almost admitted she'd never meant to start this business in the first place, which would have been a lapse in judgment since she'd have to come clean about Libby wanting her to find him a wife.

But he saved her from that mistake by making another. His mouth lowered over hers, and he kissed her so softly, so tenderly, that Ronnie had to hold on to him—and kiss him back—to keep from crying.

Turns out, she didn't do a very good job at keeping the tears at bay.

"What's wrong?" He swept her tears away with his thumb.

"Nothing is turning out the way I wanted

it to." She'd wanted a nice, simple gathering. She'd wanted to find him a mate who'd make his life more carefree. And once she'd decided to make a go of matchmaking, she'd wanted people beating down her door for her help finding them love.

"Nothing is turning out the way you want it to?" Wade's gentle smile inexplicably made her want to shed more tears. "Is that really a bad thing?"

Before she could answer, he kissed her again.

CHAPTER SEVENTEEN

"DEAR, SWEET RONNIE." Norma took Ronnie's hands Monday morning at school and gave them a heartfelt squeeze. "I heard a motorcycle gang held you hostage over the weekend and the sheriff had to rescue you. You must have been so scared."

Ronnie hastened to explain that it had been cowboys who'd hijacked her party, not her, and that everything had turned out fine.

"So they didn't bring a keg or lock you and your dog in the bedroom?" At Ronnie's headshake, Norma released her and sat in her chair. "I'm going to have to call my friend Adelaide and tell her the town grapevine got everything all wrong."

Ronnie smiled.

But the miscommunications continued.

Ginny darted into the office when she should have been at recess. "Uncle Griff says you like my dad."

"Oh?" Norma looked as if she'd won the lottery.

"No need to spread rumors, Miss Virginia." Ronnie hurried to squelch this one, hoping the rising heat in her cheeks didn't give her away.

Why did I have to let him kiss me again?

Why? Because he was a darn good kisser, that's why.

And after he'd kissed her thoroughly, Wade had turned on his boot heel and left without leaving time for any more discussion. Not about her being afraid. Or about her feeling like a burden. Or about why he was so intent upon kissing her all the time.

Well, not all the time.

He'd waved to her as he was dropping Ginny off to school today. And she'd been of two minds that he hadn't hopped out to kiss her.

It was all for the best that he hadn't.

Ronnie fixed Ginny with a level stare. "Your Uncle Griff is known to exaggerate. And you know that your father and I are just good friends."

Ginny considered Ronnie for a tad too long for comfort, those big brown eyes of hers as discerning as her father's. "If that's true, why is your face red?"

Ronnie's hands flew to her cheeks.

"Wait until I tell Piper!" Ginny flew out the door before Ronnie could stop her.

"Seriously?" Ronnie sank down in her chair, wondering aloud, "What else could go wrong today?"

A few hours later, she found out.

"Did you know that fella was going to write another article about you?" Norma asked after the last bell of the afternoon had rung. She gestured to her computer screen and an article from the *Valley Gazette*.

"Yes. He told me he was doing a series on me getting my business up and running." Ronnie came to stand behind Norma, reading the article over her shoulder.

It started out complimentary, recapping how Ronnie had a unique business idea and a plan in place to launch it. Zach mentioned her struggles to find clients, her change in pricing and her few early successes. And then things got ugly.

The atmosphere wasn't so much mixer as rave. The house was too small for the number of singles looking for love, and the party spilled out to the street.

"A rave?" Ronnie grit her teeth.

Meanwhile, Ms. Pickett was in the backyard, pairing rodeo and ranch singles with all the skill and precision of a laundress matching lost socks at the laundromat.

"He sounds like he's making fun of you," Norma said.

"Yes, he does." Ronnie took control of Norma's computer mouse and scrolled down to read more.

At one point, her star draw for women, a handsome, washed-up bronc rider, marched out of the crowd, looking unsettled. Ms. Pickett went into damage-control mode, juggling the cowboy's fragile ego while pairing up the singles most interested in finding love—admittedly, proof of her skill in the art of love.

Washed-up? Fragile ego? Wade wasn't going to be happy.

Forget Wade. Ronnie wasn't happy.

At this point, Ms. Pickett pointed out a possible match for this reporter. In the spirit of the assignment, a coffee date was made. An update on the outcome will be featured in the next installment of this series. But don't hold your breath. Although Ms. Pickett claimed the match a good one, this reporter has his doubts.

"I hope that woman stands him up," Norma said uncharitably, firmly on Team Ronnie.

"That would just prove that I'm a sham." Ronnie didn't understand it. "Zach wrote such a glowing article last time."

"Maybe he already met the woman and wasn't impressed." Norma scrolled through the article again. "Still, where are that man's professional standards?"

"Where indeed." Just as she'd half-expected—another good thing gone bad in her life. It was just supposed to be a little free publicity. He'd been the one to approach her, not the other way around, after all. "When I see that—"

The office door was flung open. "If only I would have known…" Ronnie's mother burst in. She came around the counter and hugged Ronnie. "You shouldn't have stayed alone in that house last night."

"Why not? It's my home." She held her mother at arm's length, trying to check the temperature of her upset. "Don't tell me you think I was kidnapped by a motorcycle gang in Clementine? We don't even have a motorcycle club, much less a gang."

"No, no." Mom smiled smoothly, which was a ploy considering how frantically she'd burst into the office. "I got a firsthand account of the party from Hank."

Ronnie released her mother. "Hank wasn't there."

"Oh, he heard it from Wade." And there it was. Smug satisfaction. "And then I heard it from Wade."

Wade.

It wasn't a charitable thought this time.

Ronnie's shoulders tensed.

"You should have come home last night." Mom was on a roll, moving into familiar bubble-wrapping territory. "You're an easy mark because you're overly friendly—"

"I didn't win over the sheriff when he showed up." Ronnie didn't mince words. But she didn't shout, either. She was going to win this power struggle with her mother.

"—and your door locks are flimsy."

"I have a guard dog." Ronnie moved to smoothing her mother's hair. "Brisket, remember? You sent him over."

"He's a barker," Mom said as if that explained everything. "If intruders can be licked to death, you're in good hands under Brisket's care. But this is different. Cowboys brought a beer keg to a housewarming party."

"Hey, Nell. Can you sign in?" Norma turned the clipboard with the visitor's sign-in sheet toward Ronnie's mother. "Did you see this article on Ronnie?"

Ronnie resisted clapping a hand to her forehead.

Mom dutifully signed in. She was nothing if not a rule follower. "Do you mean the article that came out last week?"

"Oh, no. This is new." Norma moved back to her desk and angled her screen so Ronnie's mother could see. "Come on back."

Mom didn't need to be asked twice. She charged back to Norma's workstation and took a seat at her desk.

Norma caught Ronnie's eye and mouthed, *I got this.*

Or she could have said, *I want fish.* Ronnie wasn't sure.

"Ronnie," Mom said after a few minutes of silence. She looked up, frowning. "I think this man is making a mockery of you."

"It felt personal." Norma nodded, smirking. "I bet you don't get as many calls today as you did last week when his first article came out."

"Phone calls." Ronnie dug her phone out of her red leather swing bag and checked her voicemail. "Thirty messages. Take that, Zach!" The jerk. She'd only had ten last week.

Norma leaned over her desk and said in her assembly voice, "I bet half of those calls are from other reporters looking to scoop her story."

"Wouldn't that be nice?" Ronnie gathered her things. She needed to go home and make cupcakes as an apology gift for the neighborhood. "Can you two just think positive thoughts?"

"No," they both told her.

Ronnie felt the bubbles her mother wanted to wrap her in closing around her. "Wait a minute. Why did you talk to Wade?"

"DAD, CAN YOU help me set up barrels?" Ginny wound her way through the garage to where Wade was getting his daily workout in.

"Barrels?" For a moment, Wade was at a loss, wondering why Ginny wanted help planting flowers in his mother's wooden garden casks in the middle of winter. In the middle of a set of bench presses, Wade racked his weights and sat up.

"Yes, the racing barrels?" Ginny stepped onto the black mats that served as padded flooring in the back corner of the garage. "And I want to ride Baby Bear."

Wade got to his feet. "Baby Bear is a pony." Ginny's pony. But still, she hadn't ridden him in a long time. They kept the pony around for Chandler's little boy to ride when he visited. "Why don't we saddle Pepper?"

"Dad." Ginny came to stand next to Wade, looking at him as if he should know the answer to his own question.

He'd bought Pepper for Ginny because she came from a long line of barrel racers. She was fast and...

She was fast.

Ginny had no confidence in her ability in the saddle.

"You can ride Baby Bear as much as you want to." Wade got to his feet and reached for his jacket and his hat. "I think Grandpa stored the barrels in the middle of the garage somewhere."

They went to look. It took them awhile. The barrels were actually in the tack room laying on their side with some saddles Tate had been washing resting on top. And then they had to find a tape measure because Ginny didn't want to practice without proper dimensions. And then they had to coax Baby Bear to the gate of the horse pasture with a bucket of oats.

It was dark and dinner time before they were ready for Ginny to ride. Wade had to turn on the arena lights. Ginny swung into the saddle. Her feet and stirrups were down too low for practicality. Baby Bear took a few steps and paused to glance back at her. Ginny urged him onward. He took another few steps and swished his tail from side to side.

"Don't bump his legs with your feet," Wade called.

"Are you sure she's your kid?" Griff joked, earning a slug in the arm from Wade. "Ow. I'm just saying that you were never afraid of anything."

He was afraid of something now. He was afraid he wasn't going to convince Ronnie to stop holding back and give him her heart. He'd stopped by the Picket Ranch on his way into town to talk to Hank about Ronnie, but Hank had gone to Oklahoma City to look at a bull, so he'd talked to her mother instead. About none of the things he wanted answers to.

"Ginny's bossy, like Wade." Ryan decided to weigh in on things. "But she's soft like Libby."

"There's nothing wrong with that," Wade said staunchly.

"Our little Ginny will be gutsier when she decides to try something for real." Tate hung his arms over the top rail the way he had as a teen. "She's just getting the lay of the land."

"You need to buy her a cuddler." Chandler pointed to Ginny. "Girls bond with horses that eat up affection. She's got to trust her mount."

"Yeah, but at some point, she's got to trust herself. And we all coddle her." Too much, Wade realized. At first, they'd done it because Libby was overly protective. But then they'd done it because they didn't want her to be lost in grief, the way some of them had been. "Especially since Libby died."

"Dinner!" Mom rang the cowbell on the front porch.

The cluster of cowboys at the arena called out that they'd be in soon, just like they used to when they were teens.

"It'll be cold," Mom called back, knowing from experience that "soon" could mean as long as an hour.

"Speaking of cold..." Griff slugged Wade's shoulder hard enough for it to be a retaliatory strike. "When are you and Ronnie going to quit dancing around each other and heat up?"

"Do I ask you when you're going to settle down?" Wade hauled back to continue their shoulder slugfest.

"That's enough." Dad stepped between them, clasping a hand over Wade's playfully clenched fist. "The next thing the two of you will be shouting is that one of you is touching the other."

"And then I'll ask for the twentieth time if we're there yet." Griff grinned.

And darn Griff, but his joke warmed Wade's heart. He and Griff broke out in laughter.

"Is anybody watching me?" Ginny called from the midst of the cloverleaf she was walking through in the arena.

They all assured her they were.

And then Wade remembered that Ginny needed more confidence in the saddle. "That's a lie, sunshine. We weren't watching at all."

His brother's stared at him, mouths agape. And then they caught on, laughing.

They spent the next few minutes watching Ginny plod around barrels.

"Hey." Griff nudged Wade with an elbow. "I was just giving you a bad time because you kissed Ronnie good night Sunday."

A kiss he'd interrupted by honking his horn.

Not that Wade was complaining. It seemed better to leave Ronnie guessing.

"I'm just touchy because she has a lot to work through," Wade told Griff. Her belief that her penchant for finding trouble would doom any relationship. Her demanding new business. Them. "It's going to take time."

And if she was open to more kisses, he could be patient.

"That's a slow burn," Dad said sagely. "Just like your mother. It took two years to convince her I was the one. And there were a lot of late-night kisses, let me tell you."

"TMI." Griff jumped down from the rail and practically ran to the main house.

"No, Dad." Wade backed into the arena with Ginny. "Just no. Ginny, enough riding for one day."

"Hey, Wade." Ryan held out his phone. "Is this washed-up handsome cowboy referenced in Ronnie's newspaper article you?"

CHAPTER EIGHTEEN

RONNIE WAS BUSY after work every night that week, acting as a dating concierge.

Turns out, nearly twenty of those voicemail messages were from ranchers and rodeo folk interested in making a lasting match.

On Monday, she went to Friar's Creek to coach a couple individually before they met for a drink at Silver Springs Bar & Grill. While she was there, she met with a rancher who was too busy to date and was a hobby taxidermist. She swung by Gary's place on the way home with a copy of a signed contract. Odelette was excited about the cross-promotion opportunity and eager to partner with Hollander saddles.

She couldn't help but thinking about Wade at Gary's place. He'd looked handsome in the clothes she'd bought for him, and she'd felt confident tucked beneath his arm. But no matter how often she thought about him or longed for another of his kisses, her mind wasn't changed. Wade was better off with someone else.

On Tuesday, Ronnie coached a nervous Willa before she met Zach for coffee at Clementine Coffee Roasters. She wanted that match to stick so bad, she nearly hung around to spy on the pair. Nearly. It didn't help that neither Zach nor Willa contacted her after their date. That really chaffed, Ronnie thought, because she had words saved up for Zach.

On Wednesday and Thursday, she spent numerous video chats with new and potential clients. Everyone wanted love. Everyone was tired of the cycle of dating sourced from those online dating apps that amounted to nothing.

She was triple-booked on Friday. First up was her video chat with Violet and Odelette.

Everyone looked fabulous. Violet was rocking a Bohemian style, including a blue paisley scarf threaded through her blond hair. Odelette wore one of her own creations, a blue denim beaded blouse threaded with silver conches. Ronnie wasn't a slouch, either. She wore a red velvet blouse with bell sleeves and dangly silver earrings beneath her earbuds.

"I'm excited about the opportunity to have both of you model for me," Odelette said, starting off the meeting in a way that settled Ronnie's nerves. "You two are like spring and summer. I'm inspired by the both of you."

And then, to close out the meeting, Violet mentioned reading about Ronnie's matchmaking in an online article.

Ronnie braced herself for ridicule.

"I wouldn't mind talking to you about that," Violet said, surprising Ronnie. "I'm cursed when it comes to dating."

"You let me know when you're ready to talk." Ronnie had learned a lot in the past few weeks about giving people space and letting them set the pace for their love futures. "I'm here. And everything I do is low-key."

They agreed to talk at the next rodeo where Cowgirl Pearl sponsored a booth.

Her second appointment was a meeting with Zach at the Buckboard during happy hour.

"Ronnie!" Zach approached her, arms wide as if about to give her a hug.

Traitor.

Ronnie held out her hand to stop him. "There won't be any hugs. Not after that article you wrote. You made fun of me and my business."

"I know. I'm truly sorry. My editor revised

the piece without telling me." Zach looked apologetic as he sat at the barstool to her left. "He doesn't think feel-good reading makes for good journalism. I'll make amends in this week's article. Promise."

Ronnie smirked, moving her plate of nachos to her right when he reached for them. "How can I trust you?" She wasn't born yesterday.

Zach stared at her nachos before speaking. "You should believe me. I went on a date with Willa as per your advice, and it worked out. We're going on another date tomorrow night."

"That's great." Ronnie sipped her lemonade. "I'm happy for you. However, you know the guidelines I use. You or Willa were supposed to text me afterward."

"I'm sorry about that, too," Zach said. "I think we both got caught up in the excitement of finding someone new and didn't want to say anything until we knew for sure."

"I suppose I can understand that. But I'm concerned about the article you're going to write next. I don't want Willa hurt." She paused to eat a fully loaded chip, letting her words sink in. Zach either had a heart or he didn't. It was best to discover it now before

Willa became more invested. Plus, Ronnie had a favor to ask of him.

"I get what you're saying here." Zach frowned slightly. "My next article will either prove I'm serious about Willa or that I'm a heartless jerk who won't fight his editor for the integrity of the piece."

"That's right." She ate another chip. Wade wasn't the only one who played poker. "I'm willing to forgive you, Zach, but I need a favor."

"What kind of favor?" he asked suspiciously.

"I heard about this really unusual date that involved a picnic blanket, fire ants and a lawsuit for pain and suffering." Oh yes. She was going to throw Tuttle Towbridge to the wolves. "Are you interested?"

"It sounds fascinating." He set his phone to record and placed it on the counter. And later, after he'd promised to pitch the silly story with the serious consequences to his editor, Zach said, "Now, tell me how the business is going."

She told him, but she spoke with more poise and carefully chosen words than she had in the past.

Thirty minutes later, Ronnie's phone alarm went off. Ronnie checked the time as she turned the alarm off. "I'm sorry, Zach. I need to get to another appointment."

"Are you acting as a buffer for a first date for someone?" Zach perked up.

She nodded. "If you have any more questions, put them in an email. I'll say goodbye here."

RONNIE INVITED ME to dinner.

Via text.

Wade knew deep down that he wasn't about to have dinner with Ronnie. This smacked of one of her blind dates.

Still, a man could hope.

And so, on Friday night, Wade showered, shaved and spritzed himself with a little cologne—all because he knew that's how she liked him to look. He put on new blue jeans, his Sunday church boots, a nice shirt and bolo tie. And then he left his winter jacket at home and headed to Barnaby's Steakhouse to see Ronnie, hoping it was only Ronnie he was going to be looking at over the dinner table.

Ronnie waited for him outside. She wore a sleek black dress, her shiny red cowboy boots and a sparkly silver jacket, the collar of which wrapped over the top of her dark hair. The prairie wind had kicked up at sundown, and she'd once told him she didn't like her hair to be windblown.

He stopped in front of her, setting his boots a little closer than was allowed. But he'd kissed her on two occasions—not to mention he fancied giving those deep red lips of hers another—if she felt the same. It was more than worth asking the question.

"You make quite an impression, cowboy," she told him after drinking in her fill in a way that had him puffing out his chest as he tucked a lock of hair behind her ear.

"And you look…" His return compliment stalled because she took a step back, reached in her pocket and thrust one of those teal-and-pink flowered business cards with introductory notes on one side toward him. "…nice and matchmakerly." He took the card and stuffed it into his back pocket, the way he wanted to stuff his rising annoyance away.

Too late for that.

"Is she inside?" Wade snapped, hoping she'd see in the neon light of the Barnaby's Steakhouse sign how much her little ruse stung. He had no doubt she could hear it in his voice. Heck, if there'd been anyone in the vicinity, they'd have heard, too.

"She is. You'll find Sandra at a table holding one of my cards." Ronnie opened the door for him, gaze sweeping the welcome mat. "You'll like her. I don't think you'll need the card to find something to talk about. She's very straightforward."

Like you, he wanted to say.

But he didn't. He thought about his father telling him he'd courted his mother for two years. He thought about how Libby wanted him to take a second whirl at love with Ronnie. And then he thought about the passionate way Ronnie kissed him back.

If he hadn't been accustomed to winning or losing in the short span of eight seconds, he'd have been more patient. He wouldn't have wanted to tug her free of that door and the expectations of some woman named Sandra. He wouldn't have wanted to kiss some sense into Ronnie.

But apparently, he'd landed on his head a few times too many. Because he didn't take the proverbial bit in his mouth and take charge of things. He remained docile and patient, intent upon waiting for the right chute to open and for the two of them to go charging through.

Wade took hold of the door above Ronnie's head and gestured she go inside first. "I'm not doing this unless you sit at the bar and watch." If he had to suffer, so did she.

"I'm going to sit at the bar and *wait*." Ronnie held up her cell phone. "They have a television, and there's an Oklahoma State basketball game on."

Marilee, the hostess, waved Wade in, smiling to beat the band. "It's not nice to be late for a date."

"Good luck, Wade." Ronnie headed for a seat at the bar where she could see the big screen and nothing of the main dining room.

Marilee led him to a slender brunette who was drinking a light beer and fiddling with Ronnie's teal-and-pink card. She didn't have the exuberance and shine of Ronnie. Or the city sophistication of Helene.

He came up to her side anyway and introduced himself.

"You are everything Ronnie promised and more." Sandra had a charming smile, but her brown hair stuck out in sharp, stubborn curls about her shoulders.

Wade couldn't rectify the two.

"Wade, can I bring you a beer?" Marilee asked, still glowing.

"Please." And quickly. He needed something to dull the pain of Ronnie setting him up with another woman. He sat down across from Sandra, wishing she was Ronnie in the worst way. "Have you ever competed in the rodeo?"

"No." Sandra's smile dimmed a little. "I'm just a fan, mostly on TV since tickets can get pricey."

Wade nodded. He hadn't been on television in quite some time. That was reserved for the bigger national events. "I compete in bareback riding. Placed third last week."

Marilee appeared with a chilled beer bottle, apparently so enthralled to be part of the date that she was cutting the regular waitress out of the picture.

"Third place gives us something to celebrate." Sandra clinked her beer glass to his. "I want to be completely up front. I'm divorced and work on the line at a beef processing plant. It's not glamorous." She nodded toward the bar. "Ronnie is so glamorous that I can't believe she called me to set up this date with someone who was formerly famous."

Wade prided himself on the fact that he didn't flinch at being labeled "formerly famous." "Ronnie probably told you I'm a widower. I've got a little girl." And that was about as far as he got on the niceties, because something was happening inside his chest. It was like Griff had wrapped those big arms of his around Wade and given him an unrelenting squeeze.

"I bet she has her mama's eyes," Sandra was saying. It was the right thing to say.

Wade began to feel guilty for not being the man Sandra thought he was—interested in finding out if they were a good fit romantically. The Griff chest squeeze lessened. His good manners kicked in.

Their waitress appeared. Sandra ordered a steak salad. Ronnie would have gone for the sirloin. Wade ordered a ribeye, feeling like he needed a bit of a splurge if he was going to survive this date without hurting Sandra's feelings. He waited for Sandra to take charge of the conversation. They talked about inconsequential things. The weather. Rising bank interest rates. The way it was hard to find a good mechanic.

Wade cut into his steak when it arrived, thinking how Ronnie had found a more down-to-earth woman than his first date. Still, he didn't plan on lingering and ordering dessert or coffee.

There was a slight commotion around the

hostess station. Rather than turn and look, Wade kept his focus on his date.

Sheriff Underwood and a deputy entered the dining room.

Wade might have assumed the law was here to get a good meal if they hadn't made straight for his table. He glanced up at them and their stern expressions. "Everything all right?"

"Sandra Jones?" Sheriff Underwood said in the same tone he'd used on Ronnie last weekend.

Sandra nodded, looking paler than a bleached sheet.

Wade almost reached for her hand in case she was about to receive bad news, like hearing her mama died or something.

"You're under arrest," Sheriff Underwood said.

Wade sat back in his chair, mouth open. Speechless.

The deputy read Sandra her rights, taking her by the arm and bringing her to her feet.

Belatedly, Wade gathered his wits, feeling a bit like he should be his date's advocate. "What's she being arrested for?"

Sheriff Underwood smiled. It wasn't pretty, that smile, and Wade supposed it wasn't meant to be. "Armed robbery. Assault. Extortion."

A guttural sound gathered in Wade's throat, but all that came out was a whispered, *"Ronnie."*

"It wasn't her fault," Sandra rushed out the words as they cuffed her. "This is all a misunderstanding. Maybe you can follow us to the station and bail me out? We were really hitting it off."

The tall sheriff chuckled.

"Not likely. Good luck with everything ahead of you, Sandra." Wade gathered his plate, utensils and his beer, and headed toward the bar. He set everything down at the bar next to Ronnie and sat next to her. "Well, that was a bust. Literally."

Ronnie glanced at him in surprise. "What? What happened?" She'd shed her coat, draping it on the bar seat to her right. All her sleek, dark hair cascaded over her shoulders in neat waves.

"They arrested Sandra," Wade said tightly, trying hard not to laugh or smile or tell her this was what happened when she tried to fix him up with another woman. "You know, Sandra. My date. The woman you thought was good enough to be Ginny's new mama.

I should have known something about her didn't jibe."

"Her…her what?" Ronnie's shoulders lowered and her expression pinched. "She was arrested. Was it parking tickets?"

Wade shook his head. "Armed robbery." Among other things. Oh, this was good. This was *"I can't wait to tell Griff"* good.

Ronnie's mouth dropped open. After a moment, she shook herself a little and laid a hand on his shoulder. "I'm so sorry. It won't happen again."

"You're darn right it won't, because that's it for me, Miss Matchmaker." He leaned toward her, lowering his head until their eyes were on the same level. "No. More. Blind. Dates."

She sucked in a breath. But this was Ronnie Pickett. Once she got an idea in her head, it was hard to shake it free. And so she recovered enough to say, "Now, Wade…"

"Don't you 'Now, Wade' me." He cut into his steak. Stopped. And took a loaded chip from her plate of beef-and-cheese nachos. "This business of yours is going down just like the imported jewelry, plasticware and cupcake businesses. At least, where I'm concerned." He shoved the chip into his mouth and frowned at her. No way was he giving her an inch in this battle. Because he planned to take a run at winning her heart.

"I've wounded your pride again," she said, placing her hands in her lap.

No. You've wounded my heart.

But that wasn't what Ronnie was ready to hear.

He took his time chewing. And his time sipping on his beer. And then his time staring at her, because it was really too much. "This isn't about my pride, Ronnie. It's about your fear of losing our friendship. And about how that's getting in the way of *this* match." He used his fork to gesture back and forth between the two of them.

She nodded, apparently bereft of speech.

Good. He hoped that meant he was making progress.

On the screen across from them, a college basketball player made a spectacular dunk. Ronnie's gaze was drawn to it and the subsequent replay.

Was she done talking for the night? "Don't you have anything more to say?"

Like maybe we should give it a go.

Slowly, she faced him again. "You know, every business and career has its challenges upon start up. Why, I remember how you struggled to place in the money once."

Wade scoffed. "You mean, in high school? I was a kid."

"I'm just starting out. Sandra…" Some of the spark was returning to her eyes. "I won't let that happen again."

"You're going to do background checks now? I don't see it." He turned his attention to his steak, knowing that he owed Ronnie for finding him renewed sponsorships but was determined not to agree to another date.

Unless it was with her.

Let her sweat a little.

RONNIE WAS SWEATING, panicking inside in a way she hadn't expected.

Why can't Wade just find a woman to settle down with?

She shoved a nacho chip in her mouth, chewing a big bite with all the care she was giving to finding Wade a wife.

And yet, I'm failing.

Ronnie hated to fail. Every time a business she'd started crumbled, she'd felt like something inside of her would break, the same something that connected her head to her backbone. And she'd kept herself together through sheer force of will, swallowing that pride Wade complained about and showing the world that nothing kept Ronnie Pickett down.

What if Zach gets wind of this?

He'd have a field day. And she…she probably wouldn't have a slew of voicemail messages inquiring about her matchmaking services.

How did I read Sandra so wrong?

Was this the first sign of the end of her matchmaking business?

Ronnie was breathing too fast and too shallow, the way she did when she panicked about something. The way she did when things went awry.

She half-turned on her barstool, watching Wade eat. He ate like he approached everything else—including kissing—with a slow, deliberate pace. He ate as if her life wasn't once more teetering on a precipice.

"You think I should stop matchmaking." Had she said that too loud? She glanced around the bar. Barnaby's wasn't the raucous Buckboard. But no one paid her any heed.

"I didn't say that." Wade offered a piece of steak to her. "Want a bite?"

"No." She sipped her lemonade, trying

to make sense of her jumbled thoughts. "I shouldn't have considered you my superstar."

Wade choked on that steak. "Excuse me?"

She waved off his upset. "It's a term Bess uses. She means it more like a marquee, a draw, something to tempt people to my services."

"Like a loss leader?" Wade's fork clattered onto his plate. "Like the toilet paper that goes on sale every third week at Barry's Grocery?"

Ronnie nodded, noting but ignoring the apparent steam coming out of Wade's ears. "I shouldn't drop your name or Tuf Patterson's," she said, realizing she was right about something. "I'm learning that big names can attract people for the wrong reasons. I'll have to warn Tuf about the woman he's meeting for a beer tomorrow night." His date might have lied to her to score a night out with the rodeo star. Ronnie's world closed in as she became lost in thought.

"Good. Thank you. Don't tell anyone I'm a client of yours. Because I'm not."

Ronnie was still half in her head, thinking about how to market her business when she started to speak, not truly considering her words. "Don't worry. I'm not giving up on finding you a wife." She'd have to be more careful. Maybe ask her next candidate for references. Her gaze drifted to the television screen and a player making free throws. "Do you know, the irony of all this is that I lied to you about starting a matchmaking service. I just did it so you'd go on some dates because I promised Libby. But then people found out and everything snowballed. And I couldn't find it in my heart to turn anyone down. Because everyone deserves a happy ending."

"What did you just say?"

"Um…" The reality of what she'd divulged sank in.

"Only you would try to pull off a ridiculous stunt like that and then get caught up in the repercussions." Wade shook his head. "And all because you thought I wouldn't go on one of your blind dates."

"Don't make it sound like you would have. You were hiding out on that ranch and keeping yourself from being ready for love again." She peered into his brown eyes as if trying to read his mind when, in reality, she was just trying to make a point. "You weren't moving on. You still aren't. You haven't even cleared out Libby's things."

Instead of arguing with her, Wade crumpled his cloth napkin and tossed it on the bar top. "Is that what it's going to take to make you feel better and listen to me?"

"Yes?" She wasn't exactly sure what he meant, but if it involved him moving forward, that would make it tremendously easier for her to find him a wife.

"As usual, you're in over your head and heading for a hard fall." Wade got to his feet, but he didn't walk away.

Oh, no. He stood right there next to her in her space, jaw working.

All that pent up energy. She wanted to take hold of it—*of him*—and give in to the impulse to kiss him.

The thought darn near stole her breath.

And then without warning, Wade bent down and kissed her forehead, followed by bringing his nose within touching distance. "I just hope I'm there to pick you up when you stumble this time."

And then he walked out on her, taking her breath and, most likely, her heart.

CHAPTER NINETEEN

"I ASKED YOU all here today…" Wade stared at the closest members of his family on the Sunday morning after his disastrous date. They all stood in his living room, having been summoned there upon their return from church.

He was at a loss for words and glanced around the room, taking in the antique coffee tables he'd been given, the comfy gray sofa he and Libby had bought together, Ginny's framed school pictures on the way next to his and Libby's wedding photograph. They'd been barely more than teenagers, flanked by Griff and Ronnie.

Back then, Ronnie was just as much a caution as she was today. Jumping into things that sparked her fancy. Trying to make everyone around her happy. It wasn't that he couldn't believe Ronnie had tried to put one over on him by creating the fiction of a matchmaking company. Or that he couldn't believe things had mushroomed into the real thing. She'd always been one to go with the flow. And she always would be.

Which was perplexing since there was a nice ebb and flow to their kisses, one she was strictly avoiding going with when his lips weren't in direct contact with hers. Sure, there was her fear about losing their friendship. But he was prepared to pursue their relationship at a slow pace.

He just needed to prove to her that he was ready to love again.

Someone cleared their throat. Ginny took his hand and gave it a squeeze—so young and yet so perceptive when it came to his emotions.

Wade ran his gaze over his family again.

Griff, Tate and Ryan, who sometimes acted like the teasing teenagers they'd been after a few years at the D Double R, reminded him that he didn't always have to be serious.

Mom, Dad and Chandler, who grounded him in faith and responsibility.

Ginny, whose well-being he tried to keep top of mind.

"I asked you here today..." Wade began again, giving Ginny's hand a little shake meant to reassure her. "...because I want to start going through Libby's things."

"Thank heavens." Mom sank onto the couch. She still wore one of her Sunday dresses, this one a cheerful lime color. "I thought you were going to tell us you had cancer."

"Or wanted to move off the ranch." Dad sat down next to her. His bolo tie sat on the coffee table.

"Or were quitting the stock company," Chandler murmured, leaning against the wall separating the living room from the foyer.

"I had no clue." Ryan glanced at his twin brother. "Did you?"

"I thought we were going to rearrange your furniture or something." Tate gave Wade that lopsided smile that told him he was joking.

"You're going to get serious about Miss Ronnie." Griff grinned, nudging Ginny. "I told you."

"Grown-ups are so confusing." Ginny pouted, frowning at Griff as she brushed her hands over the pretty yellow dress Ronnie had picked out for her. "If that's true, Dad, I just lost a bet. Now I have to do Griff's dishes all week."

"Like Griff cooks?" Tate quipped.

Wade's family erupted into side conversations that varied from teasing Griff and

Ginny to expansion of what they'd thought Wade had called them here for.

"Hey," Wade said. "Hey," he said again, louder, because no one was listening to him. And then a shouted, "Hey!"

They quieted, staring at him.

Wade nodded when he had their complete attention. "I need your help going through Libby's things. After she passed, her mother asked for some family mementos. But there's a lot around the house that was hers." Wade bent to Ginny's level. "I want you to have a say in what we keep for the house and what you keep that was hers, like jewelry and… and things." He straightened, throat suddenly thick with emotion. "But to do that, we need to divide and conquer. The kitchen. Her desk. The bedroom." Because even though he was ready to explore love with Ronnie, he wasn't ready to close the book on Libby alone.

His announcement was definitely a mood killer. There were no further jokes made. In fact, Tate glanced toward the door as if contemplating his chances of escape.

"I can help you in the bedroom." Mom got to her feet and held out her hand to Ginny. "Come on. You can look through your mama's jewelry box."

The pair went up the creaky old farmhouse stairs, talking about piercing Ginny's ears so she could wear Libby's earrings.

It's too soon, Wade wanted to say.

"I'll be up there in a minute," Wade called after them instead, sensing the trickiest emotions would be where they were headed and hoping he had the strength to hold himself together.

"Chandler and I will look through her desk." Dad stood and led the way to the small alcove where Libby's rolltop desk sat.

Wade nodded, still standing in the middle of the living room, immobile. "Put whatever you find on the dining room table, Dad."

"Okay." He gave Wade a thumbs-up.

The twins and Griff stared at Wade, waiting for their assignments.

"Can you handle the kitchen?" It was about the only thing Wade trusted the yahoos with.

"The kitchen? Really?" Tate shrugged. "Was Libby sentimental about certain pots or pans?"

Griff gave Tate a not-so-friendly shove. "Not cool, man."

"It's okay," Wade said quickly, wanting to ease the tension in them and himself. They'd each suffered loss of one form or another, and this was tough on all of them. "There's not much in the kitchen. Libby had a junk drawer that was hers and a cupboard filled with cookbooks and notebooks." Some she'd collected from high school.

Ryan nodded. "What are we looking for?"

"Personal things. Hair ties. Discarded grocery lists. Photographs and…maybe love letters?" Wade felt a blush coming on. Libby had enjoyed writing him love letters. Sometimes she'd said more about her feelings on paper than in words. "You know. Anything that you'd stumble across if you were a woman I was dating—"

"He means Ronnie," Griff interjected. "Despite his 'Jailhouse Rock' date Friday night."

"—and would feel awkward about finding." Wade gave Griff a dirty look, but he didn't put much effort behind it because his tell-it-like-it-is brother was calling things clearly this morning.

"Let the twins take the kitchen." Griff backed toward the door. "I'll go through Libby's car and her storage locker in the tack room."

"Thanks. I'd forgotten about those." Assignments given, Wade made his way upstairs with heavy steps. Suddenly, it felt as if he were losing Libby all over again, trying not to think about her absence or how he'd cope when she was gone. He'd put off this day for so long and for this very reason. It wasn't going to be an easy day, not by any means.

Mom and Ginny had dumped Libby's jewelry box on Wade's bed. They sat sorting through things.

"She had a lot of friendship bracelets." Ginny slipped a purple and pink one on her wrist, admiring it.

"That was something she and Ronnie did together," Wade explained thickly.

"These are all from Miss Ronnie?" Ginny picked through them again. "Wow. She and Mom must have been good friends."

"The best." Wade kissed the top of Ginny's head, trying not to look at the bracelets or think about high school. "When your mom told Ronnie she liked me, that was it for Ronnie. I was not in her consideration set. And considering Clementine didn't have more than a couple hundred kids in high school, the dating pool was limited to guys like your uncle Griff or Dix."

"It's hard to find a friendship like those two had," Mom said softly, perhaps knowing more about Libby and Ronnie's bond than she let on.

Wade didn't want to ask.

The pair continued to sift through the keepsakes of Libby's life.

Not wanting to recall more of those early memories, Wade went to work on Libby's dresser and closet. He boxed up most of her clothes, the things she'd worn daily as a stay-at-home mom. Finally, he was at a place where he needed his daughter's input.

"Ginny, can you weigh in on these?" He laid several jackets Libby had cherished on the bed. The soft, faded jean jacket. The navy peacoat she'd worn during winter trips to church. The white-and-black buffalo jacket Ronnie had given her one Christmas from the Cowgirl Pearl line. And then he laid out Libby's prom dresses, the four sparkly gowns she'd worn every time he'd taken her to the formal dance.

So many memories. And yet, so few. Wade's mouth was dry, but his eyes... His eyes weren't.

The room was silent. Glancing around, Wade realized he wasn't the only one shedding tears. He gathered his mother and daughter into his arms. They spent several minutes holding each other and the memories of Libby tight.

"I suppose that's enough of that." He rubbed their arms and released them.

"No good comes of keeping grief inside." Mom found the tissue box on Libby's dresser and passed out one to each of them.

"You taught me that," Wade said softly, gratefully. She'd been the one to help him go through his parents' things all those years ago. They'd cried together then, too.

His mother finished blowing her nose. "I vote yes to the jackets and no to the dresses." She sounded all business, and yet she rubbed Ginny's shoulders, giving her a smile. "But it's your opinion that counts."

Wade held his breath, wondering if his little girl was up to the task.

Ginny balled up the tissue and fingered the iridescent fabric of one gown, sniffing shakily. It took her a bit to collect herself before she met Wade's gaze. "Can I keep it all, Dad? And Mom's wedding dress, too?"

Wade and his mother were quick to reassure her that was fine.

Later that night, Wade sat at the dining room table and stared at the collection of Libby's things his family had brought to him.

Bits and pieces of his wife's too-short life. Mini photo albums. A math notebook filled with equations and his name doodled in the margins. Pins with their high school logo that had been given out during homecoming week. A cookbook notated with hints written by Libby's grandmother. That had been a wedding gift, and he wondered if Libby's mother wouldn't want to have it back. There were pictures and rodeo ticket stubs and newspaper clippings chronicling his successes. There were small stones she'd enjoyed carrying around in her pocket. For luck, she'd say. Tiny figurines—cheerful resin gnomes and mice wearing cowboy hats. Small Christmas ornaments she'd hung from doorknobs and then forgotten when they packed holiday decorations away. Sea shells from their vacations in Mexico.

What was he supposed to do with it all?

Save it for Ginny and... Ronnie.

He'd buy a special trunk and store all Libby's things inside. It didn't feel right to box them up and shove them in a closet, or worse, the garage where his chances of finding it years later were nil.

One thing he knew what to do with. He

opened the letter Libby had written him and read it silently for the third time that day.

My love,
How I wish I didn't have to leave you.

You have given me everything I ever dreamed of, a love so big and strong that I woke up every day feeling like the luckiest woman alive. How grateful I am that you shared your home with a large family, larger than my own blood kin.

But even now, as I write this, something weighs on my mind. Something we haven't discussed, something I haven't told you. And even now, it shames me to think of it.

I stole you from Ronnie.

Those brazen words. They aren't exactly true. We were fourteen when Ronnie was allowed to participate on the school rodeo team. I couldn't wait to watch her ride. She was so brave and beautiful on that horse, long hair flying behind her as free and flowing as her horse's main and tail. I wished I could be her. But I've never been an athlete. You know me. I could barely dance until you taught me down by the river!

And then one day, I showed up to watch Ronnie ride, but it was you I saw charge through the arena. You were riding a bucking bronco with only a rope and your skill keeping you on his back. I had a new beauty to admire. That very day, I asked Ronnie who you were, pointing you out. She told me your name, smiling that way she does when she's truly and completely happy. And I boldly told her that I was going to marry you someday.

I'm ashamed to say that I saw her smile falter, if only for a moment. And then she told me that if I wanted you, you should be mine to have.

Did I mention I was fourteen? Fourteen-year-old girls are fickle about their crushes. They change on the daily. I sometimes tell myself, "How was I to know if Ronnie's interest in Wade was love?" But years later, the older, wiser me knows the truth. Ronnie loved you. And because she loved me, too, she stepped aside and tucked her feelings away.

I am the worst of friends.

Why am I admitting this now?

Because I want you to be happy after I'm gone. I don't want you to hide away on the ranch, only doling out smiles to our precious little girl. I want you to live on. I want you to love again. And I want you to do it all with Ronnie.

People like Ronnie don't come along every day. Friendships falter. Trusts are betrayed. But not by Ronnie. She will always do what's right. Or what she believes is right. Even if deep down she wants something different. All those years ago, she believed that I deserved a chance to love you.

And now that I've had that chance, I want to do the same for her.

I will always have a part of your heart, Wade. But your heart is big enough to find room for Ronnie, too.

And when you do, you'll have my blessing.

All my love, Libby.

Wade carefully folded the letter and returned it to its envelope. He ran his fingers over the words she'd written on the back: *To Wade. Read after I'm gone.*

The first time he'd opened the envelope had been days after Libby died. Her words had made him angry. How could he ever love another woman, much less Libby's best friend?

Back then, he'd stuffed the envelope into the bedside table drawer and tried his best to forget about it.

And for nearly two years, he had, living a life that Libby hadn't wanted for him—closed in, closed off, shut away.

Until Ronnie Pickett had walked up to him at a rodeo and said those fateful words.

Wade Keller, you need me.

CHAPTER TWENTY

WADE DIDN'T HEAR from Ronnie for several days, which was a good thing.

He needed to breathe easy about what he was doing with Libby's things. And in doing so, he realized that the love he had for Libby would always be tied up in his growing love for Ronnie.

Growing? He'd always had a place for her in his heart, ever since they'd been two kids dealing with two different losses back in middle school. But he was letting that love set down roots in his very being. Because Ronnie was right. Loving her wasn't going to be easy. She was always going to be the person who came home with a surprise in store for him, whether that be a puppy in need of rescue or a friend in need of unwelcome love advice.

So, even though he pined for her, Wade took his time sorting through his feelings.

Still, the trail of Ronnie was everywhere

he went, like a watery wake left behind a speed boat.

"Ronnie landed me a sponsorship with True Ride Tractors and a date with the sweetest woman I've ever met," Ryan told Wade one morning. He was radiating happiness as he threw the lariat around the practice bull. "'Course, I'm not ready to settle down..." Still, his aim was true this morning, a testament to Ronnie's magic touch.

I started winning money again once she took me and my career in hand.

Wade had placed second at a rodeo the night after his disastrous date with Sandra. That had to be a testament to Ronnie's influence on him.

There were more couples than usual in Clementine Coffee Roasters when Wade went in one morning after dropping Ginny off at school. Ronnie's colorful teal business cards sat on many of the tables, the ones where people seemed to be laughing and having a good time.

It felt like Wade hadn't laughed heartily since he'd left Ronnie at Barnaby's Friday night.

There were hearts and flowers everywhere

around town touting Valentine's Day on the horizon, this Saturday, in fact.

"Ronnie's been no trouble," Lila's mother assured Wade when he stopped by her house to pick up Ginny after school on Thursday. "She explained how everything got out of hand and assured the entire block that it won't happen again."

"Thanks, but... I didn't ask," Wade said, trying not to glance down the street toward Ronnie's house. He'd been hoping she'd reach out to him.

"Miss Ronnie made us cupcakes. Here, Dad." Ginny handed him a red velvet cupcake with thick white frosting. "We saved you one."

Red velvet cupcakes were his favorite, the kind he used to order from Ronnie when she ran that cupcake business. He put it in his truck cupholder and snuck glances at it the entire drive back to the ranch, only half-listening to Ginny rambling on about her day.

It didn't look like Ronnie's matchmaking business was going to fail.

Because fixing things and pairing up lonely hearts is her true talent.

Frowning, Wade drummed his fingers on the steering wheel.

If that's true, why doesn't she realize we're made for each other?

As he pulled up into the ranch yard, his phone chimed with a text message.

Can you meet me for dinner tonight at South Siders?

Two days until Valentine's Day. What was the likelihood that Ronnie's text message was an invitation to dinner *with her*? South Siders was a fancy little café with white tablecloths and candlelight. Could this be a date with Ronnie?

Fool me once…

Wade's frown deepened. In fact, it felt etched into his face. Here he was, falling in love with Ronnie, and she was still out there trying to get rid of him.

"I'm going to ride Baby Bear around the barrels." Ginny hopped out of the truck and ran toward the barn, leaving her backpack and jacket on the truck floor.

Wade stared at the truck's cupholder and Ronnie's red velvet cupcake. Was this a peace offering?

His gut said no.

He got out of the truck and followed Ginny to the barn, planning to ignore Ronnie's message.

His phone chimed again.

Seven o'clock?

His steps slowed.

Looking forward to seeing you.

Was she?

Only a fool would believe he wasn't being set up. And who knew what kind of woman Ronnie would find for him this time. A gambler? A con artist? A down-on-her-luck door-to-door salesperson?

Wade drew a deep breath, kicked at the dirt with the toe of his boot and hesitated.

Because, darn it all, there was a slim chance Ronnie had been thinking about all his kisses and missing him as much as he'd been missing her and was asking him to dinner, not setting him up.

He'd bet Vegas wouldn't take those odds.

Wade stood halfway between his truck and the barn, torn.

And blast if he didn't have a sudden irresistible urge for sweets.

Wade stomped back to the truck, yanked open the door and grabbed the cupcake. "I am such a fool."

"Agreed." Griff came up behind him. He gasped. "Is Ronnie back in the cupcake business?"

"No." Wade handed Griff the red velvet confection. "I'm going into town for dinner tonight. Can you watch Ginny ride barrels? I need to shower and get ready."

"Hmm?" Griff's mouth was full. Red velvet crumbs clung to the corner of his mouth. "Don't tell me you're taking Ronnie to dinner."

"I'm not telling you."

Because he didn't know.

But what he was sure of was that he needed to cover his bets.

RONNIE WAITED FOR Wade outside South Siders Café looking like Wade's long-awaited dream.

She always dressed in colors as rich as her red velvet cupcakes, and tonight was no exception.

She wore flowing crimson slacks, a cream-colored tunic with roses embroidered on it, and black sandals that revealed hot pink toenails. She wore a baby blue wool duster that she'd pulled over her unbound hair, which was once more tucked inside her coat collar.

Ronnie looked gorgeous, put-together and lacking doubts. About anything, including Wade.

He wished he felt the same.

"Last-minute invitation," Wade said as he strode up to her face her in his Sunday best, including a nice thick jacket and his best cowboy hat. "That means one of two things. You were stood up or—"

"As if," she scoffed.

"—you're setting me up."

Her smile wavered. "Wade, I made Libby a promise to find you a wife after she was gone."

Wade's mouth went dry, and he wanted to turn around, get in his truck and drive away. But he stood his ground because he had one last card to play.

"You're going to love—" Ronnie hesitated before adding "—Bea. She teaches music in Friar's Creek. She's an avid college sports fan. Her parents run a small cattle operation, and she used to compete in team roping for her high school."

He gave Ronnie a hard stare, watching as the evening prairie wind tried to tug strands of her hair free. "She sounds a lot like some-one I know."

"Bea has perfect pitch," Ronnie went on as if he hadn't spoken. "She's a single mom with a little boy." She handed him her little teal-and-pink card.

Wade wanted to tear it up.

She's thought of everything.

Everything but Libby's letter.

He drew the envelope out of his pocket and handed it to her, taking her introductory card in exchange.

"What's this?" Ronnie turned the envelope over and paled in the soft light coming from the café window. "This is Libby's handwrit-ing."

Wade didn't confirm or deny it.

He let Ronnie deal with the fallout and went inside to meet the woman who the woman he loved thought was perfect for him.

WADE STOOD AT the empty hostess station at South Siders, fighting the urge to turn around and return to Ronnie.

But he held firm. He'd been making changes and progress. It was time she do the same.

For now, if this was what Ronnie wanted,

this was what he needed to do. Let the chips fall where they may.

A woman with straight dark hair sat at a table near the window where she'd no doubt seen Ronnie greet him. She raised a tentative hand, one that held a familiar teal-and-pink flowered card.

Wade raised his in acknowledgment and crossed the room to join her, removing his coat and hat, hanging them on the coat tree next to his seat. He laid his card on the table near hers, willing himself not to look out the window to see if Ronnie was reading the letter or driving away.

"This is awkward," Bea said with a nervous laugh and non-threatening smile. "I've never done anything like this before, not even on one of those dating apps. I happened to meet Ronnie while pumping gas in Friar's Creek, and she seemed so personable. I had this instant connection, as if she'd been my friend forever. And…" She blushed. "I'm babbling."

"It's okay." It was endearing.

Bea was pretty. Her hair was dark, not the midnight black of Ronnie's. Her eyes were a warm brown, not black like Ronnie's, and highlighted by minimal makeup, not the polished presentation Ronnie favored. She wore a gray dress without accessories, nothing like the flashy outfits Ronnie wore. She was Ronnie light.

"It's rare for me to get out," Bea continued, as comfortable carrying the conversation as Ronnie. "Mostly, I talk to other teachers before and after school. Don't get me wrong, I love my students." She laughed a little. "But keeping middle schoolers focused on music and not on each other is a Herculean task. And…" She drew a deep breath, giving him that smile that apologized but also told him this was who she was. "There I go again. Tell me about your daughter before I start gushing about my son."

Without meaning to, Wade began to tell her about Ginny.

And without meaning to, Wade stayed through dinner, dessert and coffee, and realized that Bea would be perfect for him.

If only he hadn't fallen in love with Ronnie.

CHAPTER TWENTY-ONE

"WHAT IS IT? What's wrong?" By the looks of him, when Hank barged into Ronnie's house after she'd left Wade on his date, he was ready to put out a fire or rescue her from an intruder. "Why did you call and hang up on me? And then you didn't pick up."

Brisket leaped up from his dog bed near the door and bounced around Hank's feet. The dog had exhibited no sympathy for Ronnie's tears after she'd read Libby's letter. He'd been excitedly trying to demolish a fuzzy squeaker toy she'd given him before she'd left to meet Wade.

Hank fended off the Labrador's enthusiasm, taking in Ronnie's face, which she knew was tear-streaked and raccoon-eyed. "Ronnie..." He joined her on the love seat, put his arm over her shoulder and let her cry some more.

She handed him Libby's letter and blotted her face with a damp, crumpled tissue. She stopped and started crying a few more times while he read it.

"Gee, Ronnie." He tossed the letter on the coffee table. "Libby was a saint."

Ronnie nodded. "And I'm the worst friend ever."

Her brother turned her to face him, holding her shoulders. "Why would you say that?"

"Because she knew I liked Wade and—"

He gave her a little shake. "And Libby didn't hold that against you. Ever."

Ronnie's gaze drifted to Wade and Libby's wedding picture, which sat next to a framed photo of the Pickett family standing on the state house steps. "But Libby blamed herself for taking Wade away from me when clearly Wade wanted her all along. I can't bear the thought that I made her unhappy all those years. It wasn't like I was bitter."

Hank released her, leaning back on the cushions. "Did you and I read the same letter? Libby thanked you for stepping aside and paving the way for a love that made her happy, as if you and the universe knew her life would be cut short."

Ronnie's shoulders sank and she started to cry again. "But I didn't know any of that."

Hank took her shoulders and gave her another gentle shake. "But you thought it. You thought it long before you read this letter. When are you going to trust that there's a love out there for you, one that won't care about disasters or messes or loves that came before? You have Libby's blessing. What more do you need?"

"You're one to talk." Ronnie yanked a fresh tissue from the box and blew her nose. "You're asking me to do what you can't. You can't trust that love will be strong enough to sacrifice a standard of living to save for a long-term dream."

"Leave me out of your wallowing." Hank sank back again, which gave Brisket the opportunity to plop his front legs in his lap and show off his new squeaker toy.

"And do you know what the worst of it is?" Ronnie went on.

"That you set Wade up with another woman?"

She nodded. She'd told him about Sandra and the arrest last weekend. "Worse. I set him up again. Tonight. That's when he gave me this."

"Ronnie, how many mistakes are you going to make with this guy?"

"Lots." She drew a shaky breath. "I've broken Wade's trust. He's so certain that people will reject him—business associates, blood relatives, women…*me*—that he created a pass-fail test. If you reject him once, he moves on."

"You've rejected him more than once, Ronnie," Hank reminded her. "And you have Libby's endorsement."

"She's perfect," Ronnie said in a lost little voice.

"Yeah, she was." Hank nodded toward the letter.

"Not Libby. *Bea*. The woman I set Wade up with. She will be easy to love, whereas I…"

"You overthink everything when it comes to love and your history, which is weird because you jump into everything else without much thought."

"That's not true." Was it?

It is!

But that only made things worse. Ronnie pounded her fist against her thigh. "Darn it."

Hank smirked, rubbing Brisket's ears. "Let's not argue. Instead, why don't you tell me if you want to take Libby's blessing and make a go of it with Wade?"

"Hank…" She didn't dare hope she still stood a chance with him. There was her repeated rejections and there was Bea.

But Wade and I had those hot kisses.

"No over-thinking," Hank said in a teasing voice that made her wonder if she should have called Bess instead. "If you had to make a choice right here, right now, what would it be?"

Wade. I want Wade.

"That's what I thought." Hank snatched Brisket's toy away from him and tossed it into the kitchen.

The old dog bounded after it. He was thriving in his new environment. It gave Ronnie hope that she could, too. An environment that included Wade.

"Maybe I should be a matchmaker." Hank stood, drawing Ronnie to her feet and giving her a hearty hug. And then he set her at arms' length. "It all boils down to the value you place on love. Do you really want to live without it? I don't think you should. Not anymore."

"Agreed." Ronnie sighed. "But it's funny you should say that." She picked up a teal-and-pink flowered business card from the coffee table and handed it to him. "Because I think you should take your own advice."

"What's this?" Hank turned the card over. "Seven o'clock reservation at Barnaby's

Steakhouse on Valentine's Day? With who? The name is blank."

"The woman you love," Ronnie said with a lighter smile, because she wasn't going to break. She was going to pull herself together and figure out these frightening feelings for Wade. Hopefully, with him. "Your date is with the woman you avoid at all costs because you don't want to disappoint her."

"Who is this date with, Ronnie?" Hank shook the card in the air, frowning.

"You'll have to show up and find out, won't you?" She hustled him toward the door.

And no matter how hard Hank pushed back, Ronnie didn't tell him she'd made a date for him with Nell Ingersoll.

"WHO SCHEDULES A rodeo on Valentine's Day?" Bess grumbled to Ronnie as they walked away from the popcorn cart. "Although I don't know why I'm complaining. I don't have a date." She pointed a finger at Ronnie. "Nor do I want one."

Because she'd been nervous, Ronnie had purchased a bag of popcorn. That might have been a mistake. Her mouth was dry, and her pulse was pounding. She should have bought a bottle of water.

Ronnie hadn't heard from Wade since before his date. And Bea hadn't returned her calls or text messages, either. Ronnie had enough business to skip this rodeo, but she knew Wade had entered the competition, and she wanted to see him.

If there was a chance...

If it isn't too late...

As if summoned by her thoughts, Wade appeared in the crowd, striding toward her in his bronc riding gear, red fringed chaps flapping with each bold step he took. Anyone who looked at him would see a confidence in his expression and a spring to his step. Not everyone would notice the shadow in his eyes or the way his jaw tensed when he saw her.

It's too late.

"I've got to talk to Wade," Ronnie told Bess. She hadn't confessed her feelings to her friend, keeping them private in case things didn't work out.

Bess took one look at Wade and said, "Good luck, hon. I believe in you." She turned and walked the other way.

Ronnie kept walking and...

Wade walked right past her.

She spun around, flabbergasted. "Wade Keller!"

He turned, pride rearing his shoulders back. He looked her up and down, a challenge replacing the hurt that had been in his eyes.

She had no idea what he was looking for, no idea what she should say, either.

Ronnie fell back on their friendly ways, holding out her bag of popcorn as a salty peace offering. "Tough draw today." He was going to ride Sucker Punch, one of the orneriest broncs the D Double R supplied to rodeos since Jouster had retired.

"I've had worse luck," he said cryptically, taking a few pieces of popcorn from her bag and putting them in his mouth.

With your dates?

With other horses?

With...me?

Ronnie swallowed. "I owe you an apology."

He raised his brows and waited.

Rodeo folk flowed around them, paying them no mind.

Ronnie swallowed again, taking a few pieces of popcorn, but keeping them in her fingers. "I lied to you all those years ago when we were in high school. We *do* suit. We suit quite well in fact. But Libby..." She trailed off. They both knew about Libby. "For the longest time, I told myself that since I couldn't have the man I loved, I shouldn't love anyone else. I'm more impulsive, unpredictable, even leap before you look than some men appreciate." Or perhaps understand. "I always had an excuse, and since my family put me in a protective bubble, I didn't challenge my excuses. I just kept fixing other people's lives and loves instead of my own."

Wade's jaw worked and he shifted his stance. But still, he said nothing. He showed nothing.

She had to ask, "Am I... Am I too late?"

"Wade Keller. Wade Keller." His name blared over the PA system. "You have three minutes to report to the chute before you're scratched."

People around them slowed. Some called his name, pointing in the direction of the chute.

"I've got to go," Wade said with regret in his voice before he turned away.

And Ronnie knew—she knew with certainty that dropped her heart to her red-booted toes—that she'd missed her chance with him once again.

CHAPTER TWENTY-TWO

RONNIE PICKETT HAD never been a quitter.

She'd lost. She lost the man who stole her heart at fourteen. She'd lost her best friend when she was twenty-seven. Oh, there were numerous other setbacks and heartbreaks. But she'd kept her head up and kept going with a smile on her face.

She wasn't going to give up now.

Ronnie sat in the stands on the bottom row by the chute where Wade was going to launch into his ride. After he'd left her, she'd lifted her chin and found a place on a bench where he couldn't miss her, not in her bright red outfit and not with her very loud voice.

"Let's go, Wade!" she shouted, clapping for emphasis.

Bess slipped next to her, staring at her face. She grabbed hold of Ronnie's hand, understanding the need for support without even knowing what had upset her friend. "Come on, Wade!"

Wade didn't look their way, not once.

Not that Ronnie wanted him to. She wanted him to concentrate on the bronc and have a good ride. She wanted him to ride for a glorious eight seconds and win the purse. She wanted him to be happy and worry-free.

Even if it meant he was happy and worry-free with Bea.

She clung to Bess's hand as her heart felt like it was breaking.

Wade set his heels at the base of Sucker Punch's neck, which was broad and mottled brown. One hand gripped his rigging, and the other hand was in the air. His torso and hips tilted to the sky. He had perfect form. And before Ronnie had talked to him earlier, he'd had a spring to his step.

"I'm sorry," Ronnie whispered, hoping she hadn't distracted him, wasn't distracting him, would never distract him again.

She leaned against Bess, who gave her another worried look.

Wade nodded, and the cowboys who'd been hovering in case Sucker Punch acted up in the chute drew back. Another cowboy yanked open the chute gate.

Sucker Punch leaped into the arena fast as lightning.

And Wade stayed on.

The beast hit his rhythm right away with a set of high, spinning kicks that made the crowd collectively gasp.

And Wade stayed on. He kept his free hand high in the air through every lunge, every spin, every bone-pounding buck.

The buzzer sounded after eight excruciatingly long seconds.

And Wade stayed on.

The crowd cheered but none louder than Ronnie.

Griff rode up beside Sucker Punch and released the bucking strap. The horse downgraded his efforts to half-hearted kicks. Griff extended an arm and Wade took it, hopping from one horse to another, riding behind Griff rather than dropping to the ground and making his exit from the arena.

"What a ride, ladies and gentlemen!" the announcer cried. "What a ride! We haven't seen Sucker Punch ridden like that in over a year."

Ronnie hadn't realized she'd gotten to her feet. She was clapping and cheering and trying her hardest not to cry.

Griff rode over to the chute Wade had just vacated.

Griff and Wade.

Wade was staring at her with an intensity that made it hard for Ronnie to breathe.

He slid off the back of Griff's horse and climbed the metal chute rails, staring right at Ronnie the entire time. He hopped over the bars and leaped to the rails on the other side before climbing up into the stands. Staring at Ronnie. Only at Ronnie.

"You are the most confounding woman," Wade said, taking her into his arms and kissing her.

His score was announced, but Ronnie didn't hear because her pulse was pounding in her ears, she was crying, the crowd was cheering and Bess was jumping up and down, screaming and pulling on their arms, pulling them apart.

Apparently Wade's score was phenomenal.
I love you!

It took Ronnie a couple of seconds to realize that Wade was shouting the words in her ear. And a couple more to realize she could shout them back. "I love you, too!"

Love. It was the darndest thing when it worked out.

Now she knew how all her clients felt when her process worked out.

When they finally let down their barriers and follow their hearts.

Ronnie laughed.

Ronnie cried.

And Ronnie kept repeating those three precious words until Wade broke into laughter and assured her that he heard her the first time.

EPILOGUE

"YOU KNOW THAT'S against the rules," Wade whispered to Ronnie a few months later as he tucked her hair behind her left ear.

"You caught me," she whispered back, tucking her cell phone into her clutch purse. "It's a message from Leo. News I am glad to get."

"Oh?" Wade caught her hand and kissed it.

"He says Tuttle dropped the lawsuit." Ronnie was ecstatic. The article Zach had written about the frivolous and petty lawsuit had been picked up by several large news outlets and apparently had generated buzz in the legal circuit.

"That's great. Oh, and hey, they're about to start." Wade planted a brief kiss on her lips.

"You're right." He'd been right about a lot of things, like how her occasional mishaps wouldn't weaken their relationship and that there were other places to dance besides the Buckboard, like on the banks of Lolly Creek under a star-lit sky.

But Ronnie had been right about things, too. Other things.

She caught Hank's eye. He stood at the altar in his blue suit, waiting for his bride to walk down the aisle.

Talk about running to the altar.

Since she'd started her matchmaking business, Ronnie had had several of her clients commit to each other with marriage proposals, but Hank had been the only one who'd decided to take it the next step so quickly. Even she and Wade had decided to wait until after the nationals in Las Vegas in the fall. Wade was winning regularly again, and they didn't want to take a break for a honeymoon while things were good.

Besides, there were still things to figure out. Like where they'd live. If they weren't horse people, Ronnie would have chosen to live in Great Aunt Didi's little house. Ginny liked it, too. But they were horse people, more so since Ronnie had begun coaching Ginny on barrels with a new little filly. But Wade had it in his head that they needed a house in line with his winning status, somewhere that was their own. Ronnie suspected he'd eventually realize winning wasn't something he needed to define himself. She and Mary were working on that. Ronnie had her eye on a nice little ranchette north of town.

Organ music filled the church as the bridesmaids began walking down the aisle. They were wearing sage green floor-length gowns.

"You did this," Wade whispered to her.

Ronnie couldn't get over the joy of whispered sweet nothings or whispered compliments from her fiancé.

She snuggled closer to Wade and sent up a small prayer of thanks to Libby. Their love and friendship had been unconditional and was something Ronnie wanted to honor in her everyday life with Wade.

The bridesmaids took their places. The wedding march began. The congregation stood and turned.

Nell Ingersoll glowed in her simple white wedding dress, the one she'd found at a second-hand store in Tulsa. Ronnie's hunch had been correct. She was the woman Hank was in love with. The one he avoided for years because he didn't want to risk losing her. And in doing so, he'd almost gotten his wish.

Nell floated past them on the arm of her father, looking beautiful and blissfully happy.

Ronnie's mother sniffed in the pew in front of them. Her father turned and beamed at

Ronnie, as if to say this was a task he'd enjoy doing for her—giving the bride away. Ronnie smiled back because she'd like that. So very much.

Ronnie took her seat next to Wade and immediately noticed something interesting.

The best man, her brother David, couldn't seem to take his eyes off bridesmaid Linda Sue Rutherford.

"Stop working," Wade whispered, his breath warm in her ear.

He knew her so well. And he needed her, too. Just as much as she needed him. Ronnie turned and planted a quick kiss on his lips before whispering, "I love you." He was her cowboy. A cowboy worth waiting for.

Wade squeezed her hand and whispered back, "I love you more."

* * * * *

For more charming romances from acclaimed author Melinda Curtis, and Harlequin Heartwarming, visit www.Harlequin.com today!

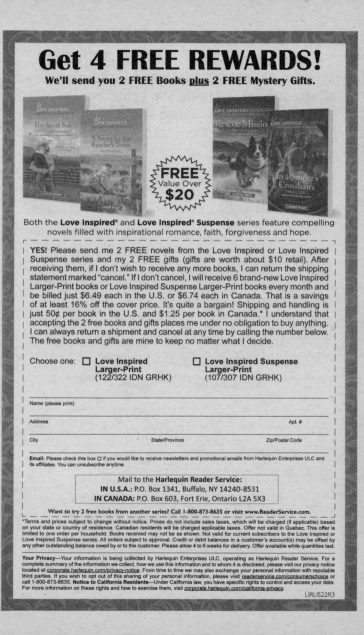

Get 4 FREE REWARDS!

We'll send you 2 FREE Books plus 2 FREE Mystery Gifts.

FREE Value Over $20

Both the **Harlequin® Special Edition** and **Harlequin® Heartwarming™** series feature compelling novels filled with stories of love and strength where the bonds of friendship, family and community unite.

YES! Please send me 2 FREE novels from the Harlequin Special Edition or Harlequin Heartwarming series and my 2 FREE gifts (gifts are worth about $10 retail). After receiving them, if I don't wish to receive any more books, I can return the shipping statement marked "cancel." If I don't cancel, I will receive 6 brand-new Harlequin Special Edition books every month and be billed just $5.49 each in the U.S. or $6.24 each in Canada, a savings of at least 12% off the cover price, or 4 brand-new Harlequin Heartwarming Larger-Print books every month and be billed just $6.24 each in the U.S. or $6.74 each in Canada, a savings of at least 19% off the cover price. It's quite a bargain! Shipping and handling is just 50¢ per book in the U.S. and $1.25 per book in Canada.* I understand that accepting the 2 free books and gifts places me under no obligation to buy anything. I can always return a shipment and cancel at any time by calling the number below. The free books and gifts are mine to keep no matter what I decide.

Choose one: ☐ **Harlequin Special Edition** ☐ **Harlequin Heartwarming**
(235/335 HDN GRJV) **Larger-Print**
(161/361 HDN GRJV)

Name (please print)

Address   Apt. #

City   State/Province   Zip/Postal Code

Email: Please check this box ☐ if you would like to receive newsletters and promotional emails from Harlequin Enterprises ULC and its affiliates. You can unsubscribe anytime.

Mail to the **Harlequin Reader Service:**
IN U.S.A.: P.O. Box 1341, Buffalo, NY 14240-8531
IN CANADA: P.O. Box 603, Fort Erie, Ontario L2A 5X3

Want to try 2 free books from another series? Call 1-800-873-8635 or visit www.ReaderService.com.

*Terms and prices subject to change without notice. Prices do not include sales taxes, which will be charged (if applicable) based on your state or country of residence. Canadian residents will be charged applicable taxes. Offer not valid in Quebec. This offer is limited to one order per household. Books received may not be as shown. Not valid for current subscribers to the Harlequin Special Edition or Harlequin Heartwarming series. All orders subject to approval. Credit or debit balances in a customer's account(s) may be offset by any other outstanding balance owed by or to the customer. Please allow 4 to 6 weeks for delivery. Offer available while quantities last.

Your Privacy—Your information is being collected by Harlequin Enterprises ULC, operating as Harlequin Reader Service. For a complete summary of the information we collect, how we use this information and to whom it is disclosed, please visit our privacy notice located at corporate.harlequin.com/privacy-notice. From time to time we may also exchange your personal information with reputable third parties. If you wish to opt out of this sharing of your personal information, please visit readerservice.com/consumerschoice or call 1-800-873-8635. Notice to California Residents—Under California law, you have specific rights to control and access your data. For more information on these rights and how to exercise them, visit corporate.harlequin.com/california-privacy.

HSEHW22R3

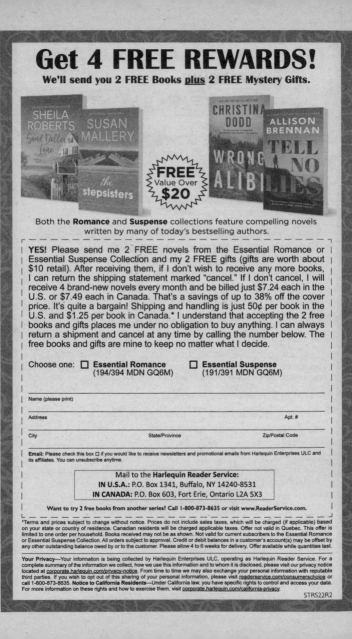

#467 HER SURPRISE COWBOY GROOM
Wishing Well Springs • by Cathy McDavid

Laurel's career ambitions keep her safe; after almost losing her business, she is cautious about letting Max and his adorable twin daughters into her life. Until she is faced with the choice to grow her business...or her family.

#468 A FAMILY FOR THE RODEO COWBOY
The Montana Carters • by Jen Gilroy

Former rodeo cowboy Cole Carter returns to his family's Montana ranch to start over. The first step: organize a cowboy challenge with animal physiotherapist and single mom Mel McNeil. But the real challenge is holding on to his heart...

#469 CAUGHT BY THE COWGIRL
Rodeo Stars of Violet Ridge • by Tanya Agler

All Kelsea wants from former rodeo cowboy Will is for him to put wind turbines on his ranch—and save her new sales job at EverWind. Until she begins feeling at home in the cozy Colorado town...and with Will, too...

#470 THE FIREFIGHTER'S RESCUE
Love, Oregon • by Anna Grace

Running kids' Cowboy Camp will be enough of a challenge for Dr. Maisy Martin without working with thrill-seeking firefighter Bowman Wallace! A childhood tragedy has left her wanting a stable, predictable life. But there's nothing predictable about falling in love...

HARLEQUIN
PLUS

Try the best multimedia subscription service for romance readers like you!

Read, Watch and Play.

Experience the easiest way to get the romance content you crave.

Start your **FREE TRIAL** at
<u>www.harlequinplus.com/freetrial</u>.